Humans Are the Ugliest Creatures
Jack Barnett

Humans Are the Ugliest Creatures

Humans Are the Ugliest Creatures

Copyright © 2020 by LHP & NOF & Jack Barnett

All rights reserved. No part of this book may be reproduced or used in any manner without written permission of the copyright owner except for the use of quotations in a book review. For more information, address:
j.s.barnett@hotmail.co.uk

FIRST EDITION
ISBN: 9798574256626

Humans Are the Ugliest Creatures

1

The Marshal and the Man in the Chair

"I came here with hope in my heart. I stood up on the hills and looked over the landscape as it sprawled out before me. Standing at the top of the ridge and watching the sun slip slowly into the horizon, an emotional response stirred somewhere inside me, the likes of which I hadn't felt since I was a child.

"The ground was bathed in deep vermillion, silhouetting all of its various protrusions. Soft yellows and pinks soared up into the sky, their ascent interrupted only slightly by circling birds and thin clouds. I stood and watched as the darkness swallowed the land. I listened as the coyotes woke and sung to the moon. The celestial vista reigned supreme, clearer to the eye than the road at high noon.

"From that day forth, my love for this land was etched on my very being. It was my sole purpose. That is to say, it was my soul's purpose. This place, and its boundless potential, was laid out before me like a detailed map. All I wanted was for it to succeed. My naivety was synonymous with my youth.

"For damn near twenty years, I poured myself into the effort of developing these lands. I went from town to town, with a smile on my face and a willing hand. There were tales of hardship and tales of success. All taking place in a landscape, which in the right light can still force a tear from my eye." He paused briefly and turned to the window. He looked down at the bustling afternoon scene playing out on Main Street and let out a heavy sigh of regret. "After all that I've witnessed out here, in this captivating place, there's one thing I'm certain of." He turned his head back to face the man sitting quietly in the chair, "We are the ugliest part of this place. Humans are the ugliest creatures."

The man in the chair smirked and raised his eyebrows. The leather of his gloves let out a creaking sound as he repeatedly balled his fists and flexed his fingers.

"You're getting too cynical in your old age, Marshal," remarked the man, while adjusting his collar.

The marshal returned to the window and made a tutting sound in disagreement.

"Cynicism is only found to be lacking, in blind men and fools," he replied as he leaned against the window frame and rested his head upon his forearm.

Marshal Ellis Andrews left his Virginia home on his twentieth birthday, lured by the promise of grand adventure and illustrious reward in the west. He had nothing to tie him down. There were no children to look after, there was no wife to keep. His mother died of consumption, and after a year spent with his perpetually intoxicated father, he could take no more. He offloaded what little possessions he had and took off for the new world.

He arrived with optimism in his eyes and good will in his heart. His years of playing peacekeeper and law maker, along with a brief involvement in the bloody civil war, molded his disillusioned view of the human species. Years later in 1869 he found himself appointed to the office of Town Marshal, in the small mining town of Good Rock. After four years in the post, his views on humankind had not softened.

He was not an imposing figure, he stood at a humble five and a half feet tall. He wore a blue three-piece suit, visibly dulled by prolonged exposure to the Nevada sun. He held a cigar tightly between his index finger and a middle finger which ended at the knuckle. Half of the digit was lost long ago in an altercation with a drunken gambler. It had since become a permanent reminder to always exercise caution. He wore a thick moustache, turned stone gray by time. The moustache sat atop a blanket of stubble, a physical embodiment of the marshal's ever-increasing apathy. His dull, steely eyes were set under a permanently furrowed brow. Upon his head, he wore an off-white hat that he rarely removed, due to his self-conscious nature and a steadily growing bald spot which ebbed away at his permanently disheveled and graying hair.

He often stared through the glass, watching over the Main Street activity and contemplating the nature of man. He found it to be meditative. It provided a short respite from the ever-churning existential turmoil, which he faced day to day. He was pulled from his quiet musings, when the man in the chair spoke.

"Marshal, as much as I enjoy these odd silences and little forays into philosophy of yours, I'm a busy man. Or I'd at least like to be," he grinned. "But I can't very well do that from here in this office."

Marshal Andrews turned to face him. His morose features hardened as he leaned forward and planted his palms on the desk.

"You don't ever get tired of it, Ed? All the running, all the bloodshed?" the marshal asked searchingly.

"Ellis, the day I get tired of it, is the day I take a nap on the railroad," he answered jovially. The marshal nodded his head in somber reflection. "So, I pry again, for the second time. Why am I here?"

The man stood up from the chair and stretched, waiting for an answer. As he lifted his arms, the pistols on either side of his hips gleamed like beacons in the night, and the brushed steel of a cleaver peered over its leather sheath and sparkled. This gesture did not go unnoticed by the marshal. He dropped his gaze to the floor, pulled a faded chair back from the desk and took a seat. He held out a hand and waved it up and down, inviting Ed to sit.

"Here," Marshal Andrews slid a piece of paper across the desk. "This is the man. Ed, it has to be quiet this time. I spent weeks cleaning up the mess you made of the last one."

Ed leaned forward and picked up the piece of paper.

"Ross Maddocks and gang," he announced as he read the paper. "And just what did they do, to earn my involvement?"

"Robbery and murder. They attempted to rob the bank in Waterston. They shot and killed five in the process. They've been identified in a small camp, just north of town," the marshal drummed his fingers on the desk and waited.

"Why can't you go after them? Going directly to your last resort seems mightily bold, don't it? A little brash even," he eased back into his chair, studying the paper.

The marshal closed his eyes briefly, clearly frustrated by Ed's questions but powerless to protest.

"You know the sheriff won't. That's almost a given these days-" he started to explain before Ed cut in.

"I wasn't meaning the sheriff, when I said *you*. Why don't *you* go after them?" Ed repeated.

He held out two fingers in the shape of a gun and pointed them at the marshal's head.

"I just don't think I have it in me to do so anymore," he explained, completely ignoring what he considered to be a childish gesture on Ed's part. "It's like there's a hydra buried somewhere under the dirt out here. You remove one head, only for another two to burst up through the ground on the other side of town."

"Well sure, Ellis," Ed agreed, squinting at the marshal, the metaphor somewhat lost on him. "Is that all?"

"Just keep it clean, Ed. I want it done nice and easy this time. That's the only way this will work. Keep it simple and you'll get your money. I won't be able to help you if things get complicated again," the marshal said, exuding fatigue as he cradled his head in his hands.

"Well, all I can do is try my best," Ed replied with a smile.

His reaction suggested that he did not share the marshal's concerns surrounding the situation. He leaned back in his chair, removed his hat and gently dusted it.

Ed Bader was three months away from his fortieth birthday. The streaks of silver hair, which scattered across his beard like leaves given to the will of the wind, were a testament to his age. His presence was commanding, and he carried with him an air which demanded immediate respect. His charcoal-black hair was thick, cropped close and slicked back, broken by a vein of gray, which crept further along his scalp with each passing year. His brown eyes spoke of a softness which many argued was not, nor ever had been, there. He wore a black three-piece suit, shrouded in a leather duster. It was said to be his cold-bloodedness that kept him from overheating in the midday sun.

Bader and his gang had made a reputation for themselves throughout Good Rock and the surrounding communities, as somewhat unsavory members of society. They ran protection rackets among whorehouses, bars and gambling joints. Whenever they wanted the payments to increase, they would stage robberies, keeping the stolen money and increasing the bill. The gang was suspected of several train robberies but witnesses never dared to come forward, if indeed there were any left alive.

They called themselves the WPC, the Western Protection Company. Members of the gang would come and go as Bader saw fit, always maintaining their numbers at around twenty. They would set up large camps on the outskirts of towns and would remain for months on end. If and when colder, wetter weather rolled in, they would disperse into the towns until it passed.

It was two years ago when Marshal Andrews first sought Ed Bader's help. A string of violent assaults took place in Good Rock over the course of a week. When Sheriff Jon Manning tried to deal with the situation and apprehend the fleeing assailant, he took a bullet to the shoulder. The injury left the sheriff incapacitated for a period of time, the mobility of his arm marginally impaired and his courage permanently depleted.

Marshal Andrews, experiencing a lack of confidence in his gun fighting ability, and not wanting to befall the same fate as Sheriff Manning, opted for an unorthodox solution. In his eyes, the whole situation had run on for too long and was fast becoming an embarrassment for the town authorities. He contacted Bader and offered him the bounty. Within four hours of acceptance, Bader returned with the wanted man's limp and lifeless body, bound neatly to the back of his saddle.

After the success and speed with which the matter was dealt with, Marshal Andrews offered Bader more bounties. Bader accepted and fulfilled his objectives, on the condition that he and his WPC were left to operate without interference from the authorities. For the marshal, it was a somewhat bitter pill to swallow, to allow those who frequently operated outside of the law to be given a free pass, but he sincerely felt that there was no other solution. The gutless Sheriff Manning was no use and at the time, he had no deputy. Without the assistance of the WPC, he felt that he would not be able to police the town. At the very least, the gang's reputation would serve as a criminal deterrent.

As Bader and his WPC men handled the removal of more outlaws and were seen more frequently throughout the town, his unit began to wear a yellow sash, tied neatly around the left arm, embroidered with the letters WPC. It was their identifier, their own version of a tin star.

Trouble arose when Bader accepted bounties on a pair of thieves, who had botched a highway robbery and slaughtered all of the passengers. The driver was wounded and later died as a result, but not before he could be interviewed and identify the men. Bader and a few of his WPC boys, located the wanted men in a quiet saloon. They were drinking at the bar, mingling among the regular patrons.

The WPC surrounded the building and trained their guns on the exits. Bader stepped forward and called for the men to surrender. He offered that if they were to peacefully emerge from the building, they would come to no harm.

The outlaws, panicked. Trapped inside and attributing no truth to Bader's words, they raised their guns at the other customers and lined them up in the middle of the room. They took the weapons being held behind the bar, unloaded the ammunition and selected two men. At gunpoint, they forced them to each hold an unloaded pistol and wait by the door. Standing behind the two innocent men, they called out to Bader that they would not be giving up without a fight. They opened the doors and pushed the two men forward. Bader's crew opened fire on them before they had a chance to protest their innocence.

The wanted men fired back at the WPC through the saloon windows. Their aim was poor and WPC casualties were minimal and non-life threatening. They returned fire, incessantly raining a storm of bullets on the building, until all activity ceased. Bader held up a fist and brought the assault to a stop.

He drew a pistol and made his way up the steps to the door. He opened the door and entered the building alone, seemly without caution. He was met with the metallic stench of blood and the dull groans of those in the throes of death.

He searched among the bodies and located the two wanted men. He gave them a sharp kick, to make sure that they were indeed lifeless, knelt down and drew the cleaver from his waist. He tore open their shirt sleeves and with delicate precision, carved a small, inch long piece of flesh from each man's left arm. He wiped the cleaver clean and returned it to its sheath. Tearing off a small piece of material from one of the men's shirts, he wrapped the flesh neatly and tucked it into his jacket pocket. He grabbed the pair by their collars and dragged them out into the street, where Marshal Andrews had just arrived.

The marshal was furious with Bader for taking such a reckless approach and displaying an almost casual disregard for human life. Bader saw it as collateral, an unfortunate instance of bad luck on the deceased's part. Marshal Andrews managed to calm things down with his superiors, so that only a couple of Bader's men were arrested and jailed to offset the wrongdoing.

The townsfolk were more fearful of Bader from then on. The marshal forbade the WPC from residing in the town. The men were not happy about the ruling, but Bader understood that if he wanted the lucrative arrangement between him and the marshal to carry on, he had no choice but to accept, so accept he did. He decreed that any WPC man who did not comply would be cast out.

"You trying your best doesn't fill me with the greatest confidence, Ed," Marshal Andrews said, finally lifting his head to meet Bader's gaze. "Just keep a leash on those dogs of yours."

"Those dogs are the only thing that keeps you in your job, Ellis," Bader answered flatly as he folded up the warrant and tucked it into his jacket. "You be sure to remember that." He placed his hat on his head and stood up from the chair. "I'll get started in the morning. I have a little something to attend to first." Marshal Andrews offered Bader a somber nod in lieu of a spoken goodbye. Bader sighed, "Ellis, things aren't that bad. Your streets are safe, and you get to take all the credit without lifting a finger."

Humans Are the Ugliest Creatures

"At what cost?" the marshal asked, blankly staring at the edge of his desk.

"A mighty cheap one, by my calculation," Bader replied. "I'll let you know when it's done," he turned and disappeared through the office door, leaving the marshal alone in his morose contemplations.

He rose from his desk and went back to the window, where he watched as Ed Bader returned to his entourage, climbed atop his horse and rode off into the distance. Every time Marshal Andrews watched Bader ride away, he wondered how harshly he would ultimately be judged. When Bader rode off, it was under the marshal's authority, regardless of whether he actually had any control over the outlaw. It was the marshal's decision to allow Bader's chaotic brand of justice to permeate the land he called home, and as he stood and watched Bader's silhouette drown in the waves of shimmering heat, he wondered just how deeply that permeation would run.

2

Stacks, the Bellamys and a New Arrival

Stacks ran the back of his hand across his brow. The beads of sweat, which were gliding gracefully along the contours of his dark, soft skin, had their paths disrupted, their contents dispersed. He closed his eyes and raised his face to the blazing sun. As its brilliant white light and consuming heat poured down on him, he focused on the feeling of warmth as it crept across his skin. He wondered about the hidden mechanisms involved, the cosmic engine which fueled processes that went far beyond his own understanding. As he stood and enjoyed the sensations bestowed by the glowing sun, he felt pride in nature.

"How lucky are we?" he asked, in absolute wonderment and awe. He turned his head and gently patted the neck of the horse standing faithfully at his side. "Luckiest there ever was, as far as I can tell," he said as he ran his hands along the mare's well-groomed chestnut coat, causing it to nicker and shake its head. "Let's get you out of this heat for a while," he told the horse.

He took the reins and walked the animal back to the stable, where he led it into its pen. After checking that the horses' troughs were sufficiently stocked, he closed the gate. Stacks rested his arms on the pen and watched the graceful creature for a while.

He thought more about nature and the creation of all things. He shook his head and grinned as the dumbfounding sense of awe resurfaced. He walked away from the pen and leant his weight against the stable doorframe, where he lit a cigarette. He looked up at the house as the door opened and his employer, Abel Bellamy, emerged carrying two glasses.

Abel's white shirt was marked by dust and dirt. The sleeves were neatly rolled up to the elbows, exposing his olive, sun worn skin. As he got closer, Stacks could see the stubble that hugged Abel's chin. It was not like Abel Bellamy to stray from his usual clean shaven and tidy appearance, but it had been a busy month on the ranch.

"Here you go, Stacks," Abel said, offering him a glass, "Martha made lemonade and you aren't missing out."

"Thank you, Mr Bellamy," Stacks replied graciously, "I wouldn't want to in this heat."

Abel smiled and took a sip. He carefully placed his glass on the floor, removed his spectacles and rubbed the lenses clean with a handkerchief.

"Damn it, I hate these things. You'd think someone could come up with something a little better than this." He put the spectacles back on his head and adjusted the thin wire arms so that they rested comfortably on his ears.

"Some days I think going blind would be a simpler solution than dealing with these things for the next fifteen years."

"Twenty years at least, Mr Bellamy," Stacks joked and offered him a cigarette, to which he politely declined with a smile and a shake of his head.

"You know, Stacks, I don't think Martha could handle another twenty years," he laughed. "I'm not one hundred percent sure I could take another twenty years myself. Maybe if I sit down a lot more I could do it. I could watch the girls get older from the comfort of my porch. Hell, as long as Martha keeps making this lemonade, I'll keep breathing just to drink it." He took a long gulp of the lemonade and closed his eyes.

"There's clouds rolling in off of the hills. As much as I love it out in the heat, I can't wait for a little relief," Stacks announced, pointing to the northern ridge.

The clouds, swollen and bulging, skulked though the sky with all the vigor of a mollusk. Abel looked up at the looming mass, tantalized by the prospect of rain.

"Is everything ready?" he asked, still fixated on the distant clouds.

"Yes, Mr Bellamy. I just got finished," Stacks replied. He lifted his glass and drank the rest of his lemonade. "Delicious, please give Mrs Bellamy my thanks."

"Stacks, how long is it going to be before you call us Abel and Martha?" Abel asked, staring up at the heavens as he adjusted his glasses.

"Quite some time yet I think, Mr Bellamy. One of the most important things to my father was respect and he made sure he ingrained it in me, I guess," Stacks politely explained.

Humans Are the Ugliest Creatures

Johnson Stacks' parents were slaves, granted freedom a decade before the Emancipation Proclamation. Looking to leave their past behind, they set out for the west. Johnson was born within weeks of their arrival and given the name of the man who had purchased his parents freedom. They had a simple existence as money was hard to come by. His father joined the Union army and fought for the freedom of others. When it was over and he returned, Johnson was old enough to find work. He had a drive to provide, not only for himself but also for his parents, who had raised him so well on so little. He took various housekeeping jobs, earning next to nothing, before he met Abel Bellamy, who offered him work on his ranch for board and a fair wage.

He was two months shy of his twenty-first birthday and at six feet tall, he stood a head taller than Abel. He was smart, diligent and took great pride in his personal appearance. He shaved daily, bathed frequently and started every day with a clean shirt.

He and Abel had been struggling to cope with the workload at the Bellamy ranch over the past month and a half. The previous ranch hand had departed unexpectedly, to take care of an ailing relative. Abel's two daughters, Elle and Fiona, had pitched in where possible, but he begrudged the idea of having to rely on them and viewed it as a failure on his part to adequately provide for his family.

"It shouldn't be too long until he arrives," Abel said, glancing at his watch. "The train should have come in a while ago. It's the coaches that aren't always as reliable."

"And when he gets here?" Stacks asked.

"You'll both come inside and eat. Martha has cooked up half a farm's worth of food. She insisted we sit down and welcome him the right way," Abel replied.

"That's too kind, Mr Bellamy," Stacks thanked him courteously.

"Then just a few light duties this afternoon. Show him around the ranch, let him get acquainted with it all," Abel finished. "Maybe with him around, I'll be able to keep Fiona from rolling about in the dirt."

"I imagine that will be harder than you think, Mr Bellamy. Little Miss Fiona ain't exactly like other girls," Stacks laughed.

"That's just my concern," Abel agreed, chuckling and shaking his head. "I don't want this life for her, but she seems hell bent on getting it."

The two men stood together in the cool shade of the stable and talked for a while longer. They spoke more of Fiona, Abel's youngest daughter, her wants in life, and what her mother would often call her unladylike pursuits. Female ranchers were not unheard of, but they were by no means common and many men, if not most, would turn their nose up at the idea.

Time seemed to stand still as they spoke. It was as though the sun had been suspended directly above them for an age. The flow of time and the lazy lumbering of the sun eventually resumed, when Stacks noticed a small black smudge on the horizon. It quivered and quaked in the haze as it made its slow and steady approach along the road.

Abel left Stacks by the stables and returned to the house. He washed his face and changed into a clean shirt, as per Martha's instructions. She was adamant that no one would bring dirt and dust to her table, especially not her husband.

As it finally reached its destination, the stagecoach's ambling advance came to a halt. Abel stood in front of the house, with his family behind him, poised to meet the new arrival. Stacks stepped forward to take the bags from the driver, but to his surprise, he was informed that there were no bags to take.

The door opened and out stepped a boy of no more than eighteen years old. His bright blue eyes seemed to shine in the sunlight as though they were precious stones. They peered out through tanned skin, which told of a lifetime spent under the sun. With a gloved hand he removed the red bandana he wore to combat the dust. The lower half of his face was carpeted with short, dark stubble. Atop his head he wore a coffee colored Stetson, which hid a thick mess of jet-black hair. He stepped forward from the coach with a burlap sack slung over his shoulder and an outstretched hand.

"Good afternoon. Billy Earl," the boy introduced himself.

Stacks clasped the extended hand and shook it firmly.

"Stacks, Johnson Stacks. Pleasure to meet you, Billy," he greeted warmly. "Want me to take your bag?"

"No, that'll be fine, thank you. This the man of the house?" he asked, turning towards Abel and the house.

Stacks nodded his head, placed a hand on Billy's shoulder and walked him along the path to where Abel and his family stood.

"Afternoon, son," Abel welcomed Billy, with a handshake and a pat on the arm. "I'm Abel Bellamy, this is my wife Martha, and my two little angels, Fiona and Elle."

"Billy," he announced himself, once Abel had finished. "Afternoon, Ma'am," he greeted Martha, tipping his hat politely.

"I hope the journey wasn't too tiresome," she replied.

"No Ma'am, it was quite pleasant, thank you," he responded and turned his attention to Abel's daughters. "Afternoon, Miss Fiona."

"Noon," she answered, as if already bored by Billy's arrival.

"Fiona," Martha barked in disapproval and wrapped her knuckles across the girl's shoulder. "Just where are your manners, young lady? You think Mr Earl here has time for your sass?"

"Sorry, Mr Earl. It's nice to meet you," Fiona forced out through gritted teeth.

"Really, it's no problem," Billy laughed and offered Fiona a wink, "and please, call me Billy. No more of that Mr Earl stuff."

She nodded her head and returned a wink.

"Good afternoon, Miss-" he began.

"Elle, it's Elle," she blurted out, interrupting him. "It's nice to meet you, Mr…" she hesitated and stopped herself, "it's really nice to meet you, Billy."

He smiled and tipped his hat, her cheeks flushed red almost instantly. She opened her mouth as if to say something, but no sound came out. She cleared her throat and reverted to a nervous smile. Fiona covered her mouth and laughed to herself, while Martha struggled to remain composed.

"Oh Jesus," Abel muttered to himself and rolled his eyes.

At seventeen, Elle was only four years older than her sister, yet the pair could not have been more dissimilar. Auburn hair flowed down past her shoulders, swaying gently in the breeze. It would shine and gleam ever so softly, when caught in the light. Two kind, round eyes as blue as the sea itself, sat nestled amongst long, delicate lashes, which she batted feverishly in Billy's presence. Her flushed cheeks brought shades of pink to what was usually soft, milky white skin.

She liked to present herself as what she understood to be a proper lady. She would style herself as best she could on the southern belles, whose fashions and lifestyles plagued her dreams. It was Fiona who first played upon Elle's fascination with the belles of the south, by awarding her the nickname Elle Belle.

At times it seemed as if Fiona's purpose in life was to exist in contrast to her sister. She was bold, headstrong and never one to admit defeat.

Her flaxen hair was cropped at her shoulders. Up until a few months ago, it fell almost to her waist. She had voiced her disapproval to her mother, but her complaints fell on deaf ears. Not being one to back down, she took a knife and levelled her hair to what she thought to be a more agreeable length, just above her shoulders, much to her mother's dismay.

She bore her father's olive skin and brown eyes, eyes which brimmed with unspent energy. Her mother and sister tirelessly tried to instill in her a more ladylike demeanor, but Fiona's disinterest was absolute. For her mother, trying to get her to wear a dress was an insurmountable task. Most days she would don a pair of beige trousers and a brown waistcoat, over a white shirt, the sleeves of which she would neatly fold up to the elbow, in the style of her father.

Fiona continued to snigger at her sister as she rung her hands and struggled to find the right words to speak. Elle shot her a deathly stare.

"Billy, I must be hungry," Elle said.

Quickly realizing her error, she gasped and shook her head. Her embarrassment at the situation caused her to blush even further.

"You must be hungry, is what I mean. From the journey, you must be hungry," she corrected herself.

Fiona erupted with laughter, while Martha watched on with a pained expression.

"Well, Miss Elle, I think you're right. As it happens, traveling does stir up quite the appetite in me," Billy replied.

As he spoke, they locked eyes and Elle instantly felt as though the air had been sucked from the atmosphere. Her chest heaved and she felt every hair on her skin stand on end as if she were in the midst of an electrical storm.

"I..." she stopped and cleared her throat, "I-" she hesitated again.

"If you'd like to come inside, Billy, I've prepared plenty enough food for everybody," Martha cut in, in an attempt to save her daughter from further embarrassment.

Fiona was sniggering and snorting, trying to hold back tears of laugher. Elle stood and smiled, unsure of what to do or say to alleviate her awkwardness. She could not understand, she was usually so confident and capable when in conversation but every time she looked into this boy's eyes, her heart launched into her throat and she choked on every word.

"Martha, Elle, I would love to. Thank you," Billy answered appreciatively.

"Your bag?" Elle blurted out abruptly.

Billy raised an eyebrow, unsure if there was more to the question. She met his gaze and felt the bones in her knees turn to liquid.

"I could carry it for you, if you want?" she finished.

"You could try," Fiona quipped snidely.

As Billy's eyes sapped the strength from her, Elle hoped he would turn down the offer.

"I'll be fine, Miss Elle. Perhaps, if a glass of water isn't too much trouble I could-" his request was cut short as Elle butted in.

"Of course, right away. I'm sorry you must be so thirsty. I'll get it right away," she babbled, clumsily brushing past Fiona and her mother, and on toward the house.

"I think we could all do with a glass of water," Abel remarked, his eyebrows aloft with bewilderment at his daughter's behavior.

Billy watched as Elle paced toward the house, fanning herself vigorously with her hands. Despite all of her nervousness and bumbling, Billy was sure that he had never seen anyone quite so beautiful. Fortunately, Billy was much more capable of controlling himself, remaining outwardly calm and collected, while inside his chest, a fire of passion roared so fiercely he feared he might bellow out smoke at any second.

Abel gestured toward the house and began walking alongside his wife. Behind them, Stacks walked beside Billy.

"After we eat, I'll show you around. It's a nice place and the Bellamys are a kind and decent family. You really lucked out with this one," Stacks told Billy and joyfully slapped him on the back.

Humans Are the Ugliest Creatures

Billy looked up at the house and saw Elle's silhouette moving past one of the windows.

"I guess I have," he said in agreement.

Fiona, who had been walking a few feet ahead of the two men and expertly eavesdropping, held back and walked with them.

"Elle Belle will be fine once she remembers where her head is, but it's me you should be concerning yourself with, Mr Billy," Fiona began, pushing her hands in her pockets and puffing out her chest. "The way I see it, you're here to eat up all my work. Me, Poppa and Stacks had a good thing going and my worry is that your presence will be in direct conflict to my goals."

Stacks laughed hoarsely and slapped his knee. Fiona stopped in her tracks, shocked by Stacks' reaction.

"Stacks, if you want to keep your job once I'm in charge around here, you'd better fall in line and start supporting my cause," she growled.

"Yes, Miss Fiona Ma'am, right away Miss Fiona Ma'am," Stacks said mockingly as he offered her a salute.

Fiona narrowed her eyes and shook her head.

"You'd better at least be funnier than this idiot," she told Billy, while pointing at Stacks. "You're already miles out in front after what you did to Elle Belle. Turning her in to a quivering mess like that, it was one of the greatest things I've ever seen," she giggled.

"Why do you call her Elle Belle?" Billy asked.

"On account of she thinks she's real fancy, with all of her airs and her graces," Fiona explained.

Humans Are the Ugliest Creatures

They reached the house and Abel politely held the door open for everyone as they walked inside.

"Fiona, stop bothering Billy," Elle snapped at her sister as they entered.

"I was just telling him about you, undoing some of the character damage you done yourself earlier," she replied. "You remembered how to use your mouth words now?" she continued to mock, speaking to her sister in a slow, monotone voice.

"Girls," Abel chastised the bickering pair.

"It's okay, Mr Bellamy," Billy said smiling, "I had a brother myself. I know how it can be."

"Here, Billy," Elle broke in, "I got you some water."

She held out the glass for him to take. He took hold of the lower end of the glass, but Elle's grip did not loosen.

"Thank you," Billy said, "it's very kind of you."

She let go of the glass and ever so briefly, the tips of her fingers brushed against his. She held her hands behind her back, looked down and smiled uncontrollably. All of this went unnoticed by Abel, who was too busy inspecting the food that his wife had laid out for them.

"Come on in, boys, and take a seat," Abel called out to them.

He pointed to the seats intended for each of them and sat down at the head of the table. Fiona walked in and took the seat next to Billy.

"You keeping an eye on me?" Billy asked her.

"You've already taken my work, you think I'm going to let you take my food too?" she said, eying him with mock suspicion.

Humans Are the Ugliest Creatures

Elle was in the kitchen helping her mother with the cutlery. She was picking up the knives and forks, at the same time as trying to look over her shoulder into the neighboring room.

"Elle, you'll break your neck if you keep twisting it like that," Martha told her.

"Like what?" Elle shrugged, feigning innocence.

"Just relax and get yourself together. Don't upset your father," her mother pleaded.

They carried everything through and finished setting the table. Martha sat next to Abel and Elle took the seat opposite Billy. The family and their two dinner guests ate together.

Billy was subject to question after question. He was asked about his childhood, his family, his interests, his plans for the future and everything else in-between. Questions came at him from everyone, everyone apart from Elle, who sat quietly in her seat and listened intently, not once taking her eyes off Billy. Abel immediately took note of his daughter's infatuation with the new hired hand, but Billy's equally reciprocated attraction was much more subtle and went completely unnoticed.

After they had finished eating, Abel and Stacks took Billy on a tour of the ranch. They showed him where everything was kept and went through the plan for the next few days. Having grown up on a ranch himself, Billy immediately understood what was required of him, and impressed Abel with his knowledge.

The ranch seemed as though it had always been there, blending seamlessly with the surrounding landscape. The Bellamy house reflected the tones and hues of its setting, red brick, clad with clay and old worn wood. The land rose up to the north, where a ridge looked out over the huddled ranch buildings below. Oblivious to the world, the cattle grazed on what little grass the hard soil of the pasture had to offer. The scene was one of total natural beauty.

Stacks took Billy to the small building, which stood in-between the barn and the house. Inside, there was a bed and some space for whatever possessions that he had brought with him. Behind the building, hidden from the view of the house, was a bathtub half buried in the ground, where they could wash.

Abel, tired from a morning's work and an unusually large meal, told Stacks and Billy to tend to the horses and sweep down the barn. Once that was done, the rest of the day was theirs to do with as they pleased. He shook Billy's hand again and made his way back to the house to rest.

As Billy watched his new employer enter the building, something in a top window caught his eye. He squinted, combatting the sun's relentless glare and focused on the window. He noticed something move. He held a hand to his brow to shade his eyes, and she was revealed.

Elle was peering at him from behind a curtain, trying to do so inconspicuously but failing. He held up a hand and waved at her. She dropped the curtain and appeared in full view. She smiled, full of joy, and returned his wave.

Billy suddenly became aware of Abel's outline in a lower window and ceased all movement. He turned his hand in the light and frowned, acting as though the whole time, he was merely inspecting it, looking for something on his skin. Abel's shadow seemed to fade into the darkness of the house as he withdrew from the window.

Billy tipped his hat to Elle, who remained in place, devoted to every moment of his attention. He returned to his new lodgings, where Stacks was relaxing and smoking a cigarette.

"You'd best put a stop to all that," Stacks told him as he walked in. "It'd be best for everyone," he said on a cloud of exhaled smoke.

"I'm sorry?" Billy asked confused.

"You don't need to play coy with me, Billy. I'm the closest thing you got to a friend here," he said as if it were an obvious fact.

Billy leaned against the door frame and removed his hat. He ran his fingers through his hair and thought to himself.

"Why should I stop it?" Billy finally spoke.

"Abel ain't going to let you and Elle be together. It's nothing personal, he just has high ambitions for his daughters, especially Elle, since Fiona seems to have her heart set on a rancher's life," Stacks explained. "I understand how those profound moments of emotion can occur. I've experienced a few myself. But this moment is one you've got to let pass by."

"And what if I can't?" Billy asked defiantly. "What if this pit of burning desire, which I feel in ways I never knew I could, doesn't extinguish? How do I carry on in the presence of that radiant beauty, when it shines brighter than the sun? I don't think I could just ignore it."

"Well," Stacks raised his eyebrows and smiled, "seems this profound moment runs profoundly deep. That bag of yours full of poetry books?"

In the house, Abel climbed the stairs and knocked on the door to Elle and Fiona's room. He turned the handle and entered to find Fiona relaxing on her bed, reading a book. Just as he suspected, Elle was standing by the window, twirling the end of the curtain in her fingers and humming a tune to herself.

"Fiona, may I have a minute with your sister?" Abel asked as he gave her leg a gentle squeeze.

She slapped her book down against her thighs in petulant protest and scowled at her father.

"Please, Fiona," he spoke sternly.

She rolled her eyes and exhaled forcefully, in an over the top and comical fashion. She closed the book, laid it on the bed and hauled herself to her feet as though she were far too weak to bear the burden of her own weight. Once the performance was over and she had made it out of the room, she closed the door and crouched down to listen.

"Elle?" Abel addressed his eldest daughter.

She stopped humming abruptly, in the middle of the melody. She was swimming so deeply in her own thoughts that she had not been aware of her father entering the room.

"I'm sorry, Poppa, I must've been away somewhere else, I didn't hear you come in," she apologized as she turned to face him. "Where'd Fiona go?"

"Who knows? That girl's head is a mystery to me," he smiled, "I don't even try to fathom it anymore, I just let it be. Elle, I need to talk to you. Come take a seat."

"What is it, Poppa?" she asked, going over the last few days in her head, trying to think of what should could have done to earn his disapproval.

"You are getting older now, and as much as I understand it, I don't like it," he began. "You're changing, your mind is changing, and everything is changing all the time." he paused, unsure of where his speech was going. Elle waited patiently, utterly confused by what he had said so far. "I saw that you took an immediate interest in Billy. I'm not sure a blind man would have misread the signals."

Hues of hot pink and red swirled across Elle's cheeks almost as soon as he mentioned Billy. He raised his hands defensively.

"I don't find this conversation particularly enjoyable myself, so let's make sure we only need to have it once. That boy is not for you," he stated plainly, "there are thousands of others out there with more to offer. This one is not the one for you."

"But Poppa, I-" she began but was silenced when he held a finger to his lips and softly shushed her.

"This is not a discussion, Elle. This is a father protecting a daughter. You're not about to throw your life away on hired help. He doesn't even own anything, he only brought with him a small bag, and that's all he has. You are Elle Belle," he explained and held her shoulders, "you deserve so much more than that. If he has any sort of sense, he'll treat you with the required courtesy and nothing more."

Her eyes brimmed with tears and her lip trembled violently as she tried with all of her might not to cry in front of him.

"But I…" she paused, swallowing hard as she choked on the words and averted her gaze, "I love him, I know it. I can feel it in every inch of me like liquid fire. I know it's crazy, Poppa, but it's real, I swear it. I've never felt anything like it in my life," she babbled.

"I have said my peace," he sighed, "maybe your little heart will ache for a time but soon you'll see what folly it all was, and you'll laugh. You will thank me, Elle," he finished adamantly.

She lurched forward, wrapped her arms around her father and wept as hard as she ever had.

"Please, Poppa, please," she begged him, "you don't understand! Please!"

He untangled her arms from around his neck and stood up.

"I'm sorry, Elle, but the answer is no," he told her bluntly.

As he approached the door, Fiona, who was eavesdropping throughout, ran and hid in another room. He opened the door and looked back at Elle, who had buried her face in the bedding and was sobbing freely. He took no pleasure from it, but he remained steadfast in his conviction. She would endure a brief period of heartache but would later reap the rewards of a brighter future, and as far as he was concerned, he was duty bound as a father to deliver it.

As he left and descended the staircase, Fiona emerged from her hiding place and went to comfort her sister. She sat by Elle's side on the bed and lifted her head into her lap. She ran her fingers through her sister's hair and sang a lullaby.

"He doesn't understand," Elle said, blubbing through the tears.

"It's alright, he doesn't need to. I don't know what you're feeling but if it's as real as you say, then what use are Poppa's words anyway?" Fiona told her. "It's the same way you all tell me I can't have certain aspirations. They're mine to have and I'm going to have them. Same goes for you. You are Elle Belle and no one else is in charge of what you feel."

Elle stopped her sobbing and listened to his sister's words. She was surprised to hear her speaking in such a way. She instantly felt terrible for all of the times that she had made fun of Fiona's choices and told her that she was wrong.

"I'm sorry if I have been unkind to you, Fiona," Elle apologized.

"It's alright," Fiona shrugged, "I don't need anybody's approval, I can get there all on my own if I have to. I'm Fiona Bellamy," she puffed out her chest and tried to flex her muscles, "I'm the strongest and the toughest there ever was or ever will be."

The pair of them laughed together. When they fell quiet, Elle seemed to stare blankly at the ceiling.

"It hurts," she said softly, "like a knife plunged so deep it's pierced my very soul."

"Oh, it will be alright, Elle Belle. Together, we'll figure something out," Fiona said optimistically.

Humans Are the Ugliest Creatures

3

The Western Protection Company and Ross Maddocks

Bader closed one eye and rested a steady hand on the horizon. By his approximation, there was around two hours until sundown. He thought the estimation generous, since the sun was already a glowing orange orb, hanging lazily to the west. Bursts of pink and red hued the atmosphere, like the entails of fireworks streaked across the sky. The beauty of it stuck him. Was this what the young marshal had seen, that captivated him so? Just as his mind began to wander and his thoughts puzzled the splendor of the natural world around him, his focus was pulled by something much more immediate, something much uglier.

Dried blood covered the back of his glove. He turned his hand, surveying it in the dying embers of the day. When he balled his hand into a fist, the blood cracked and flaked over the ridge of his knuckles. He blew against the back of his hand and watched the paper-thin flecks float in the warm evening air like confetti.

"Dixon, get over here a minute," Bader commanded.

Lyle Dixon obediently followed his orders and approached him.

"Yes, Boss?" he asked and awaited instruction.

Bader spat on the back of his hand and commenced wiping it back and forth across Lyle's tattered and worn jacket. The WPC recruit stood stoically as the blood was cleaned from the glove and smeared across his clothing in broad brushstrokes of dulled red.

"Don't you hate it when this happens?" Bader said though a wide grin. "You can never quite get it clean enough. Blood seems to stain things to their core." He finished cleaning his glove and patted a flat palm against Lyle's jacket. "This jacket for example, it's ruined now. Take it off."

Lyle untied the yellow WPC sash from his arm and stuffed it into his pocket. He took the bloodied jacket off and held it out to Bader.

"Why are you offering it to me? You think I want that?" he asked incredulously. "Over there, take that jacket, the blue one. It should be clean enough."

Lyle turned to where Bader pointed and spotted the jacket that he was referring to. He walked over to it and tugged at the collar, much to Bader's frustration.

"Jesus Christ, Lyle, watch his head or you'll ruin that one too!" he bellowed.

Lyle flinched at Bader's raised voice and nodded his head timidly.

"Ok, Boss," he said, "sorry, Boss."

"Never mind sorry," Bader dismissed the apology, "just watch the head. You angle it the wrong way and all sorts of blood is going to pour out and soak that jacket."

He watched as Lyle carefully pulled at the jacket and tried to maneuver the dead man's body. The dead man's head bobbed gently where it hung over the edge of the porch. There was a gaping hole in the underside of the skull, which pooled with viscous claret, slowly thickening in the heat.

Lyle quickly turned his head back and forth, repeatedly shifting his focus from the jacket to the head. Each time he tried to adjust the jacket, the head would move slightly, lolling lifelessly and tipping the balance of the ruby liquid, causing him to lose his nerve.

After tentatively tugging from various angles to no avail, he slipped his hands under the shoulders of the jacket and raised his arms, in an attempt to slip the garment from the body. Unfortunately for Lyle, the effort completely backfired. As he raised his arms, the shoulders lifted with him and so too did the head, which flopped forward, drooping like a sunflower at the end of summer. As it did, what can only be described as a deluge of gore poured out from the underside of the deceased's mangled jaw. Shocked by the speed of which it all happened, Lyle pushed the body away, lost his balance and fell backwards into the dirt. The jacket was doubtlessly ruined, along with the gray shirt that Lyle wore.

"Lyle, you dim witted simpleton!" Bader chastised. "Look what you've done. What's wrong with you? Ruining a perfectly good jacket like that, anyone would think you were ungrateful."

The nearby members of the WPC erupted in fits of laughter.

"His skull must about two inches thick I reckon, Boss," Roy Willis chimed in.

Bader immediately shot him a reproachful look, which told him in no uncertain terms that it was not his place to speak.

"Lyle, quit squirming and get up," Bader said calmly.

"I'm sorry, Boss. I tried to get it so that it was easier, but I don't think that I could…" his excuses trailed off into silence as Bader held a palm in the air.

"Roy, take off your shirt and give it to Lyle," Bader instructed, without looking at the man.

"My shirt?" Roy questioned. "But, Boss, why the hell should I have to hand what's mine over to that wretch, just on account of him being-"

"Because that's what I told you to do!" Bader barked. In a show of dominance, he gripped Roy by the neck and proceed to shout merely inches from his face, "Now take off your God damn shirt and hand it over, before I decide to strip you down to nothing, tie you to my horse and make you walk back!" He took a step back and watched on with a feverish intensity in his eyes as Roy reluctantly complied.

"This ain't making no sense," Roy complained as he unbuttoned his shirt. "Ain't me who should have to suffer for another man's stupidity."

"I suffer your stupidity every day. Maybe this will teach you a thing or two about compassion and charity," Bader said plainly as he took the shirt from Roy. He approached Lyle and handed him the garment, "here, put this on. We'll find you another jacket soon enough."

Lyle removed his bloodied shirt and donned Roy's. It almost fit him better than it had Roy. He retrieved the yellow sash from his pocket and tied it around his arm. He struggled with the knot, causing the fabric to fold and crease. Bader brushed Lyle's hands away and straightened out the sash, retying the knot neatly.

"Thanks, Boss," Lyle said gratefully.

"Don't be blind to the lesson at hand," he called out to everyone present. "We are a community and if you are willing to work to the best of your capabilities, then you are valued and shall be treated as such. Hell, if we don't at least try to look after each other, what are we even doing?" he let the question hang in the air and mounted his horse. "Everybody, saddle up. We're out of here in five minutes."

Bader and his WPC returned to their camp as the sun hovered half swallowed by the horizon, and the violet and blue stains of the night sky faded into focus. The camp was located a short ride from Good Rock, just beyond a hill which looked out over the town. It was encircled by trees, nestled in a crater-like feature, where the earth rose on all sides.

Several fires burned and meals were being prepared. Tents were pitched erratically throughout the camp, a colorful jungle of canvas. The horses were hitched at the back of the camp, where there was enough free space for them to graze.

Two small shacks stood in the center of the camp, built from a patchwork of wood, tin and iron. The slightly smaller shack was Bader's prime residence, where he slept and stored supplies, while the larger shack housed his three most trusted men. Those three men were White Price, Frank Kelly and Wilbur Woods. They were the longest serving and longest surviving of the WPC, and the only members of the group who Bader trusted to act without direct supervision.

As soon as they arrived at the camp, Bader disappeared into his shack to rest, while the other men relaxed around the fires and ate. His three generals sat at the center most fire, with several other members, enjoying bowls of stew and chunks of stale bread.

"So how comes your name is White? I ain't heard of that before," asked Clyde Simmons, one of the WPC's newest and youngest recruits.

White Price chuckled to himself and dropped his bread into his bowl. He was a burly, barrel chested man with a rugged, slate gray beard, which he stroked as he spoke.

"See, I was born Wyatt," he paused to pick something from his teeth, "and one time, this sheriff took me in to stand trial and when I told them my name, I guess they heard wrong. Like you said ain't too many people called White, so they tend to remember the name."

"Sure it ain't your momma and poppa was just too dumb to spell Wyatt?" Wilbur Woods speculated gruffly.

Wilbur was the oldest member of the WPC, he wore an eye patch over his left eye, which he lost to a broken glass, years ago in a brawl. His gnarled and scared skin meant that young Clyde found it difficult to look him in his remaining eye, without experiencing a profound sense of unease.

"Shut your mouth about my parents you old invalid," White snapped at Wilbur.

"Maybe he's secretly a savage called White Buffalo or something," Frank Kelly mused, drawing laughter from the surrounding men.

Frank Kelly seemed the most approachable of the three, he was the youngest, the most presentable, and always wore a smile on his face. He had soft green eyes, framed by mutton chops and a moustache, which were groomed with the utmost precision. He was a well-liked member of the WPC, despite the violence and ruthlessness he was famed for.

"Kelly's so funny he ought to have a show in town," White snorted sarcastically.

All the men laughed again, all the men but Roy Willis. With a surly look across his face, he pulled his jacket tight across his bare chest and folded his arms.

"Something wrong, Roy? Little cold tonight ain't it? Maybe you should be wearing some more clothes," Kelly laughed.

"You shut up," he growled. "You should've stepped in and stopped him. It wasn't right what he did, making me give my shirt to that oaf."

Kelly pulled a hatchet from his waist and threw it, burying it into the ground at Roy's feet. He moved so quickly that the axe was already stuck in the ground before anyone had a chance to react.

"Watch that tongue of yours, Roy," Kelly threatened, the reflection of the flames dancing in his eyes, gave him a look of hell fueled fury. "I will not stand for it. I will not," he continued, "if you really have a problem with the boss, you can take it up with him. But I warn you, if I hear you running your mouth off like that again, I'll cut your damn tongue out and toss it in the fire. You understand me?"

Kelly waited but only the soft crackling of the flames filled the air. "Do you understand?" he repeated himself, visibly clenching every muscle in his body.

"Yes," Roy replied, without looking up, "I get it."

With that, he rose from his seat and left the fireside to sulk alone in his tent. The others continued to talk and make fun of one another, the majority of which was good natured, however in a camp of men like such, scuffles were an unavoidable occurrence.

Bader did not emerge from his shack at all that night. Someone dutifully brought him a bowl of food and left it in front of the door. No one saw the door open but in the morning the bowl was empty.

The sun rose up from where it slumbered beyond the horizon and set about purging the cool air, restoring the familiar arid heat which the landscape knew so well. The birds sung their greetings as the first sunrays bathed the trees in golden light.

A short walk away from the camp, Bader knelt at the side of a creek. He splashed water over his face and sat back with his feet resting in the water. The sky was clear, and he could already tell just how punishing the day's heat would be.

He pulled a small folded cloth from his shirt pocket and carefully unraveled it, revealing a small piece of cured meat. He ate it slowly, nibbling at it bit by bit as he sat listening to the sounds of the surrounding scene. He tried to identify the call of each bird as it sung. He listened to the soft and soothing sounds of the flowing creek. Daybreak was his favorite point in the day, when he was rested and could envisage all of the day's potential laid out before him.

Humans Are the Ugliest Creatures

He returned to the camp, where only the most eager of the WPC had risen from their beds. The rousing scent of fresh coffee filled the air, along with the sizzle and pop of eggs as they were cracked onto skillets. Bader strolled through the camp, whistling and casually tossing his hat in the air and catching it. He took a seat by the fire, where Clyde Simmons was pouring a cup of coffee.

"Morning, one coffee, please," he requested politely, "and once that skillet gets going, I'll have two eggs."

Clyde handed over a cup of coffee and Bader thanked him. He held his hand over the skillet and felt that it was hot enough to begin cooking. He picked up an egg and went to crack it but froze as Bader held out a hand, signaling him to stop.

"Crack an egg like that and you'll be picking shell out of your teeth for hours," he told him. He reached across and took the egg from him, "watch closely, there's a reason some people call me The Cook." With one hand he cracked the egg into the skillet and tossed the shell in the fire. He nodded at the iron pan, "you try."

Clyde picked up an egg and cracked it on the skillet, just as Bader had. He tried to split the shell in two with one hand but applied too much pressure and crushed half of the shell in his palm. Bader laughed as the golden yolk split on impact.

"That one's yours," he told him, "try again."

Clyde picked up another egg and made a second attempt, only this time he was more delicate. He could not do it with the speed that Bader had, but he nonetheless managed to do it.

"Good job. You learn fast. It's Clyde isn't it?" Bader asked.

He did in fact know the boy's name. He made a point of knowing all the names of the WPC members.

"Thank you, Boss. Yes, it's Clyde. It's Clyde Simmons," he replied. "It's a nice morning ain't it?"

"It sure is, young man. It will be a warm one today. Make sure to bring some water with you," Bader told him.

"Bring some water, Boss? Sorry but I don't follow," Clyde replied, his confusion plain.

"I'd like you to stick close to me later on today, when we ride out," Bader explained. "It'll be good for you."

"Of course," Clyde accepted the offer and his eyes lit up like fireflies. "Thank you, Boss. I won't let you down."

"I know you won't," Bader smirked. "I think those eggs are about done."

He held out a bowl for Clyde to serve the eggs. Once he had finished eating, he stood up from his seat and took a refill of coffee.

"Thank you for breakfast, Clyde. I'll see you later."

Bader left the fire and walked over to the shack where his generals slept. He held his ear to the door but all he could hear was the unmistakable sound of deep slumber. He opened the door and crept inside.

The three men slept side by side, in folding wooden cots. He stood at the end of the beds and one by one, he kicked the base of each of them. Kelly and Wilbur both shot bolt upright and drew their pistols as though they were mechanical toys, made entirely of gears and springs. They breathed a collective sigh of relief, when they saw that it was Bader standing before them, a mischievous smile creeping over his face.

White did not respond to Bader's first attempt at waking him. When he kicked out again, the bottom leg of the cot buckled, and the bed collapsed. White was left in a heap on the floor, fighting to get out of his blanket, while the others hooted and howled with laughter.

"Well, I've never known someone to be so resilient while awake, yet so damn venerable while asleep," Bader laughed.

"Darn it, Boss. One day you're going to give one of these two a heart attack," Kelly joked, deflecting his own anxiety from the rude awakening.

"Only one of us is trembling," Wilbur mumbled, holding out a steady hand.

"Kelly, Wilbur, I need you with me today. White, you'll stay here and run the camp," Bader informed them.

Wilbur nodded and got to his feet.

"Sure thing, Boss," Kelly confirmed.

"So, you don't even need me?" White asked, exasperated, sitting on the floor still half wrapped in the sheet.

"Not on the job, no," Bader clarified.

"Then what in the hell did you need to break my bed for?" he asked crossly.

"I thought it was funny," Bader replied flatly as he made his way out of the shack. "Wilbur, Kelly, get dressed and eat something," he called back to them over his shoulder. "I need you raring to go before noon. We're taking ten."

Unbalanced and still groggy from sleep, Kelly pulled on his trousers and stumbled through the door after Bader.

"Boy, it's getting warm already," he muttered, placing a hand above his eyes, shielding them from the ruthless glare of the sun breaking through the trees. "You said it's us and ten, Boss?"

Bader nodded his head as he lit a cigar and billowed thick smoke into the air.

"This a big one?" Kelly asked, scratching his head.

"Could be," Bader shrugged and flicked the spent matchstick away. "I'm not taking chances on it. It's a bounty, there's always risk with a bounty. You'll likely be fending for your life, so prepare accordingly."

Bader turned, walked back to his shack, took a seat on a bench and tried to enjoy his morning cigar in the shade.

Thirteen WPC men rode out of the camp at eleven in the morning. The sun had continued its steady ascent into the vast, open, blue sky, which soared so endlessly above. It beat down heavily, warming their backs as they rode toward Good Rock.

The journey was not a long one but they took it at a leisurely pace. Bader sent Wilbur Woods on ahead, with instruction to locate and scout the camp where Ross Maddocks and his gang were supposedly hiding in plain sight. In Bader's mind, he could not decide if Maddocks choosing to stay near the town was decision born out of confidence or idiocy. As the ride went on, he was leaning more and more toward the latter.

The WPC waited patiently for Wilbur to return. They were arranged in two by two formation at the side of the road, allowing enough room for townsfolk to pass by freely. As people rode past, Bader would tip his hat, smile politely and call out greetings. He saw his WPC as doing a service for the people of Good Rock. It was by no means the ideal scenario and sometimes things inevitably did go wrong, but it was a means to an end and overall, he believed that the town was safer with him and his men than without them.

"It's important that people see you, Clyde. It's all about building respect," Bader told the young recruit. The pair were sat atop their horses at the front of the group. "All these men behind us, they see you up here with me, believe that. You are earning respect right now, from men you've never even spoken to, and all without lifting a finger." Bader paused to cough and spat a wad of phlegm into the dirt. "Excuse me," he apologized. "You see, respect is a funny thing. The initial chunk of it is all appearance based. The way you carry yourself, the way you dress, first impressions mean a lot. Then you open your mouth and the words that come out either further the initial respect or diminish it entirely. Finally, it's the actions."

He fell silent, dismounted his horse and stood in the road. A stagecoach slowly trundled toward them and came to a halt where Bader stood. He raised a hand to the driver.

"Good morning," he smiled and gestured toward the sun. "Another lovely day, isn't it?"

The coach driver studied the group nervously and nodded in agreement.

"Sure is nice, Mr Bader," he replied.

"I apologize for the inconvenience, but the road is closed for a short while, you'll need to take another route out of town," Bader informed him.

"Absolutely, Mr Bader," the driver said anxiously, "no problem at all. I wish y'all a good day."

With that, the driver turned the coach around and headed back down the road from where he came. Bader returned to his horse.

"That is the type of respect I'm talking about, Clyde," Bader told him.

"Looks like fear to me," the man behind Clyde sniggered.

"Kelly, if you'd please," Bader said, closing his eyes in frustration.

Kelly, who was sat next to the chuckling man, smiled and threw a punch, connecting forcefully with the man's lower jaw. The power and shock of the strike sent him tumbling from his horse, where he landed in an uncomfortable heap on the floor and groaned. Kelly shook the pain from his hand and laughed, igniting a chorus of laughter from the rest of the WPC behind him.

"Fear and respect run a thin line out here," Bader explained, returning his attention to Clyde. "Due to the nature of the work we do, sometimes that line can be a little hard to see. Have no doubt, these people respect us for the service we provide but they fear being on the wrong side of that service. That's why it works."

Clyde listened intently and nodded his head. He was genuinely grateful that the legendary Ed Bader had taken an interest in him.

It was not long before Wilbur returned from his scouting. He had found the Maddocks camp, situated ten minutes south of the town's edge. By his count there were five men. The camp had a good view of the land on all sides and would be tough to approach unnoticed.

Bader rallied the WPC and they rode out to the Good Rock limits. Just beyond the southern side of the town, there was a small stream surrounded by woodland, it was from this spot that Wilbur had seen the criminal camp. Bader,

Humans Are the Ugliest Creatures

Wilbur and Kelly dismounted and lay low at the edge of the trees, surveying the target.

"Well, you're right about one thing," Bader muttered, "there's no sneaking up on them once we break these trees."

"Boss?" Clyde spoke and the three men looked over their shoulders to where he stood.

Frank Kelly jumped to his feet.

"Just what do you think you're doing? Fall back in line right now, boy!" he shouted at Clyde, his temper quickly dyeing his skin a shade darker.

Clyde flinched at Kelly's anger but bravely stood his ground. Bader angrily pounded a fist against the dirt.

"Rein it in, Kelly, and get back over here," he ordered. He pointed a finger at Clyde, "this had better be good."

"There's a…" he started nervously, shaken by the confrontation. He cleared his throat and composed himself, "There's a train track what runs across the clearing, between here and the camp."

"Go on," Bader encouraged.

"Well, it's closer to them than it is to us. If we wait until the next train comes through, then once we're covered, we head toward the camp as fast as we can. We time it so we break across the tracks just as the train passes and take them by surprise," Clyde finished and stood waiting patiently.

Bader turned to face the camp and assessed the plan.

"It could work," Wilbur grunted.

"I think you're right," Bader said, with a grin spreading slowly across his face. "You think fast, kid. Don't ever lose that," he told Clyde.

The boy's shoulders visibly slacked as relief washed over him.

"Good work, boy," Kelly praised him, wrapping an arm around his shoulders, "real nice."

He turned away from Clyde and snatched a rifle from another WPC man's hands, delivering a swift boot to his shins when he did not immediately release the weapon. He returned to Clyde and presented the gun.

"Here's your reward, kid. You lead the line with us."

Clyde took the gun from Kelly and studied it.

"Glad I could help," he said, wide eyed and full of apprehension.

"You grasp this opportunity with both hands," Bader smirked, from the floor where he lay. He pointed at the rifle in Clyde's hands, "that is what all this is all about."

They lined up in formation at the edge of the woods. They were organized with five at the rear and four in the middle, led by Bader, Wilbur, Kelly and Clyde at the head of the unit. They waited patiently for the next train to come by. Luckily, the WPC did not have to wait for too long. After about an hour, they heard the unmistakable whistle of an approaching steam train.

"This is it, boys!" Bader called out to his men, looking back over his shoulder. "Everybody, on me. When we break past the track, we rain hell down on them!"

The men responded with a rousing cheer. Bader held an arm up in the air, instructing them to hold position. He waited until the train blocked their view of the camp and then charged forward. All of his men immediately followed, charging toward the train in rigid formation. They rode hard to give themselves the best opportunity that they could.

Bader drew his rifle from the holster as he neared the tracks, and all those behind him followed suit.

The last carriage cruised past Bader in a blur as his steed leapt forward and cleared the tracks. He was the first man out into the open and the first man to start shooting. His first shot went awry and alerted the camp of the imminent danger. His second shot ripped through its intended target's neck, filling the surrounding air with a fine crimson mist as the man dropped to the floor.

Kelly and Wilbur, leading others behind them, kept low on their horses and pressed on ahead of Bader, launching a pincer assault on the camp. Kelly bore left, drawing two pistols and laying down heavy fire. Most of his bullets buried into the dirt, but it kept the men in the camp suppressed while the rest of the WPC advanced. Wilbur, who had flanked to the right, was the first to dismount and enter the camp. He immediately took out one of the robbers, with a clean shot to the head.

Clyde pulled up next to Bader and took aim with the rifle. He fired three shots before one connected, catching one of the targets in the leg and sending him spiraling to the ground. Clyde watched as the injured man struggled to his knees, only for Kelly to jump from his horse and bury a hatchet into the back of his skull.

Bader rode forward, casually taking shots at any sign of movement. A hand appeared from within a tent and began firing blindly. Kelly watched as one of the WPC men took a bullet to the shoulder and fell from his horse. He pulled the axe loose from the dead robber's skull and sprinted toward the wildly firing gun. With a powerful swing of his arm, the hatchet took the hand off at the wrist. The man stood up in the tent, screaming and disorientated, trapped in the canvas, until Wilbur silenced him with another headshot.

Humans Are the Ugliest Creatures

Bader made it to the camp just as the sole surviving enemy slipped away the chaos and attempted to escape.

"Hold your fire!" Bader commanded, while he took aim at the fleeing coward.

He watched as the man raced across the arid soil, each step sending a plume of dust and dirt up into the air. Some of the men looked on with confusion and concern as they saw the man escaping. Bader aimed steadily and muttered to himself.

"Oh no you don't," he said, and as he spoke the last word, he pulled back on the trigger, heard the crack of the rifle and watched as the man managed one more step, before crashing face first into the dirt. "Will someone make sure we've got our man. Wilbur, I saw you. You'd better pray you haven't turned his face into a crater."

"I know I didn't," he said indifferently.

"Boss, we got company," Clyde said as he drew his pistol.

"Put your gun away before I put you away!" Kelly growled at Clyde.

Clyde nervously fumbled his gun back into its holster.

"Let the boss handle this. Just be ready," Kelly told him.

Two men on horseback approached the camp, where the WPC had already begun lining up the bodies.

"Just what in the hell is going on?" the older of the men barked as he dismounted. "Who's in charge here?"

"That'd be me," Bader replied, with his hands firmly planted on his hips.

Humans Are the Ugliest Creatures

The second man descended from his horse and stood next to the first. They both held their jackets open to reveal sheriff and deputy badges pinned to their chests.

"Sheriff Turner of East Ridge," the sheriff announced with pride, "and this here's my deputy."

Bader leaned back and raised his eyebrows in mock awe.

"My goodness, I must be blessed," he gasped.

"You are responsible for this bloodbath?" the sheriff asked.

"You've got it mixed up, Sheriff, this is a morning's hard work," Bader joked.

He pulled the bounty papers from his pocket and handed them to the sheriff. He snatched them from Bader's hand and glanced over them.

"Do you know how much work I put in to tracking and plotting to take these boys? We had a plan! And we was about to execute that plan, before you rode in, all guns blazing, and slaughtered them all!" the sheriff raged.

He held the bounty papers in both hands and tore them to pieces, cursing Bader and his men. He scattered the now worthless documents to the wind. Bader sighed and squinted against the sunlight, as he watched the little squares of paper rise and fall on the air, until they all settled down gently in the dirt.

"Drop your weapons. You're under arrest," the sheriff announced as he and his deputy drew their pistols and trained them on Bader.

Almost instantly, the two men found themselves the subjects of twelve gun barrels as the WPC men fanned out and circled them.

"I really wish you hadn't done that," Bader said, shaking his head.

He lifted his guns and the cleaver from his belt, placed them on the ground and slowly raised his arms in surrender.

"That's a good start, now tell your men to lower their weapons," ordered the sheriff, adrenaline coursing through every vein in his body.

Bader remained silent, while twelve guns stayed trained on the lawmen.

"They aren't lowering their weapons," Bader said and moved his finger in a circular motion, "this is my insurance policy. It ensures you won't pull that trigger." Bader took a step forward.

"You have orchestrated a slaughter out here and you will stand trial. I don't want to shoot you," Sheriff Turner explained.

Bader locked eyes with the lawman and took another step, testing the sheriff's resolve.

"Then lower your weapon," he reasoned and moved forward again, so that the barrel of the sheriff's gun was less than an inch from the WPC leader's sternum.

Beads of sweat raced along the sheriff's cheeks as the tension rapidly mounted. He could feel the blood in his neck, thick and hot as it churned through tightened veins. The cavity in his chest seemed smaller, less able to accommodate his breath. It required more physical effort to steady the muscles, which wanted so badly to shake and tremble, than it did to hold the pistol at arm's length.

"It would be ideal if we could resolve this without any more bloodshed," the sheriff proposed as he lost his nerve and began to lower his weapon.

Humans Are the Ugliest Creatures

As soon as he started to lower his arm, Bader made his move. He surged forward, taking the sheriff by surprise. In one fluid movement, he drove a knee into the sheriff's ample gut and pulled a knife from the boot of his raised leg. He forced the blade up through the soft underside of the sheriff's jaw and into his skull.

There was no resistance offered from Sheriff Tanner. The lawman staggered and gargled as Bader pulled him close, using his body for cover. The deputy took one shot at Bader, which buried into the sheriff's back. The single shot served as a catalyst for the surrounding twelve weapons, which inevitably all opened fire on the deputy. He died instantly, the flesh of his torso pulped. Bader held his hand up, ordering the men to cease fire. He laid the sheriff's body on the floor and pulled his knife loose.

"No more bloodshed is always ideal," he addressed the dead man as he wiped the blade clean on his jacket, "but it's just not always realistic."

He tucked the blade back into his boot and retrieved his guns and cleaver. The cleaver gleamed and sparkled in the noon sun as he turned it. He knelt down next to the body and tore the sheriff's sleeve up to his elbow. He took the cleaver and very carefully cut into the arm, removing an inch-long piece of flesh. He wrapped it in a cloth and placed it in his pocket. Sighing, he patted the dead man's chest. He stood up and whistled, getting the attention of the WPC men.

"Wilbur, take the men back to camp. Kelly, you stick with me. We'll have to straighten this out with the marshal. Clyde, I want you to stop by the marshal's office and tell him to get out here."

Wilbur nodded and rode away, with the rest of the men following behind him. Bader and Kelly dragged the bodies and lined them up together, keeping both Maddocks' and Sheriff Tanner's bodies separate.

The pair rested in a small patch of shade, under a withered and dying tree. Clyde followed his orders obediently and before long, Marshal Andrews could be seen emerging from the woodland beyond the train tracks. He rode slowly and cautiously as he advanced on the camp, which frustrated Bader as he had by now grown tired of the heat. When the marshal eventually arrived, he climbed down from his horse and approached the two men.

"Afternoon, gentlemen," he greeted, in his usual somber tone. "This is not the normal procedure. It's been troubling me on the ride over."

"Death is the usual procedure of life," Bader quipped.

The marshal ignored the comment and looked across to the bodies, which had been neatly lined up.

"We got into some trouble, Ellis," Bader started. "We're going to need your help."

"Trouble?" the marshal scoffed as he made his way to where the bodies lay. He studied them briefly and raised a hand to his face. "That's East Ridge's sheriff," he spoke from behind his hand as it begun to tremble.

"Was East Ridge's sheriff," Kelly corrected him, with apparent disinterest.

"Do you think this is a game?" the marshal snapped and stormed over to where Kelly stood. "A man risks everything to protect the people of this land and you gun him down."

"Ease up, Ellis," Bader said, placing a hand on the marshal's shoulder. "Kelly, shut your mouth and take a walk."

Kelly stepped back and returned to his spot under the tree. The marshal wore a look of fury as he stood with Bader.

"Listen, Ellis, it wasn't meant to be like this. I tried to pacify the man, but he wouldn't have it. He was downright unreasonable. He even tore up the bounty papers. I can still claim it, right? That is Ross Maddocks laying right there."

"Ed," Marshal Andrews sighed in utter exasperation, "there's no way around this. The massacre at the saloon was enough, but this," he paused and shook his head in disbelief, "this is something entirely different."

"Now hold on, Ellis, what happened here and what happened there were-" Bader began but was cut off.

"You've killed a town sheriff, Ed. What am I supposed to do?" he asked. "I should never have turned you loose out here again, I've been too complacent. I might as well have just pulled the trigger myself," he muttered grimly and stared down at the ground. "I won't lie for you, Ed," he said looking back up, "a man has to draw a line somewhere, he has to!"

"A man can also get his tongue cut out," Kelly offered a passing threat.

Bader spun and moved toward Kelly, gripped him by his collar and lifted him to his feet.

"Get out of my sight and pray that I don't shoot you in the back as you ride away," he growled through gritted teeth.

Kelly shook himself free of Bader's hold and did as he was told, wearing a petulant scowl across his face. Bader returned to the marshal and placed an arm around his shoulder.

"Ellis, as miserable as you are, I enjoy your company and you've granted me lucrative opportunities, which I'm grateful for. I wouldn't ask you to lie for me, but I'm sure there's some way we can straighten all this out."

"It's over, Ed," the marshal said plainly as he shrugged Bader's arm away. "There's no burying this. Bounties will be issued in the morning for you and your men. I'm sorry but my hands are tied. I'd advise that you flee the state, flee the county at the very least."

"You know me better than that, Ellis," Bader smiled.

"Then more bloodshed, to end more bloodshed," the marshal muttered gravely.

Bader, realizing that Marshal Andrews was not to be swayed, sighed and accepted his position. He looked off at the horizon and shook his head in disappointment.

"Well then, Ellis, I guess this is the conclusion of our dealings. I'll send someone by for the Maddocks reward later. I trust you'll honor it," Bader said, climbing up onto his horse. Marshal Andrews offered a disinterested shrug, "see, I knew you would," Bader finished happily. "See you around, Ellis," he called over his shoulder as he turned his horse and set off to reconvene with the rest of the WPC.

In the heat of the midday sun the marshal stood alone. Surrounded by death, he scuffed at the blood-soaked soil and hung his head in shame.

4

Billy, Fiona, Sheriff Manning and a Bounty

Billy and Elle lay by the fire, naked but for one another's embrace. It was the third night running that Elle, with the aid of her cunning sister, had snuck out from the Bellamy house to meet with her love. The air was cool but not cold. They lay together, enjoying the heat of their bodies against each other's skin, as much as that of the flames. They laughed as they tried to count the fireflies dancing above the grass. They planned their future together, detailing what each aspect would look like and how they would make it work. The happiest moments of their days were when they met, and the worst were when they parted.

"Isn't it wonderful," Elle reflected, looking up at the sky.

"Isn't what?" Billy asked.

"That you could've gone to any ranch, in any place but you came here," she laughed and shook her head in astonishment, "every time I think about it, I just know how lucky I am."

They lay in silence as they thought about their fortuitous meeting. It was as though they had always been linked by some invisible force, each one a missing part of the other, gently tugged and guided through time and space, until they finally made one another whole again.

"This isn't enough for me," Billy admitted, while he twirled Elle's hair around his finger. "I need to be with you more, all this sneaking around won't do. Do you think Mr Bellamy would ever-" Elle cut in before he got a chance to ask the question.

"Poppa won't allow it. Believe me, I've tried to convince him but he won't budge on this one. I know he thinks he's doing what's best but he's breaking me in two," she lamented.

"What if we were to go?" Billy suggested.

"Just leave everyone?" she mused apprehensively, "I don't know, Billy. I don't know if I could."

"It might be the only way."

"Even if it was, what would we do? How would we survive without any money?" she asked. "I'm not trying to poke holes in the idea, but we got to consider these things. It wouldn't be that easy."

"I know, Elle Belle, I know. Those are the parts I ain't quite worked out yet, but I will, don't you worry, I will," he smiled at her reassuringly. "Then we can be together whenever we want. Hell, maybe even under a roof!" he said and leaned down to kiss her.

They stayed together by the fire for a few more hours. The time came for them to part ways as the night sky prepared to give way to the green hues of dusk and the birth of a new day.

When the next day arrived, Elle was tired. After three days with very little sleep, despite her sister's best efforts, she was struggling to conceal the effects from her parents. She told them that she was fine, but they were convinced that she had come down with a possible illness. They confined her to her room and prescribed plenty of rest.

No matter how weary she was, she still made it to her window to watch over and admire the man she loved so dearly. She waved to Billy and blew a kiss. He returned her wave and smiled, while Fiona watched on and grimaced. When Elle faded back into the room in search of rest, Billy took a seat on a nearby tree stump and lit a cigarette.

"Part of me wishes you two would run away now," Fiona said as she approached Billy. "At least then I wouldn't be forced to watch this." Billy looked around, concerned that someone might overhear. "Don't strain your neck, there's only us," Fiona told him tiredly.

"How'd you know about that?" Billy asked her.

"Elle Belle told me," she explained, "but don't worry, I ain't going to tell nobody. I just want to help. She's always been dramatic but what she's going thorough now is something else, and I know if it were me acting that crazy, I'd want her help."

"Thank you, Miss Fiona, I-" he started to thank her, but he was interrupted.

"Quit calling me Miss Fiona, Jesus! You still call her Miss Elle when you're lying with her?" Fiona spoke over him.

Humans Are the Ugliest Creatures

"No," he replied, a little shocked by what he was hearing.

"Well, quit it with the Miss stuff. It's just Fiona, okay?" she finished.

"Yeah, sure that's fine by me," he laughed, still thrown by her boldness. "So, you want to help, did you have any ideas?"

"Nope, not yet but we got some time to come up with one. Poppa wants you to go to town, to pick up some groceries and he wants me to ride along with you. He said he was tired of my yammering and that you, being a quiet man, could do with the company," she clarified.

"How thoughtful of him," Billy muttered, "you ready to go?"

Instead of answering him, she turned and ran into the house. She reemerged a minute later and placed a wide brimmed hat on her head.

"Now I am," she announced.

Billy stood up and took the hat from her, turning it in his hands as he examined it.

"This yours?"

"It was my poppa's, from when he was about my age," she told him, squinting in the harsh sunlight. He returned it to her, and she promptly put it back on her head. "It's mine now though, and I look better wearing it than he ever did, I assure you that."

"I can believe it," he laughed, "let's get going."

The pair saddled up and rode side by side toward Good Rock. They took the longer scenic road though the woodland and followed the creek. They spoke about the adoration that Billy and Elle had for one another, until Fiona mocked him and made retching sounds. Then they discussed Fiona's future and how she was adamant that she would be leaving her family home to look for work.

"Just like you, Billy. I'll leave home carrying nothing but a small bag on my back," she told him as they rode alongside the creek.

"Is that right?" he humored her.

"You bet it is. Maybe I'll get myself a job for a nice family, just like you did, and I'll fall in love with somebody and they'll wave at me from the window," she carried on.

"A strong boy ain't likely to be hiding away by the curtains, blowing you kisses," Billy joked.

"Well, handsome boy, pretty girl, it don't matter much to me. So long as we're in love," she replied plainly.

"You think…" he paused, thrown once more by how forthcoming and sure she was for a young girl, "you think Mr Bellamy would be alright with that?"

"That's exactly the reason I'll be away. Then he can't tell me how to dress, how to speak, how to think. He ain't in my head, living my life. I got to make my own choices. I know he means well and wants what's best for us but all he's going to do is drive us away," she explained.

"Yeah, your sister said something similar," Billy said, lifting his hat and scratching his head. "It's a shame though, Mr Bellamy seems like a nice man."

"He's blind to it. Some days I think Momma sees what's happening, but then other days she's just as bad," she trailed off. Before Billy could formulate a response, she stood up in her saddle, "let's pick up the pace a little. Last one to get there has to carry everything back!" she shouted as she kicked her heels and sped forward.

They raced along the road toward the town. Fiona led the way for most of the remaining distance. Billy managed to pull up alongside her but at the last moment, she surged forward and was the first to pass the town's initial buildings. She stood up in the saddle, cheered for herself and made fun of Billy for coming second. She leaned down, hugged her champion horse and whispered her thanks in its ear.

"You ride well for a young girl," Billy commented.

"For a young girl?" she echoed, questioning his phrasing.

"You ride well, Fiona," Billy corrected himself, rolling his eyes.

"Well, maybe when we get back you tell Poppa that, and maybe next time he'll let me go out riding," she said.

"Wait," Billy held up a hand, "he doesn't know you're out here?"

She shrugged indifferently and marched her horse on down the road.

"Fiona?" Billy called after her.

"I asked to go, he told me no, so I said I was going for a walk," she told him as she turned in the saddle, "now let's move on please, I don't want to talk about him anymore."

Billy shook his head in disbelief but decided that there would be time enough to deal with her dishonesty later. For now, he would be better off to just to get the groceries and go.

Humans Are the Ugliest Creatures

The sun was already two thirds of the way to high noon. Fiona thought that she could feel her skin pulse as the blazing orb poured heat down on her. She pulled at her collar, inviting in the cool air. She watched Billy and wondered how it was that he seemed so unfazed by the heat. She knew she had to toughen up. She would never be respected as a rancher if she was unable to handle a little bit of sunshine. Through narrowed eyes, she looked up to where the sun hung so placidly and let it know, in no uncertain terms, that she was not one to back down.

"What are you doing?" Billy interrupted her. "Let's get this started. Where's the store?"

Still squinting, she slowly turned to face him and raised an eyebrow. She tilted her head to the side and studied him.

"Never mind," she sighed, drawing it out. "Follow me," and with that, she trotted her horse on down the street.

Main Street was the busiest street in town. A boardwalk ran the length of the street on either side, providing access to the town's many stores and businesses. At the time of their visit, the main thoroughfare was dry and dusty, but after a prolonged spell of rain, it was near impossible to ride through from one end to another and come out clean.

The town was a hive of activity, the air rich with the sounds of a busy community. In the middle of the street, the town hall loomed large over the other buildings, rivaled only by its opposite structure, the Good Rock Grand.

The Good Rock Grand was the more eye catching of the two buildings, its soft pastel pink colors made it stand out from its drab neighbors. Ornate pillars, adorned with carved flowers, held up a wide balcony that looked out over the bustling street.

The town hall had recently been painted after a public consultation, but the intended pale-yellow color was not delivered, so they had to make do with a dull olive green. If you were to ask around the town, most of Good Rock's residents would have told you that they much preferred it the way that it used to be.

As the pair passed the town hall, Billy noticed a tired looking man with a sullen expression and furrowed brow, standing at one of the windows. Fiona caught him staring and followed his gaze up to the window.

"That's Marshal Andrews," she informed him. "Poppa says he lives under a cloud and that he ain't too much fun to converse with."

Billy raised his eyebrows in response but did not reply.

"The store is over there," she pointed, "just past the Grand. The Grand is where all the fancy people stay when they come to town. Elle Belle used to try and stand around outside, pretending she was one of them," she giggled and Billy laughed with her.

They passed the hotel and hitched their horses in front of the grocery store.

"Since you were dishonest in needing to come out here, you can be the one to go inside," Billy said and handed her some money. "Pick up something for your sister to make her feel better, some tobacco for me and Stacks, some liquor for your poppa, and then you grab whatever you want. We'll get some flowers for your momma too, before we leave," he finished.

She took the money from him and skipped into the store.

"And make it quick. I don't want to be here all day," he called after her.

Humans Are the Ugliest Creatures

He remained outside, leaned against the wall and lit a cigarette. A small gathering of townspeople on the other side of the street pricked his interest. A man walked out in front of the crowd. He stood taller than most, dressed in a dark gray suit. Pinned to his lapel was a sheriff's badge, gleaming in the sunlight. His bald head was hidden under an open crown hat. The bristles lightly dusting the lower portion of his face were a mottled brown and gray. He raised an arm to the crowd and in his hand, he held a poster.

Billy stepped down into the dusty road and approached the gathering. They watched as the sheriff took a hammer and nailed the poster to the wall.

"Some of y'all know who this is," he declared, turning to face the crowd. "For those of y'all who ain't so savvy, this here is Ed 'The Cook' Bader."

Billy peered over the woman in front of him and got a glimpse of the poster. There was a depiction of the man drawn in the center, and it read:

"Urgent notice, $1000 Reward! $1000 reward to any person or persons, who capture Ed Bader, alias The Cook. Wanted for the murder of Sheriff Tuner and Deputy. Deliver dead or alive to the nearest US Marshal's office. Satisfactory proofs of identity will be required."

"I also have here in my hand, notices for four-hundred dollar rewards for Ed Bader's WPC generals, White Price, Frank Kelly and Wilbur woods," the sheriff boomed. "There is also a further twenty-five dollar reward, for each identifiable WPC member brought in. Don't go getting any ideas, we know who these men are, so sticking a yellow sash on someone's arm and bringing them in will only land you in jail." He proceeded to nail the other posters to the wall, one by one. "Y'all have a good day and keep it peaceful," he said as he turned and retreated back into the shade of his office.

As the crowd slowly began to disperse, Billy made his way to the front and stepped up onto the boardwalk, to take a closer look at the posters.

"Typical of that so-called sheriff to offer out his dirty work," he heard a woman say from behind him.

"Wait, you actually expected him to do anything about this?" a man replied incredulously. "Shame it wasn't him that was gunned down instead of that East Ridge sheriff."

Billy studied the illustrations on the posters, trying to imagine what the men were like and how he would measure up to them. He was pulled from his contemplation when he heard someone calling his name. He turned and saw Fiona standing behind him, struggling to hold two paper bags full of purchases.

"Billy, you want to stop daydreaming and help me with these?" she said, trying to hold a bag out to him. "You did lose the race after all."

He took a bag from her and she breathed a sigh of relief. She tilted her head and examined the posters behind him.

"This what you were looking at?" she asked, staring at the posters.

"The sheriff just came out and tacked them up," Billy said. "You heard of any of these men?"

"Sheriff Manning came outside?" she asked, her mouth agape and eyes wide with wonder.

Billy shrugged and nodded, baffled by her reaction.

"He doesn't tend to come out much is all," she laughed. "I don't really know these men. Poppa doesn't talk about those things much and if he does it's only with Momma and Stacks. I know who the WPC are though. They're the men with the yellow sashes on their arms. Poppa said they're above the law."

"Well, it doesn't look that way anymore," Billy muttered. "Wait here, stay put" he said, turning to face Fiona.

"Wait here and stay put?" she snorted, making her disbelief at his audacity plain, "I don't think so. I'm coming with you."

"Fine, come on then," he conceded, knowing full well that arguing with her was not an option.

They walked together along the boardwalk and entered the sheriff's office. Sheriff Manning was sitting at his desk, sipping tentatively from a steaming cup of coffee and looking over some papers. Billy stood in the doorway and patiently waited for him to notice their presence. Fiona, who was not nearly quite as enduring, stamped her foot on the floor. The sheriff looked up at them startled, and smiled with relief when he perceived no threat. He stood up from his seat and gestured at the two chairs in front of his desk.

"Good morning," he greeted. "It is still morning, isn't it?" he asked, suddenly unsure of himself.

"It was morning last time I checked," Billy said, looking toward the window.

"Well, welcome nonetheless," he smiled. "You, I know. You're one of those Bellamy kids. But you, I'm not sure I recognize," he finished, holding a hand out to Billy.

"The name's Billy Earl, Sheriff. Pleased to meet you," Billy introduced himself and shook the sheriff's hand.

"Sheriff Jon Manning," he announced proudly.

"Manning the coward," Fiona said under her breath.

"What was that, little girl?" Sheriff Manning snapped.

"Little girl?" she protested loudly, getting to her feet.

"Fiona, that's enough," Billy told her reproachfully.

She dropped down noisily as she returned to her seat and folded her arms. She glared at the sheriff, who readily returned her scowl.

"What was it you folks came in here for?" Sheriff Manning finally asked.

"Information," Billy said simply.

"You'd like some information, or you got some to give?" the sheriff probed.

"I'd like some," Billy clarified, "specifically about the nature of those men on the posters you just nailed up."

The sheriff pursed his lips and instantly looked uncomfortable.

"Hey, Young," the sheriff called over his shoulder. "Young, get out here and fetch me another coffee."

A young Asian man appeared from the back of the building and took Sheriff Manning's cup.

"This is Young, my deputy," he introduced the man.

"Yeun," the deputy quietly corrected him.

"Yeah, Young," he repeated, shaking his head in confusion. When Deputy Yeun left with the sheriff's cup, the sheriff leaned in and whispered, "He's Chinese. He doesn't make a whole lot of sense, but you toss a coin in the air and he'll shoot it from twenty feet away."

Billy smiled politely and waited for the sheriff to return to the matter at hand. After a few moments of awkward silence, the sheriff realized that he had allowed himself to get distracted.

"I apologize," he started, "things get away from me sometimes. Now, those men you want to know about, Bader and his merry band of marauding mercenaries. All you need to know about them is that they are danger. Truly treacherous, more devils than men really. Bader leads the gang through violence and terror. His generals perform a similar role. They say even death is afraid to take Wilbur Woods. I heard he claimed over a hundred men in the war. White Price is a giant of a man, with the strength of a thousand, but none too bright. Frank Kelly is unhinged to say the least. Rumor has it, he engages in amorous friendships with some of the other men, sort of like they did in ancient Greece," he paused and looked at Billy, suddenly excited, "you like ancient Greece? I got a book around here somewhere, I think I left it in the back-" he started to get to his feet, when Yeun returned with the coffee.

"Sheriff, I'm not so concerned with Greece right now, maybe another time," Billy interrupted him.

Sheriff Manning shrugged off Billy's disinterest and smiled. He took the coffee from Yeun and returned to his chair.

"These men," Billy continued, "they are just men and all men, as far as I'm aware, share the same mortal weaknesses. How long would it take to pay out those bounties?"

"A matter of days, four or five maybe" the sheriff replied, "but son, you're missing the point. These aren't just men. These are the worst of men."

"All men bleed, all men die," Yeun said simply, in a heavy accent.

"That's enough out of you, Young," the sheriff barked.

"Yeun," the deputy corrected again.

"Damn it, I know your name," he growled in frustration, waving a hand and silencing him. He turned back to Billy and straightened his jacket, "Looking at you, I don't think I'm going to be changing your mind none, but believe me when I tell you that walking away from this while you're still breathing, is the real reward. You go up against Bader and he will cut you down, I guarantee it."

"You know that from personal experience?" Fiona questioned.

"You really ought to keep that little girl in check," Sheriff Manning warned Billy.

Fiona shot up from her chair and laughed at the sheriff dismissively. Unable to spend another moment in the company of the sheriff, she strode across the room and left to wait outside.

"No manners that child," he muttered as he uncorked a bottle of whiskey and topped up his coffee. "Look, Burt-"

"It's Billy," Billy interrupted.

"Right, right, of course it is," he mumbled irritably, "this is not a playground. It ain't like it is in the picture books. People get hurt, people die, and lives get ruined. You seem like a smart enough kid, you've probably got options, only thing this road leads to is death."

Billy leaned back in his chair and scratched his head.

"I thank you for the concern but with all due respect, you don't know much about me, Sheriff. I consider myself to be a fortunate and downright competent man," Billy said proudly as he stood up and made his way to the door, "I got drive and love's true purpose in my heart."

"Okay, sure sounds nice," Sheriff Manning yawned, "we'll see if any of that matters when you're lying in the dirt, with a great big hole in your chest and your lungs are slowly filling up with blood."

He waved his dismissal, having completely lost interest in the young man. Billy turned and left the office to find Fiona.

"Some people can't be helped, Young," the sheriff addressed his deputy, who remained impassive. "Some people seem to be just yearning for death."

Billy found Fiona outside the sheriff's office, studying the reward posters. She was standing with her hands planted firmly on her hips, her fingers shaped like guns. She squinted at the posters and pretended to draw and shoot at each one. She turned to face Billy and tipped her hat back.

"I think you can do this, they don't seem so tough in the pictures," she observed. "The sheriff's a coward, I wouldn't listen too much to him. I've never heard of him confronting anyone. Poppa said he got hurt bad one time and he hasn't been the same since."

"Why doesn't he step down?" Billy asked.

"He'd be humiliated even more than he already has been, I suppose. Plus, I don't think they've got anyone else to step up. Heroics are in short supply here," she shrugged. "So, you think you're going to do this?"

"It's a lot of money, Fiona," Billy told her, "enough for me and your sister to go wherever we want. We could get married and have a life together. Hell, maybe one day, when you can spare a few days away from your ranch, you could even come visit," he laughed. "I'll talk to Elle Belle about it and see what she thinks."

"Big, brave, strong man going out to fight for her in the name of love," Fiona sung, clasping her hands together and twirling, mocking her sister. "I'm sure she will love that," she said, rolling her eyes.

"Promise me you won't speak about this to anyone else, okay?" Billy insisted, placing a hand on her shoulder.

"I swear everyone thinks I'm simple," she replied and pushed his hand away, "of course I won't say nothing."

"Well, let's head on home then," Billy smiled and patted her on the back. "And you can be the one to explain to your poppa, how it is you ended up out here," he added.

She flounced and scowled as he said it but eventually agreed. They made their way back across the street to the horses. Billy sent Fiona into another store to buy some flowers for her mother. When she returned, they unhitched their horses and rode on out of town.

By the time they made it back to the Bellamy house, it had just gone noon. Abel was sitting on the porch, enjoying the sunshine and sipping a glass of water. Stacks was nearby, lying on a small patch of grass, smoking a cigarette.

Billy and Fiona pulled up and took the horses to the stable. When they approached the house, Fiona began to explain where she had been. Abel stood and held up a commanding palm, instructing her to stop.

"Fiona, I don't want to hear it," he said in a tired voice, "go inside, your momma will deal with you."

Fiona hung her head and obeyed her father. Glumly, she entered the house and disappeared from sight.

Humans Are the Ugliest Creatures

"Mr Bellamy, I-" Billy began, before being silenced by the same authoritative hand.

"Not another word, Billy," Abel started. "I don't for one second think you'd have taken her off if you knew I was against it. I know how she is, she has a persuasive nature and a tendency to muddy the truth," he smiled.

"Miss Fiona picked these out. There's flowers for Mrs Bellamy, some fruit for Miss Elle, a bottle of bourbon for you, and I think some candies in the bottom, she picked those out for herself," Billy explained as he presented Abel with the grocery bags.

"You paid for these out of your own money?" Abel asked, surprised. "This is very generous, Billy. I'll see that your reimbursed for at least half, on account of little Fiona's imaginative interpretation of the truth. I'll make sure the candies get to her but only after I leave her to sulk for a while. Thank you for taking care of her."

"I think it was more a case of her looking after me," Billy laughed, "she's an impressive rider, Mr Bellamy."

"You really think so?" he probed suspiciously.

"Near enough better than me," Billy confirmed.

Abel scratched his chin and pondered over it for a few moments, while staring absently into the distance.

"Glass of water?" he offered.

"No, I'm fine, thank you," Billy replied.

"I suppose we've been stood around long enough. The work won't get itself done," he said chirpily.

Inside the house, Fiona had been confined to her room. She sat down heavily, which caused her sister to stir from her slumber. Elle sat up in her bed, with her head full of the haziness of sleep. She rubbed her eyes and greeted her sister with a halfhearted wave. It looked as though it took all of her might just to lift her hand. She ran her fingers through her hair, which was matted and knotted from sleep. Yawning, she got up and joined her sister, picking up a hairbrush along the way. Fiona watched irritably as Elle tried to brush her hair, using the absolute minimal amount of effort possible. Eventually she grew tired of it and snatched the brush from her hand.

"Give it here," she snapped, "I never seen anything so pathetic." She held the small wooden brush and began to tease the knots from her sister's hair. "Keep still. Surely you got the strength to hold your head up at least."

"There's dirt on your britches," Elle said mid yawn, "what have you been doing?"

"Billy took me into town," Fiona smirked.

Elle spun around to face her sister, her eyes suddenly wide and alert.

"What? What do you mean? Why? Where did you go? What did he say? Did he speak about me? Why did he take you and not me?" she fired question after question as though they were uncontrollably falling from her lips.

Fiona put her hands on Elle's shoulders and firmly turned her away, so that she could continue brushing her hair.

"I lied and told him Poppa asked him to take me to town," she confessed. "That's why I'm up here now, I'm not allowed back down. I brought you back some fruit but I think Momma has it downstairs."

"But did he talk about me," Elle snapped.

Fiona responded by tugging hard against a knot, causing Elle to stiffen with pain.

"I'm sorry. Thank you for thinking of me," she apologized.

"Just watch it, Elle Belle," Fiona warned. "I'm sure he said something about you at some point," Fiona toyed with her sister. "If only I could remember what it was."

"Fiona, please tell me," she begged.

"Alright, lighten up. Of course, he spoke about you. He damn near wouldn't stop, I thought I was going to vomit," she laughed and earned herself a cold glare from her sister. "He said how there was fire in him or something, only it moved like a river and it was all because of love, I think? He was carrying on like a poet, I was just watching the birds overhead. I knew all I needed to know by that point, so I stopped listening. He loves you, Elle Belle. There's no doubting it. I don't know why exactly," she teased, "but he sure does."

Elle turned and hugged her sister tightly.

"Thank you, Fiona," she said as her eyes moistened, "I hope one day you meet someone who makes you feel this way. It's as though my bones are melting inside, every time I think of him."

"Sounds awful painful to me," Fiona shrugged and they both laughed.

That night, Elle met with Billy again in secret. The sky was clear and the moon shone brightly, illuminating their path. The trees and cacti, which lined the trail, were dark and silhouetted against the glittering stars of the night sky. Elle shivered as the cool breeze struck her skin. Billy chivalrously removed his jacket and draped it over Elle's shoulders. He put his arm around her and pulled her in closer as they walked. Instant warmth and a profound sense of safety washed over her.

They stopped by an old tree and rested against its trunk. As Billy took her hand, she felt a lightning bolt shoot through her arm and jolt her heart. She wondered if there would ever be a time when she would be able to look him in the eye and not blush. She hoped there never would be.

"Elle Belle," Billy said confidently, "I want nothing more than to be with you and I'm willing to do whatever it takes to make that happen. I have a plan."

5

Billy, Stacks, the WPC and a Violent Drunk

Billy and Stacks were finished with work for the day. Abel had granted them the following morning, so that they could go into town and enjoy a few drinks. The pair of them cleaned up and rode away from the ranch, under the glowing gaze of the evening sun. Several small clouds labored across the deep blue sky as the stars slowly shifted into focus. They followed the road at a leisurely pace, the anticipation of the first drink ever-growing.

"What do you know about Ed Bader?" Billy questioned Stacks, breaking their silence.

"Ed Bader," Stacks said as he thought to himself. "Ed the Cook?" he asked, somewhat thrown by the abruptness of the question.

"Yeah, a few people have called him that," Billy mused, "why?"

"I heard he eats people. He's all kinds of crazy," Stacks explained, "him and his crew."

"I'm going to kill him," Billy announced casually.

"What?" Stacks exclaimed, wide eyed in disbelief.

"I'm going to kill him and whoever else in his gang that I can, and I'm going to collect the reward," Billy said as if it was the simplest task in the world.

Stacks laughed for a second, assuming that Billy was joking.

"Jesus Christ, you're serious, aren't you?" he asked.

"I am, Stacks," Billy nodded, "I'm going to get the money, and then me and Elle are going to run away to be together. I might need your help."

"My help? You want me to help you kill Bader," Stacks scoffed. "Look, I don't say nothing about you and Elle running around at night. As far as I'm concerned, that's help enough," he finished.

"You want to stay here, right? Meet someone, maybe raise a family or something? Can you do that and honestly say you'd feel safe with those men running around, doing whatever they want?" Billy said passionately.

"Maybe you're right about that. Maybe we would be better off without criminals being responsible for the law but I really think you're underestimating the men you're up against," Stacks told him, with genuine concern.

"Maybe you're underestimating the man they're up against," Billy laughed and killed the conversation. "Let's pick up the pace and get that drink. I'm damn near as parched as the desert floor."

The two men rode on into Good Rock and hitched their horses across the street from the saloon.

The Silver Boot Saloon was Good Rock's liveliest watering hole and boasted a full house almost every night. The bar ran the length of the back wall, with small round tables occupying the space in-between. On the right-hand side, there was a small stage, barely large enough to fit the upright piano.

A short man, in a comically large top hat, was providing the evening's entertainment. He was sitting at the piano and singing songs which he knew to be popular with the regular patrons. Two saloon-girls stood at either end of the piano and danced halfheartedly as he played.

The atmosphere was, as ever, lively and merry. By the time Billy and Stacks arrived, the evenings proceedings were in full swing. The clientele was made up of a cross section of townspeople. There were storekeepers, bank tellers, prospectors, ranchers and fur trappers, all mingling together, all contributing to the joyful din.

Billy and Stacks entered the building and headed through the crowded room towards the bar. Billy ordered a beer, while Stacks opted for a glass of bourbon. They took their drinks and found a couple of empty seats in the corner of the room. As the singer finished a song, they applauded and stomped their feet against the floor, chanting and cheering until he started to play again.

"So now that you've met Miss Elle," Stacks started, "what do you think, when you look up and see those two pretty girls in red, dancing on that stage?"

Humans Are the Ugliest Creatures

"I don't see them," Billy replied honestly, "I've barely even noticed another woman since I met Elle. You can't see the stars twinkling while the sun is up," he said smiling.

"You must be crazy or blind," Stacks laughed, "because those are about the prettiest women in town."

"Well, maybe you need to travel out of town a little more often and see what else is on offer, because there's plenty more than that. You go far enough and you might even find a girl and not have to part ways with your money for some attention," Billy joked.

Stacks punched Billy's arm and laughed.

"You got it all wrong, Billy, these women end up paying me for my services," he replied, finding his own joke funnier than Billy's.

He took two cigarettes from his shirt pocket and offered one to Billy. Billy lit his and leaned back in his chair, resting the back of his neck against the cool glass of the window. The room was stifling, even with the gentle breeze from the nearby entrance. As he smoked and sipped at his beer, he surveyed the room, watching the guests as they hooted and cheered at the end of another song.

It was not long before Billy noticed a man standing near the bar. He was dressed in a dark waistcoat and a green shirt, his left arm adorned with a yellow sash. He studied the man as he sipped from his glass and watched the performance. He clapped to the rhythm of the music and slapped his hand against the bar. He had a thin, well-groomed moustache and a small tuft of hair on his chin.

"You know who that man is?" Billy asked, keeping his eyes locked on him.

"Have you not been listening?" Stacks said, expressing his annoyance. "I've been speaking to you for damn near five minutes and you've drifted off in a daydream. Do I know who that man is," he muttered to himself, in a mocking tone, before pointing to himself and asking, "Do you know who this man is?"

"I think it's about time you had another drink. You need to loosen up," Billy laughed.

"I do accept apologies in the form of bourbon, thank you," Stacks said, returning to his usual calm and contented demeanor. He squinted trying to get a good look at the man who had caught Billy's eye. "I don't know who that is," he finally said, "I don't think I've seen him around before." He looked back at Billy and tapped his arm, "you see that yellow? He's WPC. That means you stop your staring before you start something. They aren't even meant to be in here anymore."

"Ease up, Stacks," Billy said reassuringly, "no one's starting anything. Let me get you that drink."

He stood up from his seat and started to work his way through the crowd. He got to the bar and positioned himself behind the WPC man. He ordered a bourbon for Stacks and another beer for himself. He turned to face the stage, rested his elbows on the bar and leaned back.

"Good show tonight," Billy announced.

The WPC man turned his head slightly and briefly looked at Billy. Unimpressed with what he saw, he offered a lazy shrug in response.

"What do you think about the piano player?" Billy asked.

Again, the man was virtually unresponsive.

"The girls are not too bad either, I reckon if-" Billy continued.

Humans Are the Ugliest Creatures

"Listen, you got your drink, now get out of here," the man cut in, interrupting Billy.

"Sorry," Billy apologized, "I saw you with that yellow sash on and I couldn't resist. You boys are like heroes around here," Billy praised.

The man did not respond but proudly puffed out his chest.

"Must be like a badge of honor," he continued, "I'd wager there are real feelings of pride when you tie that sash on in the morning."

The man clenched his jaw and started to tap his foot against the floorboards.

"Kid, I don't know what you want from me," he snapped irritably, "go stand somewhere else."

"How'd you get to be a WPC man, anyway?" Billy carried on. "I think I got what it takes. If you tell me where I could find Ed Bader and the camp, maybe I could join up, get a yellow sash of my own."

The man spun and grabbed Billy by the throat.

"Who the hell are you?" he snarled. "Walking around asking your stupid little questions, you're likely to get put down kid! Is that what you want?"

Billy got a hand to the man's fingers, where they gripped tightly at his throat. He bent one back forcefully enough, so that it snapped loudly and remained upright, at a ninety-degree angle to the back of his hand. The man howled in pain as he released his grip.

A second WPC man, who was visibly intoxicated, lurched forward from the crowd and took a swing at Billy. Just as he threw the punch, Stacks barreled into the man's back, sending him crashing to the floor. The first man got to his feet and pulled a knife from his boot. The dim light of the oil lamps gave the blade a dull, yellow sheen as he drew it up.

Billy reacted before the man had a chance to use the weapon. He kicked out at the man's hand, three times in quick succession, causing him to lose his grip on the knife and drop it. Stacks stood over the drunken man, making sure that he was not a threat, while Billy delivered a heavy blow to the first man's stomach. He threw another punch and connected squarely with the man's jaw. Having gained the upper hand, Billy held the man in place by his collar.

"Where's Bader?" Billy demanded. "You tell me where he is, and you'll get to live!" He shook the man violently, "Tell me!" he ordered.

The man spat at Billy in response. As he raised his hand up to hit the man again, someone from behind him took a firm hold of his arm and held a knife to his throat. Billy froze in place and Stacks instantly threw his hands up.

"And just what the hell do you think you're doing?" came the deep voice from behind him. "Turn him loose before I loosen your neck," he ordered.

The entire room fell silent as everyone focused their attention on the scene. When Billy let go, the man got to his feet and picked up his knife.

"Let me cut him open, White! Let me cut him open right here!" he shouted, rage coursing through him.

Billy stiffened at hearing White's name. He was suddenly aware of the gravity of his situation.

"Put that away and get out of here. You can tell the boss about the mess you've caused," White instructed authoritatively.

Humans Are the Ugliest Creatures

The man began to protest but lost his nerve when confronted by White's silent intensity. With a thunderous scowl, he cradled his injured hand and left quietly.

"You, step forward," White commanded, pointing at Stacks.

The ranch hand complied, stepping over the drunken man and standing in front of Billy. White placed a heavy hand on Billy's shoulder and spoke close to his ear.

"I'm about to let you go. When I do, if you move or speak in a way that I don't deem appropriate, I will gut the pair of you where you stand. Are we at an understanding on that?" White threatened.

"Yes," Billy said flatly.

White slowly lifted the blade away from Billy's throat and nudged him forward to where Stacks was standing. White studied the two men and stroked at his beard.

"Lucky for you two, we're on the shortest of leashes," White said, picking up Billy's hat from the floor and tossing it to him. "Don't mistake this for kindness. Get out," he finished.

Billy and Stacks looked at each other unsure of whether or not to move.

"Get out, before I change my mind about it," White reiterated menacingly.

The pair of them made their way to the front of the building and headed outside. White tucked his knife away and ordered another drink. The singer resumed his piano playing and the jovial sounds of the evening returned as though they had never left.

Stacks and Billy headed back to their horses. Stacks stormed on ahead, fueled by anger at Billy's naive carelessness. Billy stopped and planted his hands on his knees as he trembled with nerves and tried to catch his breath.

"On another night, they'd have killed us, Billy," Stacks raged. "Am I supposed to lose my life because you're too ignorant to be subtle, or even understand what it is you're up against?"

"I'm sorry. It won't happen like that again. You're right, I shouldn't have done it the way I did in there," Billy apologized, finally regaining control of his body.

"Billy, you seem like a good man and of course I want Miss Elle to be happy, but I've only known you for a week or so and I'm not going to lay down my life for you," Stacks explained. "If you want to get a drink, that's fine by me, but if you want to go beating on WPC men, then you're on your own, you can count me out."

"Understood," Billy confirmed, "I'm sorry I dragged you into all that. It wasn't smart." He offered his hand out to Stacks, who grasped it and shook it firmly.

"I think it would be best for you to lay low for a while," Stacks suggested, "those boys know you're thinking about that reward, which spells trouble. We can pick up a bottle from the Grand and head back."

"Maybe you're right about that," Billy said, looking back at the Saloon. "Come on, let's get out of here."

They hopped up onto the boardwalk and headed down Main Street to the Grand, where they purchased a bottle of bourbon and some tobacco. The pair returned to their horses and began the ride through the night to the ranch.

Back at the Silver Boot, since the disturbance had taken place, White Price had been drinking in silence. He sat alone at a table and stared vacantly at the opposite wall. The drunken WPC man stirred on the floor next to him, where White had left him to recover. He leaned back in his chair and repeatedly snapped his braces against his chest in time with the music. He stopped and smiled when he saw a man standing in the doorway, entirely dressed in black. He picked up his drink and crossed the room.

"Evening, Boss," he greeted and handed Bader a glass of bourbon.

He tossed the glass back and drank the dark liquid as though it were water, placing the glass upside down on the nearest table, when he was done.

"I hear you stopped one of our boys from spilling someone's guts tonight. Good work, White," Bader told his general, with a grin.

"That's right, Boss," White confirmed as Bader gave him a congratulatory pat on the back.

"So, number two is on my trail already. Looks like I'm not quite as popular as I once thought," Bader jested, feigning dismay. "Maybe he didn't hear how quickly I put down the last one?"

"You planning on putting this one down too, Boss?" White asked excitedly.

"I'm not sure yet. In an ideal world, I'd like to clear my name and get back on somewhat friendly terms with Good Rock. Go back to picking up easy money bounties and not have to keep looking over my shoulder all the damn time," Bader explained. "That just won't be possible if I have to keep killing people. When they raise a gun at me, sure, that's different. But otherwise, I think I ought to show a little restraint. That goes for all you boys as well, which is why I came down to commend you for your actions tonight," he said, smiling. "So, who was this kid?"

"I don't know," White answered, slowly stroking his beard, "I didn't recognize him, but I reckon I know that nigger he was with."

"White," Bader said reproachfully, "we live in a new world now. You know I won't stand for intolerance. There's equal value in every man. You just need to make use of it."

"Sorry, Boss," White apologized, "that man, he works at ranch a little ways from town. Bell or Bell-May or something like that?"

"Thank you, White," Bader said, tipping his hat, "that might be just enough to go on."

"I thought you said you wasn't going to kill him?" White asked, wearing a puzzled look.

"I'm not going to kill him," Bader grinned, "but he must be deterred nonetheless." He placed a hand on White's shoulder, "go back to your table, have another drink. I'll talk to you tomorrow."

White nodded his thanks and waded through the crowd, back to his table.

Bader lit a cigar as he made his way along the boardwalk. He watched the smoke dance and curl up into the night, where it faded to nothing. He stopped outside the town hall and looked up at Marshal Andrews' office window. Light flickered and shadows swayed back and forth across the walls. Bader threw a coin against the window frame and whistled loudly. The marshal appeared at the window to see Bader looking up at him, hands planted in his pockets, grinning ear to ear, with a cigar clenched firmly between his teeth.

Marshal Andrews opened the main door to the building and let Bader into the entrance hall. Bader took one look at the marshal and was troubled by how exhausted he looked.

"Jesus, Ellis, do you ever leave this place?" Bader asked, "you look as though you haven't slept for days."

"What is it, Ed? You shouldn't be here," Marshal Andrews said, choosing to ignore Bader's concern.

Even for his usual glum self, his demeanor seemed much more dower that evening. Bader went to place a hand on the marshal's shoulder, but he pulled away.

"Are you sure you're alright?" Bader pressed.

"You have two minutes, Ed," the marshal replied quietly, without meeting his gaze.

"I need a favor, Ellis," Bader said, cutting to the chase, provoking a scoff and shake of the head from the marshal.

"And why should I do that for you?" Marshal Andrews challenged.

"After all we've been through, you can't grant me one little favor?" Bader smiled. "Sure, it was a business arrangement, but every relationship has a personal element. That's what makes us as people special."

"There's nothing special about people," the marshal muttered somberly, before sighing and finally relenting, "what is it that you want, Ed?"

"Just some information," he grinned, "there's a ranch not too far from Good Rock, Bell-May?"

"Bellamy," the marshal corrected him.

"They got a couple of ranch hands?" Bader asked.

Marshal Andrews sighed again, this time much more deeply.

"Yes," he confirmed, "one was in Sheriff Manning's office, inquiring about the price on your head."

"You see, Ellis," Bader hooted, "this is how friendship works."

"Ed, I swear it, if you do anything unprovoked, you'll have Pinkerton agents so far up your ass, not to mention the National Guard," the marshal warned.

"Relax, Ellis," he laughed, "there's no way that-" he fell silent, interrupted by the sound of gunfire.

Bader drew his gun and entered the adjacent room. He made his way toward the window, cloaked by darkness. A man was standing in the middle of Main Street, holding a rope tied to a bloodied body. He wore a blood-stained shirt and a sombrero which hung low over his shoulders. He was visibly drunk and finding it hard to maintain his balance.

"Sheriff!" the man called out and fired a shot through the window of Sheriff Manning's office. "Marshal!" he shouted and fired a second shot at the town hall. "Anyone else in this stinking town, who wants to lay claim to slaying my brothers!" he slurred venomously.

He looked around, waiting for any type of response. He spotted Deputy Yeun moving in the sheriff's office and fired again.

"I swear to God, if someone doesn't come out to face me, I'll kill everyone in this town! I already got one of them right here and he won't be the last!" he raged, spitting profusely as he shouted.

He turned and fired two shots at randomly targeted windows. Bullets spent, he threw his gun down and drew a second pistol.

The windows along Main Street gleamed and twinkled as the light from the moon reflected in the eyes of anxious onlookers, peering above window frames. Bader stood and passed Marshal Andrews, who was cowering next to a chest of drawers.

"Jesus, Ellis," he muttered disdainfully, "this will cost you another favor." With his pistol behind his back, he made his way to the door and called out to the gunman, "I'm coming out, don't shoot."

He nudged the door open, testing the gunman's resolve. When he saw the man's arm was limp and his gun was resting lazily at his side, he pushed the door open and stepped out onto the boardwalk.

"You ain't the marshal," the gunman called out as Bader rested his shoulder against a pillar and studied the man in the street. "You ain't even the sheriff!" he shouted.

"That's quite an observation," Bader said sarcastically, "my turn. You're a Maddocks boy," he grinned, "you've got that same simple look about you. The look that made it easy for me to identify your brothers, right before I killed them."

"You?" the man seethed, stumbling forward and lifting his arm.

"Don't raise that gun," Bader warned halfheartedly. "I warn you, don't raise that gun."

Just as the man raised the weapon, Bader, quick as lightning, straightened up and fired a shot, causing the man's knee to explode in a violent burst of blood and bone.

"I told you," Bader smirked as the man fell to the floor, writhing in agony. He stepped down into the street and approached the man. "At least your brothers managed to put up a bit of a fight before getting gunned down."

The man drooled and fought against the pain as he tried to crawl along the ground to retrieve his gun. He gripped handfuls of dirt and dragged himself forward.

"That's the spirit, but I wouldn't do that if I were you," Bader mocked, standing over the man, watching intently as he edged closer to the weapon. "Please don't pick up that gun," Bader protested unconvincingly as he took aim at the man's head.

Marshal Andrews made it to the door and watched as the gunman grasped the handle of his pistol and rolled onto his back. Bader fired his gun, killing the man instantly. He looked up to see the grim, pale faces of the townspeople, watching from their windows. Seconds later, the sheriff and his deputy appeared on the boardwalk, as did the marshal.

"After all that I've done for you people," Bader called out to anyone in earshot, "the protection service I have provided to keep you safe, a price is put on my head. I wonder, who will you turn to now? Who will be your salvation? See how long you fair on your own. See how many die next time." Bader turned to address the supposed figures of authority, standing together on the boardwalk, "see how long it is before you're on your knees, begging for my help."

Bader holstered his gun and turned to walk away, feeling a profound sense of injustice and wrongful persecution. How could a town, for which he had risked his own life and the lives of his men to protect in the absence of authority, be so quick to demonize him? As far as he was concerned, the East Ridge sheriff was collateral damage and the blood was on the hands of the cowardly Sheriff Manning and Marshal Andrews.

Deputy Yeun ran inside the sheriff's office and picked up a rifle. He returned to the boardwalk and took aim at Bader as he walked away. The marshal stepped out in front of him and laid a hand on the rifle, forcing Yeun to lower it. Yeun looked up at the marshal questioningly.

"Ellis, what the hell are you doing?" Sheriff Manning hissed angrily. "He's right there in the open."

"You take that shot and the WPC will raise Good Rock to the ground," the marshal explained as he took the rifle from the deputy's hands and unloaded it.

Bader climbed atop his horse and turned to look back at them. He saw the marshal holding the open rifle over his shoulder, while the sheriff and his deputy dragged the bodies from the street. He tipped his hat, waved and turned to ride away.

Marshal Andrews watched as Bader's figure merged with the surrounding darkness and was eventually swallowed by the black of night. The marshal stood and stared at the bloodied and broken bodies. Once again, he was confronted by a crushing sense of the fragility and worthlessness of life, an inescapable dread that plagued him relentlessly.

6

Bader, Billy and a Thief

It did not take long for Bader to locate the Bellamy ranch. He took White Price and Wilbur Woods along with him. White was there to identify Billy, while Wilbur was to be left behind to stake out the Bellamy ranch and wait for the opportune moment to strike. After the brawl in the Silver Boot Saloon, Bader had decided that something needed to be done.

Wilbur spent day after day laying on the ridge, under the shade of a tree, watching over the ranch. He watched as Billy worked, keeping track of his movements through a telescope. He made detailed notes on Billy's interactions with others, as well as the comings and goings of the family and other visitors to the ranch.

Humans Are the Ugliest Creatures

He allowed himself a series of short naps during the day. At night there was no time for sleep. Wilbur was too busy roaming the hills, following Billy and Elle during their clandestine rendezvous. He would find vantage points and map the routes taken by the secret lovers. Wilbur was a master of stealth, with his careful movements and the cloak of night, he was never once seen nor heard.

On the fourth day of observation, Wilbur's patience was beginning to be tested by the persistent heat. The arid, cracked soil beneath him seemed to radiate and mirror the heat of the sun above. He had removed his thick leather duster and untied a tattered red neck-scarf, but it was not enough.

He decided to leave his post and ride to a nearby stream, where he walked out into the middle and lay down, immersing himself in the cool water. He could feel every inch of his skin pulsing as the water gently flowed around him, lowering his temperature. The weak current pulled at him lightly as he allowed himself to float. With the sun as hot as it was, he knew that he would be bone dry long before dusk arrived.

When dusk completed its slow, inevitable transition into night, Wilbur was ready to make his move. He packed his gear and rode his horse toward the ranch, where he hitched the steed to a low hanging branch. He took cover, crouching behind a tree near the ranch's edge, while he waited for Billy to follow the same path that he had followed each night on his way to meet with Elle.

Wilbur remained as still as possible in the rapidly cooling night air. There was no wind to sway the branches. There was no breeze to stir the grass. There was not a sound to be heard near or far. There was only Wilbur and the calm of night.

Humans Are the Ugliest Creatures

He heard Billy's movements long before he saw him. He drew his gun and watched as his target followed the path, walking up the rise toward his position. He waited for Billy to pass by, watching him the way an animal watches its prey. He slowly got to his feet, moved silently through the grass and then he was right behind him. The first noise Billy heard was the click of the gun as Wilbur pulled back on the hammer.

"Don't move a muscle, don't say a word or I swear to God, I'll kill you and then I'll kill everyone in that house," Wilbur warned, his gravelly voice close to a whisper.

He checked Billy over for weapons and confiscated a knife. He pressed the gun barrel against the back of Billy's head and pushed him forward.

"Move it. Over there, by the trees, that's my horse."

Billy complied obediently and remained silent throughout.

"We're going for a little ride," Wilbur told him, "put your hands behind your back."

He did as he was told and stood quietly, while Wilbur knotted a rope around his wrists. He gripped Billy's legs and lifted him up, helping him onto the horse. Once he was in the saddle, Wilbur joined him and turned to face him.

"You don't need to be knowing how to get where we're headed, so I have to cover up your eyes," Wilbur explained. He lifted a small burlap sack from a saddle bag and placed it over Billy's head, completely obscuring his vision.

As Billy's world plunged into darkness, he felt a biblical flood of fear wash over his body. He trembled in the saddle and could only breathe in short sharp breaths, which caused the sack covering his head to balloon. He was amazed that he managed to keep his balance as they started to ride. He

Humans Are the Ugliest Creatures

leaned back and shook his head from side to side, trying to loosen the sack. He moved it in such a way that he could see a very small portion of the ground to his left. He could not see much as it was a dark night, but he kept a close watch on the ground, trying to draw a map in his mind. He looked out for landmarks or changes in terrain and tried to memorize them as they went, but it proved useless and he soon gave up.

Billy's thoughts raced as they rode. Where were they headed? Were these to be his final moments? He knew that his captor was a WPC man, he had seen the yellow sash. Had the events in the Silver Boot sealed his fate? Was he to be buried in some anonymous corner of the desert?

Whatever thought it was that raced through his mind, he always circled back to Elle. Despite his perilous situation, he spent a great deal of the ride worrying about his beloved Elle Belle. She would be alone in the dark, worrying about him. What if she thought that he had abandoned her? She would be heartbroken and full of despair. Such thoughts of her possible anguish and fear, were harder for him to stomach than the very real possibility that he could be killed at any moment.

"May I speak?" he eventually asked, assuming they were far enough away that the Bellamy family would be safe from harm.

"You may not," sounded Wilbur's gruff voice.

"Where are we headed?" Billy carried on, but Wilbur gave no reply. "What's going-"

Billy's questions were cut short, when he received a blow to the head and fell from the horse. He landed heavily on his shoulder and lost all the air from his lungs. He felt a pair of hands reach under his arms and lift him to his feet.

"I told you not to speak," Wilbur said calmly. "Get back on the horse. It's not too far now." He helped Billy back up onto the horse and they rode on.

The whole journey took around two hours to complete, but to Billy it felt as though they had been riding for days. For the last ten minutes of the ride, Billy could hear the sounds of people. The din of laughter and chatter floated on the air, filtered and distorted by the nearby trees. As they rode closer, he could also hear the crackling of fires and whinnying of horses. The various noises steadily grew in volume and clarity, until they finally came to a stop.

"We're here," Wilbur announced gruffly.

He climbed down from the horse, put his arms around Billy and guided him to the ground. He placed his hand on Billy's head and lifted the sack away. Billy blinked as his eyes adjusted and he studied Wilbur's gnarled face. He got a better look his captor in the light, the facial scaring and the eye patch were too distinctive, too uncommon to be coincidental. His likeness on the wanted notice was near perfectly accurate. There was no mistaking that his captor was Wilbur Woods.

"Go on," he said, pushing Billy on into the camp.

Billy looked around at all the men, he counted fifteen at first, then nineteen but there could have easily of been more. Wilbur took Billy to an iron post, rooted in the ground near one of the campfires, and pointed at the ground.

"Sit," he commanded.

Billy followed the instruction and sat on the floor. There was a steel chain attached to the pole. Wilbur picked up one end, ran it around Billy's waist several times and fastened it in place with a lock. He took a knife from his belt and cut the rope that bound Billy's hands.

"The boss will see you in the morning," Wilbur informed him and handed him a flask filled with water.

Billy nodded thanks and took a drink from the flask. When he looked back up, Wilbur Woods had disappeared into the depths of the camp. He leaned back against the pole and slouched down, until the chains were no longer pressing into his back. Not a single man in the camp so much as looked at him or acknowledged his existence. After a few hours of resisting sleep, he finally gave in and closed his eyes.

Billy woke as someone stood over him and whistled flatly. He stared up at the figure, whose face was distorted by shadow. The morning sun blazed brightly behind him. Billy held up a hand to shield his eyes and squinted hard against the light.

"Rise and shine, kid. It's another beautiful day," the man spoke joyously. "How about you sit up straight, so I can loosen them there chains."

Billy pressed the heels of his hands into his eyes and tried to rub away the last of sleep's hazy grip.

"Where are we?" Billy asked as he sat up.

The man wagged a finger at him and shook his head.

"I'm sure there will be time enough for questions later. First thing's first, we have to establish the ground rules," he smiled. "Lean forward a little so I can get at that lock."

He leaned over Billy, undid the lock and stepped back, allowing Billy to untangle himself and get to his feet. He got his first good look at the man standing in front of him. The well-groomed, neatly trimmed moustache and surrounding facial hair, gave him away as the unpredictable Frank Kelly.

"What's your name, kid?" Kelly asked.

"It's Billy Earl," he replied, "and you're Frank Kelly."

"That's right," Kelly said, sounding impressed. He winced as he studied Billy's face. "Wilbur give you that? He's not known for his patience," he chuckled.

A large violet bruise stained the right side of Billy's head. He ran his fingers over the bruised area and felt the dull ache pulse through his skull.

"It's not so bad," Billy muttered defiantly.

Kelly placed his hands on his hips and nodded encouragingly.

"That's the spirit," he said smiling, "now, as I mentioned, the ground rules. You'll want to pay attention to these. Firstly, there are twenty armed men walking around here. They carry pistols, shotguns and knives. You name a weapon, likelihood is, someone here is wielding it," he laughed. "While holstered, these weapons and their carriers are near enough harmless. They are under strict instruction to remain so, so long as you behave that is." He placed and arm around Billy's shoulders, "Should you choose to misbehave, if you're lucky, it will be the guns that come out and they'll be targeting this region," he waved a hand over Billy's chest and head. "If you ain't so lucky, it'll be the knives that come out and you'll have twenty men coming at you, trying to stab and fillet whatever parts of you they can get at," his soft smile slowly mutated into a menacing scowl. "You can be sure of it that I'll get to you first and when I'm done, I'll cut the life out of everyone back at that ranch of yours."

Billy tensed and stared forward, remaining silent. Kelly patted Billy on the chest and lifted his arm away as an affable smile returned to his face.

"Now that we have that covered. It's about time you met the boss. Follow me," he said cheerfully.

Kelly led Billy through the camp and stopped at one of the fires, where a man was seated by himself, eating what appeared to be a small rasher of bacon. Billy studied the man, his black clothes, the flecks of gray in his beard like snow on a dark night. As Billy approached, the man leaned back and his sly grin developed into a board toothy smile.

"Good morning," he beamed.

"Boss, this here is Billy Earl," Kelly announced.

Billy stood in silence and watched the man.

"Well, big bad Billy Earl, I've heard about you," he smiled fondly. "Take a seat, I'm the man you've been looking for. I'm Ed Bader," he said, pointing to a space on the log bench, next to where he sat. He held out the food that he was eating, "hungry?"

Billy shook his head.

"I suppose it's not for everybody. I'll get someone to fix you something later," he shrugged.

Billy did as he was instructed and took a seat. Bader waved a dismissive hand toward Kelly and he promptly walked away, leaving the pair of them alone by the fire.

"Am I going to die here?" Billy asked, looking into the flames.

"We'll see about that," Bader replied cheerfully. "I brought you in today so that you could learn a little more about us, a little bit more about me and hopefully a little bit more about yourself," he winked and finished his food.

Billy watched Bader's movements, the ease and confidence with which he spoke. Both his strength and physical ability were visually evident, he was nearly doubly as broad as Billy. He opened his arms wide and stood up from the bench.

"What do you think of the place?" he asked. "Personally, I think it's impressive."

"It's a campsite," Billy said, turning his head and surveying the camp.

"You're not thinking big enough, Billy boy. Aside from the tents and shacks, what do you see?" Bader asked, watching Billy as he took in their surroundings.

"Men," he said quietly.

"That's right, men," Bader chuckled. "Get up. Walk with me," he instructed.

Billy walked alongside his captor and listened as Bader greeted every man they passed by name.

"One thing I've learned is that people are relatively simple creatures. I find that there's a base, emotional driving force behind all actions." He paused and held up four fingers, "Fear, hate, greed and love. Think about them. What drove you, the night you walked into the Silver Boot put hands on one of my men? What was it that fueled you with such foolish bravery?"

Bader stopped walking, turned to face Billy and waited for an answer. All Billy offered in response was a resigned shrug.

"I'm going to need a little more than that," Bader grinned. "If White is to be believed, you aren't exactly the quiet, timid type."

"What drives you to do all of this?" Billy asked abruptly.

Humans Are the Ugliest Creatures

Bader leant back and blinked repeatedly, acting overly surprised.

"There he is," he pointed at Billy and laughed, "coming out of your shell at last. What drives me?" Bader mused. "I did ask you first but if it will get a dialog going, I'll go along with it." He paused and thought for a few seconds before answering, "That's a very broad question and one that has an answer, but that answer comes later."

"You kill dangerous men and take money for it. All the while you hold the town, which you claim to protect, by the throat," Billy surmised.

"That's one way to look at it," Bader conceded, "but you never saw this town before my choking hand of salvation gripped it. It was chaos. Sheriff Manning hides behind his desk and the marshal pouts at his window. It was a lawless place. I cleaned it up."

"You took it over," Billy argued.

"Took it over?" Bader scoffed. "Banned from frequenting the town. A price on every man you see's head. That sound like a takeover to you? This is the reward we get for cleaning things up in Good Rock. Makes me madder that a hot hornet the more I think about it."

"Then why not leave?" Billy asked.

Bader chewed his cheeks and shook his head slowly.

"Oh no," he said slowly, "I'd sooner burn it all the ground. Return it to the chaotic mess I found it in." Bader began walking again and Billy followed. They moved through the camp and stopped at another campfire, "Morning, Clyde," Bader greeted cheerfully, "how are those eggs coming?"

"Morning, Boss. They're much better," the boy replied.

Humans Are the Ugliest Creatures

Bader held out a hand and was given a plate of eggs and beans.

"Eat this. You look like you need it," he said as he handed the plate to Billy.

Clyde stood and brushed the dirt from his oversized trousers. He held out his hand as he approached Billy.

"Morning, I'm Clyde," he introduced himself. "You a new recruit?"

Billy studied the boy standing in front of him. Noting his greasy hair, wiry physique and the uneasy, awkward way in which he carried himself.

"How old are you?" Billy finally asked.

"I'm sixteen," he replied uncertainly, "I mean I will be sixteen later in the year."

"You see, Billy," Bader started, "I found Clyde by himself. He didn't have anything. I picked him up and gave him a purpose, gave him a reason to get up in the morning."

Clyde stood proudly as Bader spoke.

"Take a seat, Clyde, finish your food," Bader dismissed the boy.

He placed his hand on Billy's back, edging him forward as they began walking again.

"Is this why you brought me here? Is this what I'm supposed to learn? That you're a good person, you save young men, you look after the town?" Billy questioned. "I don't buy it. You pick up a young kid, you put a gun in his hand and make him kill for you. That's not saving someone. You kill other outlaws, while amassing a small army of your own. You do whatever you want and terrorize whoever you please. If you're trying to prove you're a good man, you're a long way off," he finished angrily.

"I see my gracious hospitality has been wasted on you," Bader remarked crossly. He took the plate from Billy's hands and threw it to the floor. "Since it looks like were about done talking, I guess it's time for the real lesson to begin," he barked.

He gripped the back of Billy's neck and pulled him forward. He marched Billy into the center of the camp, near the shacks and another campfire.

"Kelly!" he called out to his general.

Kelly immediately stood and awaited instruction.

"It's time," Bader growled.

Kelly smiled sickeningly and nodded his head.

"Alright boys, gather round!" Kelly boomed and kicked out at some of the men who were slow to comply. "Now, God damn it! Move your lazy, worthless asses!"

It took just under a minute for all the men to congregate. Bader stood out in front of them and smiled. Maintaining a firm, commanding grip on Billy's neck, he forced Billy down onto his knees.

"You stay there, and you pay attention," Bader instructed fiercely.

He let go of Billy, raised his arms in the air and waited for silence. As the murmuring died down and the men fell quiet, Bader slowly lowered his arms and addressed them.

"Every man here wakes up in the morning and ties a WPC sash around his arm. It's worn with pride. It commands respect! It's a God damn honor!" he boomed across the crowd and stomped his foot, emphasizing each word. The men hooted and cheered in response.

As Billy knelt and watched, he could feel the sweat rolling down his back. Even in the shade of the shack, shielded from the sun, there was an inescapable heat which seemed to increase with every sentence Bader spoke. The WPC men were captivated. All eyes were focused on Bader, even Billy struggled to look away.

"The only thing I ask in return is loyalty," he continued, "that's all. Be loyal to me, be loyal to each other. Regrettably, it would seem that for some people, despite what we provide, loyalty is too much to ask," he paused and whistled.

White and Wilbur emerged from the back of the crowd and stood either side of a man at the front. When Bader signaled to them, they gripped the man's arms and hauled him forward. The man struggled as they forced him down to his knees in front of Bader. He kept resisting but White and Wilbur's hold remained firm. Kelly stepped closer and delivered a sharp blow to the man's stomach. He instantly went limp and began coughing as he tried to regain his breath. Another man suddenly lurched forward from the crowd.

"Turn him loose," he shouted, "he ain't done nothing!"

Kelly drew his pistol and pointed it at the protesting man.

"You need to simmer down, Wade," he hissed, "stay back if you know what's good for you."

Wade Willis stopped in his tracks and watched on helplessly. The man on his knees spat into the dirt.

"Please, Boss, I didn't do it! You don't need to do this," he began.

Bader silenced him with the wave of a hand and knelt down close.

"Roy, you made your choice," he sighed, "these are the consequences." He stood and addressed the crowd, "You all know Roy Willis, he ain't exactly a newcomer. However, what you don't know is, somewhere along the line Roy made a choice. He chose to steal what wasn't rightfully his. He stole from me and therefore he stole from you. That cannot go unpunished."

Bader drew his gun and fired with such speed that anyone who blinked might have missed it entirely. The bullet buried into the right side of Roy's chest. White and Wilbur let go of Roy and watched him slump backward, groaning and wheezing as he tried to pull in air.

Bader holstered his gun and dropped to one knee. His cleaver seemed to glow almost iridescently as it was unsheathed. With brute strength, he held Roy's arm firmly in place and carefully sliced into the skin, removing a small piece of flesh. Billy watched on in horrified bewilderment as Bader took the flesh and tossed it into a skillet, which had been heating over the fire. It sizzled and crackled loudly as it landed on the hot iron.

Kelly lowered his gun and Wade rushed forward to his brother's side. Bader sheathed the cleaver and made his way over to where Billy was still kneeling silently. His eyes stayed fixed on the morbid scene as Bader crouched down next to him.

"You see, it was greed that drove Roy to steal from me. Fear made him struggle and lie about it. Love caused his brother to protest," he paused and rose to his feet, "and hate made me do what I did." He returned to the skillet, picked up the cooked meat and took a bite.

"Please, Boss, he's in pain," Wade begged as the slowly dying Roy gargled and coughed up blood.

"I know," Bader said dispassionately as he finished the piece of meat, "that's the point." He casually made his way back to Billy. "What you need to take away from all this is that, whatever it was which drove you to come after me, it's not enough. It will never be enough," he warned ominously. "It's been a pleasure meeting you, Billy," he grinned. "Clyde, come over here," Bader barked.

Clyde stepped forward from the crowd, wide eyed and nervous.

"Ready your horse, you're going to ride with Wilbur and take Billy home," he instructed, placing a hand on the boy's tense shoulder.

While Clyde left to prepare the horses, Billy's hands were tied behind his back and the sack was once again placed over his head. Billy stood and listened while he waited. He could hear Bader speaking nearby.

"My hand was forced, you know that," the gang leader muttered softly as he rested a comforting hand on Wade's back. "Talk to White later and he'll help sort out a proper burial."

"Thank you, Boss," Wade nodded gratefully as he fought back tears.

Bader patted a hand on Wade's shoulder and turned his attention to the crowd.

"Make sure you give Billy boy a real nice send off!" he called out happily.

As Billy was led through the camp, the WPC men whistled and spat at him. Some of them even threw punches and kicks. Three times Billy was knocked from his feet as

Humans Are the Ugliest Creatures

he walked. He knew he had to get up and keep walking, the whole ordeal would be over soon. There was nothing he could do in the way of retaliation. He had to grit his teeth and take the punishment. He was still breathing at least. The time for revenge would come another day.

Bloodied, bruised and exhausted, Clyde and Wilbur lifted him up onto the horse. Wilbur climbed up after him and waited for Clyde. Wilbur nodded to Bader, who grinned wickedly and returned the gesture.

They rode for around an hour, before the pace slowed to a near stop. They were at the base of a hill, near several trees, whose branches loomed above them and shaded them from the harshness of the sun. A gentle breeze moved through the dry grass, causing it to sway and fill the air with a soft rustling sound.

Wilbur lifted the sack from Billy's head. The left side of his eye was swollen and darkening, while dried blood stained the corner of his mouth. Billy squinted as he adjusted to the light.

Just as he turned his head to survey his surroundings, Wilbur thrust the palm of his hand against Billy's chest. Billy hit the ground with a thud and rolled over to see Wilbur wielding a blade. It was Billy's knife, which Wilbur had confiscated when he was first taken captive. Wilbur threw the blade down at the ground next to Billy. The soil was too hard and dry, so the knife bounced and passed dangerously close to Billy's head.

"What are you doing?" Clyde asked, utterly confused. "I thought we were taking him back."

"Shut up, boy," Wilbur growled, "throw me your gun."

Clyde drew his gun and obediently handed it over. Wilbur began emptying the bullets from the gun, throwing each one at Billy as he did. Clyde watched on completely baffled as to what Wilbur was doing. He finished throwing the bullets and addressed Billy.

"The boss wanted you to know that you can't avoid consequences. There's no running from them," he said gruffly, "and this is a direct consequence of your actions so far. It's all on you."

Wilbur flicked the barrel back into place, raised his arm and shot Clyde. The bullet hit just above his temple, killing him instantly. Billy felt a fine mist of blood moisten his skin as Clyde's body wilted and tumbled from the horse. Billy's chest heaved, where he lay on the ground. Wilbur tucked the gun into his jacket and spat.

"If you continue down this road, the consequences will be much worse. No one else need die because of you," he warned.

Billy watched as Wilbur turned and rode away, leaving him alone with the dead boy. He lay still for a while, until he managed to calm himself down and regain control. He shuffled backward, picked up the knife and cut himself free of the ropes. Once free he rolled Clyde's body over and saw the gaping hole in the side of his head, which was already beginning to attract flies. Billy slumped back and cursed Bader, angered by the senseless loss of life. Just as he knew Bader had intended, he felt a great deal of guilt over the boy's death.

He took a flask of water from Clyde's horse and drank the few remaining drops. Kneeling down, he began loosening the earth with his knife, with the intention of digging a grave for the boy. In his weakened condition, the task proved too strenuous and ultimately Billy had no choice but to give up.

"I'm sorry, kid," he mumbled to himself as he got to his feet.

He left the body at the base of the tree and climbed up onto Clyde's horse. He looked out at the vista beyond the trees and could see Good Rock in the distance. From the angle of the town, he knew roughly where he was in relation to the ranch and more importantly, he now knew the general direction of the WPC camp.

All Billy thought about as he rode was seeing Elle again. He'd be back soon to relieve her of any heartache. He could not wait to hold her, to kiss her. He imagined their future together and more than ever he believed it was possible. Bader's attempts at intimidation had only served to embolden him. He knew who the man was now. He had seen him, and he understood him. He was just a man, they were all just men and all men can die.

7

Billy, a Rifle and the Funeral

Fiona was washing dishes alongside her mother. She had been holding and absentmindedly scrubbing the same plate for several minutes, while her mother lectured her. What it was that she had done to earn the scolding, she was not entirely sure, nor for that matter did she care.

She watched through the window and followed a white-tailed kite as it glided gracefully through the endless blue of the sky. A small soap bubble rose up from the sink and slipped through the air, floating on invisible currents. Fiona closed one eye and angled herself until it looked as though the bird in the sky was trapped in the bubble. The bubble eventually burst and the bird was free once more. She looked back down at the plate in her hands and sighed.

When she lifted her head, she saw the horse and its bloodied and bruised rider, trot into view.

"God damn it!" she shouted, dropping the plate in shock and pointing through the window.

"Fiona!" her mother hissed. "You'll clean this up right now! And watch your mouth, little lady! Have you even listened to a word I've said?"

"Jesus, Momma, it's Billy!" she bolted from the kitchen and nearly crashed through the screen door as she left the house in a frenzy. "Poppa! Poppa!" she called to Abel as she sprinted down the path towards Billy.

Abel was swinging a pickaxe, trying to uproot a tree stump and was frankly too busy for his daughter's mischief.

"Stacks, get your lazy ass out here!" she yelled and pounded a fist against the side of the barn as she passed.

Stacks slowly emerged from the barn, lighting a cigarette and wondering what all the commotion was about. When he saw what Fiona was running towards, he went cold all over and the cigarette fell from his gaping mouth.

"Mr Bellamy!" he called, running halfway to the house. "Mr Bellamy, Billy's back and he's hurt!"

Abel, realizing that he had mistakenly ignored his daughter's shouts, dropped the pickaxe and moved quickly to the front door of the house.

"Martha, fetch some towels," he calmly ordered his wife as he rolled up his sleeves.

"Poppa, is it him?" Elle was stood halfway up the stairs, her eyes already red and threatening tears. Abel sighed, causing her to gasp and cover her mouth, "is he okay? Poppa, tell me is he okay."

"I don't know yet but from far off, he looks a little rough around the edges," Abel admitted.

Elle shuddered and lost the strength in her knees. She shakily sat on the step and found herself struggling to breathe. Tears began to stream down her cheeks as she shook her head and quietly mumbled to herself.

"Calm down, I'm sure he'll be fine, just keep back and don't get in the way," her father instructed, dismissing her reaction as ridiculous.

"I will not," she growled defiantly as she steadied herself and got to her feet.

Clumsily, she rushed the rest of the way down the stairs and brushed past her father. She barged through the door and fell to her knees, her strength failing her once again, when she saw Stacks and Fiona helping Billy down from the horse. She bent forward and buried her face in her dress, sobbing uncontrollably.

"Darn it, Martha, will you control this girl," Abel called back into the house as he tried to lift Elle up from the floor, "she's hysterical as all hell out here."

Elle went stiff and pulled back from her father, trying to free herself of his grip. She wiped the tears from her eyes and watched as Fiona hitched the horse, while Stacks helped Billy walk toward the house. She snatched her arm back from Abel, rose to her feet and stumbled unsteadily down the path as quickly as she could. When she reached Billy, she tucked her head under his free arm and took the rest of his weight.

"Afternoon, Elle Belle," Billy muttered and forced a smile, "you don't know how glad I am to see your face again."

"Oh, I think I've got an idea," she replied softly, wiping her eyes as they welled up again and she struggled to hold back the tears. "If it's anything like what I'm feeling, it feels pretty damn good. I knew you wouldn't leave me like that."

"Leave you?" he chuckled, "Elle Belle, someone would have to kill me to keep me away from you."

"You keep doing what you're doing, and someone just might," Stacks cut in abruptly.

Elle shot him a cold stare.

When they made it to the house, Abel took over from Elle and Stacks. He helped Billy inside and sat him down on a chair. Elle and Stacks stood side by side in the doorway and watched closely as Abel looked him over. Fiona pushed them apart and squeezed in through the middle.

"What happened, Billy? Where'd you go? How'd you get all beat up?" Fiona rambled, full of adrenalin.

"Back it up, Fiona," Abel snapped. "Let me check him over first."

Abel turned Billy's head from side to side and wiped away the blood with a warm, wet towel.

"I got abducted by some bandits. I couldn't sleep so I got up for a cigarette and a walk. They took me by surprise on the road," Billy said.

Stacks and Elle glanced at one another, both of them understanding exactly who the so-called bandits were.

"They beat on me, when I didn't have nothing to give them and I wouldn't lead them back here," he explained.

"That was mightily brave of you, Billy. Thank you," Abel said earnestly. "Fiona, would you give us a minute, please?"

"You must be crazy if you think I'm going anywhere," his youngest daughter guffawed.

Abel pressed his face into his hands, in frustration at Fiona's constant rebellion.

"Fine," he sighed, dismissing her and turning back to Billy. "A lot of this is not your blood, Billy," Abel spoke quietly.

"The men who took me got into a disagreement and shot at each other," Billy lied. "One of them took a bullet and I guess I got some on me. To be honest, I hadn't even noticed. I was just focused on getting back. I took the dead man's horse and rode as best as I could."

"What happened to the other bandit?" Abel asked.

"He bolted after shooting the other man," he explained. "I waited to make sure he was gone, I checked my tracks many times along the way, just to make sure that no one was following me."

"Okay," Abel nodded, satisfied with Billy's explanation. "We'll get you cleaned up and then it's probably best you get some rest. You need to let all that bruising heal."

Once the rest of the blood had been cleaned from his face, Stacks helped Billy up from the chair and they made their way to their living quarters.

"I'm glad you're okay, Billy," Elle told him as they passed her.

When the door closed behind them, she clenched her jaw and fanned at her eyes, blinking profusely. She tried as hard as she could to be strong and shed no more tears.

"He'll be alright," Martha said as she passed Elle, causing Elle to latch onto her mother and hold her tightly.

"I don't know what I'd do if he wasn't," she whimpered.

"That's enough of that kind of talk," her mother scolded her, lifting her arms away. "Fiona, take your sister upstairs. I think she needs a lie down just as much as poor Mr Earl." Fiona nodded and took her scowling sister's hand, "and don't you come back down neither. You know you're still in trouble."

Fiona mimicked Elle's glare and the pair of them climbed the stairs and went to their room.

Stacks laid Billy down on the bed and helped him take off his shirt. A look of concern spread over his face, when he saw the mottled purple bruising across Billy's torso.

"Damn, Billy, they did a number on you," he remarked.

"They went easy on me," Billy corrected him, "I think I got off lightly. I wasn't expecting to leave with my life."

"So, have you learnt your lesson now? Are you done with this hero nonsense?" Stacks berated, shaking his head.

"Not at all. I'm surer than ever that I can do this," Billy told him.

Stacks looked up at the ceiling and laughed.

"You're going to get yourself killed," he said flatly.

"Not if I get some help," Billy countered. "I need a favor form you." Stacks began to protest but Billy waved at him dismissively, "I'm not going to ask you to do anything stupid," he assured him. "What I need is for you to speak to Deputy Yeun. Talk to him for me. As far as I can tell, he's the only one around here ready for action. I need a rifle, a good one."

"Billy, look at yourself," Stacks started.

"Stacks, please, there's no talking me out of this. My mind is made up," Billy explained.

"Fine," Stacks relented and nodded his head. "But I don't know how much English he speaks. How's your Chinese?" he joked, relieving some of the tension. "Just tell me, what the hell are you planning?"

"I know one of the roads they use and that's where I'll be," Billy answered simply.

Billy slept for the rest of the afternoon and into the evening. He awoke to a light, tapping sound, coming from the window near the door. He struggled against the soreness and stiffness of his body and climbed out of the bed. He picked up a gun from under his cot and waited by the entrance.

The tapping continued to sound. Billy opened the door just enough the see who was outside. Elle was hunched low by the corner of the building, tapping and looking over her shoulder back to the house. When she turned her head back to the door, she fell down in shock at seeing Billy holding the gun. He held his hands up innocently, placed the gun back under the bed and picked up a jacket. Elle got up from the floor, giggling to herself and tucked her head under Billy's arm.

They walked a short distance from the building and sat down at the base of a tree. Elle cradled Billy in her arms and kissed the crown of his head.

"I was frightened, Billy," she whispered. "When you didn't show, I didn't know what to think. I waited around for a while, but I was scared out in the dark by myself." Billy reached up and held her hand while she spoke, "I couldn't understand why you didn't show. I stayed up all night wondering about it. I racked my brains trying to figure out what it was I did or what I said. I don't think poor little Fiona got a wink of sleep."

"You don't need to worry about that now, Elle Belle," Billy comforted her.

"Then, when I knew you weren't there in the morning, my heart sunk even further. I damn near collapsed when you came back. Firstly, on account the relief I felt, and then because of the state you were in," she explained as she softly stroked his hair.

"Well, I'm back and I'm on the mend," he said confidently and sat up to face her. "I know what I have to do. It won't be long now and we'll be away together. Everything we've talked about-"

"All of our hearts dreams," Elle added, cutting in.

"That's right, it'll be me and you, Elle Belle, and I won't let nothing get in the way of that, you can count on it," he finished.

As promised, the next day Stacks went to Good Rock to speak with Deputy Yeun. Yeun took the most powerful rifle that he had access to and gave it to Stacks. Through broken English and a thick accent, he explained that however much he wanted to help, he was forbidden by Sheriff Manning to be directly involved. The sheriff feared the inevitable backlash that would follow if an attempt on Bader's life failed. Yeun did not want to risk his life as well as his livelihood, but was happy to do what little he could in providing a gun and bullets.

Stacks thanked the Deputy, returned to the ranch and presented Billy with the rifle. The metal of the barrel gleamed and sparkled in the sunlight, while the polished wood of the stock seemed to glow. Billy picked it up and studied it. It was the biggest gun that he had ever held, and the weight was something that he would have to get used to quickly.

Billy was supposed to be resting and recovering. Abel had relived him of his work duties, until such time as he had recuperated. Stacks left the door to their building closed, so that everyone would assume Billy was inside. While no one was watching, Billy snuck out and took the gun out to the hills to practice.

With a piece of chalk, he marked three circles on a tree. He stepped back twenty paces and dropped down on one knee. He took his time, closing one eye and aiming at the target. He tried to block out the steadily building heat of the sun, and the tickle of his sweat as it tracked and weaved along the back of his neck.

He exhaled slowly and pulled back on the trigger. The loud clap of the rifle was followed by a screeching burst of startled birds and a dull thud as the bullet drilled into the tree. Billy approached the target and inspected his shot. There was a small hole, two inches higher than the outer chalk circle. He frowned and picked at it, trying to see how deep the bullet went.

"If you lay down on the floor when you aim, you'll take a better shot," a voice suggested.

Billy turned to see Fiona standing behind him.

"Damn it, Fiona, you sneak up on people like that and one day you're going to give someone a heart attack," Billy said, clearly startled and irritated.

She shrugged, unimpressed by his reaction to her advice.

"What are you doing out here?" he asked.

"I came to watch you shoot," she answered. "You need to do better than that, and you will if you listen to me and lay down."

Billy brushed past her and returned to the spot from where he fired. He got down to his knees and took aim at the tree. Fiona knelt down at his side.

"I'm telling you, Billy, you need to lay down flat," she insisted.

He gave her a dismissive glance and targeted the tree. He fired again and once more the bullet hit the edge of the outer circle.

"You're too tense," Fiona observed.

"Too tense?" Billy repeated, shaking his head. "What do you know about it?"

"Plenty!" she snapped and snatched the rifle from his hands.

She lay down on the dusty ground and tilted her hat forward, shading her eyes from the sun. She took careful aim and lay as still as she could. She breathed in deeply through her nose and held her breath. Billy watched the tree as she pulled the trigger. A bullet cut through the air and crashed into the chalk line of the center circle.

"How'd you learn to shoot like that?" Billy asked, wide eyed.

"I used to take Poppa's rifle out and practice shooting bottles," she answered, brushing the dirt from her knees.

"He let you do that?" Billy questioned, raising an eyebrow.

"No," Fiona snorted with laughter, "of course not but I managed to sneak off and do it four or five times, before I was caught. Enough for me to get some good practice. This is a nice rifle," she said, studying it, "you do what I just did, and you shouldn't have a problem, even from far away."

Billy followed Fiona's advice and lay down on his stomach.

"Now, rest on your elbows and get comfortable. Take slow and steady breaths, while you aim. Close your eye and focus on staying still. When you're ready, hold your breath and pull the trigger," she advised competently.

He lay still as he concentrated. When he was sure of his aim, he did exactly as she said and held his breath as he fired. The bullet impacted the tree almost exactly where Fiona's had. She bounced on the spot and hooted and cheered for Billy.

"Well, I'll be damned," Billy muttered as he got to his feet.

"See, I told you," she said smugly.

Billy chuckled to himself and reloaded the rifle. He carried on practicing, following Fiona's guidance. It was not long before he found a position which offered him comfort as well as accuracy.

When he was done, they made their way back to the ranch. Fiona returned to the house and Billy snuck into the stable. He readied a horse and when the coast was clear, he led it from the barn and rode away from the ranch.

He headed for the spot where he had been dumped by Wilbur Woods and witnessed Clyde's death. When he passed through, the body was gone. All that remained was a dark stain on the dry soil, where the dirt had swallowed the blood.

From there, he rode on in the direction that Wilbur had fled. He dropped down the hill and carried on riding until he came to a dusty road, which ran all the way to the town. He stared up at the undulating landscape and at the hills to the west. There was no other road that ran out of Good Rock on this side of town. With what he knew and his approximate understanding of the camp's location, he was sure that he was looking at the WPC's road into Good Rock.

He surveyed the area and looked for a vantage point. He needed a spot where he would be able to watch the road and make a quick, quiet escape.

Behind him, high up on the hill, there was a small outcrop of rock, sheltered by some trees. He trotted up and hitched the horse, out of sight from the road. He lay down amongst the tufts of grass in-between the trees. From where he hid, his view was clear, but he harbored some doubts about his ability to shoot at such a range.

Looking at the surrounding landscape, there was no alternative. He wondered about moving further up the road, beyond the curve of the hill, but he did not know the land and decided that it was too much of a risk. Past the hill, the terrain seemed to plateau and would be far too open. Where he lay, he was concealed and knew his escape route.

The road mostly stayed quiet. One coach, followed by three solo riders, passed through during the first hour but nothing after that. It was around the two-hour mark, when he heard something in the distance. The faintest sounds of music carried on the winds. It did not take long for the source of the sound to reveal itself.

Figures appeared, steadily rising over the shimmering horizon of the hill. Billy counted nine men as they seemed to emerge from the ground. One man led the group on foot, playing a violin as he walked. Behind him, six men bore a coffin atop their shoulders. At the rear of the party, two large figures rode side by side. Billy knew that one of these two men was Bader, while the other was likely to be White Price, but as all of the men were dressed from head to toe in black, it was difficult to tell who was who from where he lay.

The violin sung out and filled the air with melancholic melodies, becoming ever clearer as they neared the closest point in the road. Billy studied them intently as they passed by, trying to pick out any distinguishing features, but from his angle he could not tell them apart. He watched their body movements as they rode and their mannerisms as they spoke, but it gave him very little to go on. Still unsure as to which man was his target, he lay the rifle down and watched them ride on past his position. He knew that they would likely be returning at some point and that he would get another chance.

The group moved at a slow pace along the road, marching to the rhythm of Lyle Dixon's violin. The simple wooden coffin rocked gently from side to side as though it were at sea. The afternoon sun was not as strong as it had been during the morning, nevertheless the men could feel themselves sweating under their layers of black. Bader and White smoked cigars as they rode behind the procession.

"I helped Wade with this because you asked, Boss," White started, "but I have to admit I don't agree with it. Roy was a thief. He doesn't deserve it."

Bader puffed on his cigar and let the smoke billow out, shrouding his face. He switched it from one side of his mouth to the other several times, before holding it between his fingers.

Humans Are the Ugliest Creatures

"Maybe it's best if you take the rest of the journey to puzzle over your misgivings," Bader suggested, staring off into the distance.

White nodded and the pair returned to silence.

They reached Good Rock, in what Bader considered to be good time, veered left at the top of Main Street and headed to the church. They passed by the front and entered the graveyard, where a pastor stood waiting near a freshly dug grave. The men carefully lowered the coffin onto a set of ropes, ready to be let down into the ground. Bader and White climbed down from their horses and hitched them to the gates.

The graveyard was large for a town the size of Good Rock. The rows of tombstones and wooden crosses spoke of the inescapable violence of the land. They ranged in shape and size and, lacked any organization, a chaotic sea of monuments to the dead. An iron fence ran in a ring, enclosing the graveyard in the growing afternoon shade of the church and trapping the tumble weeds as they wandered aimlessly.

The pastor paced back and forth, mumbling prayers to himself, while the men grouped together and waited patiently. Once the funeral party was accounted for, the pastor turned to face them and raised his hands high.

"Just as each day has an end and each season has its end, so too does each of us," he called out, closing his eyes and looking up to the sky. "The Lord is my shepherd," he said somberly as he lowered his head and looked across the men. "Inevitably, some men stray from the path and thus stray from the Lord's guiding grace. Roy Willis was one such lost soul, frightened, out in the wilderness. He failed to see that ever present love, which binds us all. Give thanks to the God of heaven, for his steadfast love endures forever. It breaks my heart when men are blinded to it, for they will not know the love, which is there before them. Take solace that in death he will surely know it, there is no doubt."

The pastor held out a hand and gestured to the ropes, which lay underneath the coffin. The pallbearers stepped forward and each of them took hold of a rope. They planted their feet and carefully lowered the coffin into the ground. The pastor stood at the head of the grave, held his arms out and recited a poem

"To everything there is a season, and a time to every purpose under the heaven: a time to be born, and a time to die; a time to plant, and a time to pluck up that which is planted; a time to weep, and a time to laugh; a time to mourn, and a time to dance; a time to get, and a time to lose; a time to keep, and a time to cast away; a time to rend, and a time to sew; a time to keep silence, and a time to speak; a time to love, and a time to hate; a time of war, and a time of peace." He lifted his head and looked at the rough and rugged group of men, "If I might, I would like to ask you men, who are all God's beloved children, join me in the recitation of-"

"Jesus Christ," Bader muttered under his breath and rubbed his forehead, "I think that's enough, Pastor, thank you," he said as he stepped forward. "Good service, well done." He tucked a dollar into the pastor's shirt pocket and turned to face his men. "I know there has been a lack of understanding around this," he announced and pointed behind him at the grave. "I have heard the disgruntled whispers, on more than one occasion today. Allow me to explain it to you, so that you may pass it on the next time you hear someone complaining." He patted his hand against his bicep as he spoke, "look at your arms, all of you. Take a look and tell me what you see?"

"A yellow sash," Lyle replied proudly, from where he stood cradling his violin.

"That's right, a yellow sash. The very same yellow sash tied around Roy's arm. That means something. Yes, he stole, and he paid the price for that treachery, but that does doesn't mean he was never one of us," he explained sternly. "Most of you are all each other has, you are a family. You do right by one another."

All the men nodded their heads as he finished. Satisfied that they had understood, Bader picked up a shovel and sprinkled earth over the cheap wooden box. He turned and threw the shovel to one of the men.

"Dutch, help Wade with the burying. We'll head back when you're done," he instructed.

The two men filled the grave and patted down the topsoil, while Lyle stepped forward and played a lament on his violin. Wade stood at the side, closed his eyes and said a silent prayer for his brother. Bader and White climbed up onto their horses and waited at the gate. When everyone was ready, they rode out of Good Rock and started back to the camp, following the same road they had taken earlier.

* *

Billy saw them coming from far away. He had hoped that with the group riding towards him, he would have a clearer view of their faces, but with the sunlight waning and the land's shadows developing, he regretted not having taken his chances the first time around. He removed his hat and assumed his firing position. He shut an eye and took aim at the riders as they made their steady advance.

"Where are you?" he muttered aloud to himself. "Where are you?" he spaced out each word, switching his aim back and forth between the two men. "There."

He held his breath and squeezed the trigger. A shot rang out, a thunderous clap reverberated around the hills. He watched his target slump forward and fall from the saddle.

The contours of the landscape distorted the origin of the sound, causing the men to draw their weapons and spin in all directions, firing at even the slightest perceived movements.

Billy grabbed his hat and took his leave during the commotion. Somewhere in his body a dam burst and he was flooded with adrenaline. He had done it, he had killed Ed Bader. He and Elle would be free to elope. He felt lightheaded, as though he was floating an inch from the ground. He felt every muscle in his body shake and tremble as he mounted his horse and fled.

Perhaps it was the rush of adrenaline, the thrill of success, or the disassociation he experienced as he pulled the trigger and made his escape. It could have been any one, or all of these distractions, which caused him to miss the solitary figure who broke away from the panicked WPC group. The man stood staring up at the hill, consumed with absolute fury. With a clear line of sight, he watched Billy as he got up and ran.

"Hold your God damn fire!" he boomed at the other men, keeping his eyes on the hill.

The WPC guns fell silent and all that could be heard were the anguished groans of the wounded man. The men rallied around him anxious for instruction.

"You, go get Kelly!" he barked at one of the men. "You two, get him on that horse. We've got to get him patched up!"

8

The Lovers, a Death and a Consequence

When Billy returned to the Bellamy ranch, the moon was a bright gaping hole in the sky, triumphantly glowing with pride at having drained the light and killed the day. He held his hand against his chest and looked up at the milky white circle as it bathed the landscape in pale silver. He considered how truly lucky he was. He felt his heart beating through his chest and wondered if it were at all possible that somewhere out there in the vastness of the country, there could be a happier man than him. As he veered away from the path and over a small rise, he saw Elle waiting for him. He knew then for certain, that it was not possible for a happier man to exist.

Humans Are the Ugliest Creatures

She was waiting alone, near the tree where they would frequently meet as secret lovers. She was wearing her favorite dress. It was deep blue in color and whenever she wore it, people would comment how it brought out the color of her eyes. She was sitting beside a fire, with her knees pulled up under her chin, rocking back and forth restlessly. As he approached, she stood up and ran to greet him. He climbed down from his horse and was almost bowled off his feet by her eager embrace. She kissed him hard, and then pulled back sharply. She put her hands on his head and twisted it left and right, looking him over for any sign of fresh injury.

"Hey, calm down," he laughed, taking her hands, "I'm fine. No one even knew I was there."

"I was so worried. Fiona kept telling me you'd be alright, that she'd seen you shoot but I couldn't help it," she blurted out, pressing her face into his chest. "I stayed at the window from the moment you left, and as soon as night fell, I came out here to wait."

"I did it, Elle Belle," Billy said softly.

She pulled back quickly and covered her mouth, while her eyes sparkled and danced with excitement.

"That's right," he laughed, "all of our dreams are about to come true."

He pulled her back in and held her in his arms. The soapy, flowery scent of her hair filled his nostrils as he kissed the top of her head.

"What do we do now?" she asked, holding handfuls of his shirt tightly.

"We wait until morning, then go speak to Sheriff Manning and Marshal Andrews and they will be able to confirm it," he said smiling, "and then we can collect the money and be on our way."

"Billy, this is so amazing. I believed in you always, but I never thought it would happen so fast," she paused to wipe the tears from her eyes. "I can't wait to start our life together. It's all I think about. Poppa will come around to the idea. I figured once we settle down, I'll write him and let him know that I'm safe, and that I do love him, but I have to live my life for me and not anybody else."

"He'll learn to accept it, I'm sure," Billy reassured her, "your momma too."

"I think she'd be alright with it. She just goes along with what Poppa says anyhow. She's too busy trying to keep Fiona in line to worry about me," she giggled. "Fiona causes me trouble to no end, but she can be the kindest, sweetest person. I'll miss her terribly, Billy. Promise me we will come get her from time to time so that she can visit."

"I promise, Elle Belle," Billy said as he stroked her hair, "hell, we owe a lot to little Fiona. She's helped out wherever possible, every step of the way."

They stood in silence for a while, holding each other tenderly.

"Leaving with you is all I've thought about since you arrived," Elle told him, breaking the silence, "and now it's real, I'm realizing just how much I'll miss them."

"You aren't having second thoughts, are you?"

"Goodness, no," she laughed, "quite the opposite. I feel like I'm standing on coals. I know I'll miss them all, but I also know that I don't need them. I've got it all right here," she said confidently.

"That's good," he said, smiling as he brushed the hair from her eyes. "I never could've guessed how drastically my life was about to change as I stepped out of that coach and onto your ranch. In all of my wildest dreams, I've never seen something so perfect."

She blushed and pushed her face into his hand as she giggled.

"I love you, Billy Earl. I love you with all my heart, so much so that sometimes I swear it even hurts," she told him.

"I love you too, Elle Belle," he replied truthfully.

They kissed passionately under the stars. They lay with one another next to the fire and both felt as though they were the only two people in the world.

* *

Frank Kelly was pushing his horse to its limit as he tore across the land, leaving a trail of dirt and dust floating in his wake. He strayed from the road, opting for a quicker route, dodging and weaving to avoid colliding with trees and bushes.

"Come on boys!" he screamed to the men behind him, his face flushed red with rage. "Keep up or I swear, when were done I'll hobble the lot of you myself!"

He focused his attention directly ahead of him, coursing from the WPC camp to Good Rock as fast as he could. There was not a single cloud in the sky above them. The moon's softly shining light cast away the black of night and washed the land in a deep blue hue, as though they were riding at the bottom of the ocean. Far reaching shadows crept across the ever-arid soil, like the long, withered fingers of giants, occasionally spooking the horses and causing them to leap over the imagined threats. The surrounding country was deathly silent, save for the heavy beating of hooves as the men demanded more and more of the animals.

They made it to the town in what Kelly was sure was record time. He jumped out of the saddle before the horse had stopped moving and stumbled forward as he struggled to stay upright.

"All of you, wait out here and watch the horses," he commanded breathlessly. "The first man to cause trouble, will be the first to lose his life. Don't move until I come back," he threatened them vehemently, his wide eyes darting franticly from man to man.

He sprung up onto the boardwalk and barged past two armed WPC men, who were guarding the door to Doctor Foulds' office. As he entered the building, he was met by shouts and groans of agonizing pain. It took the combined force of three men to hold the injured man in place on the gurney.

Doctor Foulds was a wiry, thin man with a tuft of white hair at the base of his chin. He adjusted his spectacles as he nervously approached the patient with a pair of forceps. Large sections of his white shirt were soaked through with the wounded man's blood. To look at him, it would be easy to assume that he was the patient. The doctor wiped a cloth at the source of the blood flow, a hole at the base of the man's ribcage, almost an inch in diameter.

"Hurry it up, Doc!" one of the men snapped at him.

Kelly moved into the room and picked up a small towel from a side table. He stood at the top of the gurney and pulled the towel across the injured man's mouth.

Humans Are the Ugliest Creatures

"Bite down," he instructed, "here comes the hardest part."

Doctor Foulds lifted the cloth from the wound and inserted the forceps. The WPC men holding the man in place, bucked up and down as he writhed in pain. It was as though someone was scrambling his insides with a branding iron. With every one of the doctor's movements, waves of searing pain wracked his body. The doctor looked up anxiously, sweat streaming from what felt like every pore on his body. He angled the forceps up and down and side to side, fishing around inside the man, doing his best to retrieve the bullet.

"Hold him still, I need him still!" the doctor barked in frustration.

One of the men drew his pistol and held it to the doctor's head. The doctor froze in place. He shuddered and felt he knees go weak with fear as the man leaned in close.

"Not another peep until you're done, Doctor," he snarled.

Doctor Foulds closed his eyes and took a deep breath, trying as best as he could to remain calm and focused. As he continued his search for the bullet, the wounded man seemed to tense every muscle in his body and growled into the gag. He arched his back to the point where it looked like he might snap in two and then fell silent as he slipped into unconsciousness. The doctor mopped the sweat from his brow and continued his attempt to save the man's life. After a few more minutes of prodding and digging for the bullet, the doctor put down the forceps and stepped back.

"I'm sorry," he said firmly, "it's just too deep. Even if I could get it out, the damage done is too great."

He stumbled back and pressed against the wall as the man with the gun stepped forward. He placed a hand on the doctor's shoulder and sighed. Doctor Foulds held his hands up to his face.

"Please have mercy, I tried. I," he stuttered, "I did all I could."

"Thank you, Doctor," the man said quietly, "I know you did." He stepped away from him and looked at the wounded man, whose big chest heaved with every labored breath. "Can you fix up that whole at least?" he asked.

"I'm afraid it won't accomplish much," the doctor muttered nervously, "he has already lost a considerable amount of blood."

"Doctor, even if it buys us half a minute it's worth it," the man replied, without turning to face him. "Will he wake up again?"

"I couldn't say. It's possible," Doctor Foulds told him honestly as he slinked past him.

He picked up a new cloth and dabbed at the blood, trying to stem the flow, but it was no use. He looked over his shoulder to see the man's stern face looking back at him, causing him to choke on his words. He turned back to his patient. Feeling as though he had run out of options, he balled the cloth and pushed it into the wound. He picked up a needle and started to stitch the wound closed. When he was finished, he dressed the wound in a fresh bandage. It was not long before the clean bandage was stained with a growing crimson blotch. The injured man stirred where he lay as Kelly lifted the gag from his mouth. His eye lids fluttered and he murmured something incomprehensible.

"What did he say?" the man asked Kelly, brushing the doctor aside.

"I don't know," Kelly replied, "I couldn't make sense of it."

Kelly leaned his head down and held his ear close to the dying man. He mumbled again, coughed and clenched his jaw.

"I think he's praying," Kelly offered.

"Praying? You sure about that?" the man questioned. "Doc, you got any morphine or something for him?"

"Morphine?" the doctor's eyes widened and he shook his head. "I did but we were robbed of it last week. I'm waiting on some more, but it's been slow to arrive."

"Robbed?" the man asked in disbelief, "just what in the hell is going on in this town?" He shook his head and sighed. He approached the dying man, who was feverishly babbling to himself, and laid a hand on his chest. "Don't worry about a thing. You rest easy now. You hearing me?"

"You're a real hero," Kelly told him. "They'll be talking about you for years to come. You're one of the best."

The man continued to murmur, his eyes unable to fix on anything in particular.

"I sure hope it ain't too painful now," Kelly said quietly, "I think you're probably past the worst of it."

The dying man's head trembled as he repeated the same word over and over.

"Sorry, sorry, sorry," he mumbled rhythmically.

He coughed heavily and his eyes rolled up into his skull. His body gave one final shudder as his chest filled with air for the last time. All the men in the room watched on sorrowfully as Kelly gently brushed the dead man's eyelids to a close. He stepped back from the body and held his hat in his hands.

"This is a dark day in our history," a man addressed the room. "One that we will carry with us always. Death must not be shied away from. Look at it," he pointed at the deceased, "know it and do not forget it. It comes for all of us, one by one. It can't be avoided. But this death, this death is an insult to the great man who rests before you. A coward's bullet ended him. The very same coward who took poor, young Clyde's life and did God knows what with the body, robbing us of the chance of a burial," he seethed. He folded the dead man's arms across his chest and looked around the room at the other men. "The great White Price has died, and he will be avenged," he announced coldly.

"What's the plan, Boss?" Kelly asked eagerly.

"He wants to send us to hell? Well, we're going to bring hell to him!" he roared, provoking raucous cheering from his men. He turned to Doctor Faulds, "Doc, I'll make that sure you are compensated for this inconvenience."

The doctor nodded timidly, while the WPC men followed their leader through the doors and out onto the street. They mounted their horses and paused, awaiting instruction. Bader held his hand up, commanding silence.

"Check your guns over, boys, check them good. Tonight, we ride for White and we make his death mean something. On me!" he ordered.

He turned his horse and rode on up Main Street and out of town. Kelly rode close behind him and the WPC men obediently followed.

As they raced out of Good Rock, Marshal Andrews, racked with anxiety, emerged from his home and crossed the road. He clumsily climbed up onto the boardwalk and stood in the doorway of Doctor Faulds' office. The air was heavy with a sickly iron scent. He looked down at the floor, sticky with blood, and saw White's lifeless body resting on the gurney. He stepped forward and placed a hand on the doctor's back.

"Doc Faulds, are you alright?" he croaked. "What happened here?"

"I'm fine," the doctor replied through puffs of smoke, "a little shaken is all. They barged in and took over. This man here, Mr Price, he'd been shot. He took a bullet to the abdomen, I tried to retrieve it but I couldn't. Even if I did, he had already lost too much blood." He paused and gave the marshal an accusatory look, "Didn't you hear the commotion, Marshal?"

"I did not," he said sheepishly as he scratched his cheek.

Doctor Faulds shook his head disdainfully, not for one second believing the marshal's lies.

"Do they know who shot him? Did they say where they were going at all?" the marshal pressed.

"Mr Bader seemed to know who the gunman was but he neglected to mention the name. They're headed to wherever they believe he is," he finished. He exhaled slowly and closed his eyes, "Marshal, if you are quite done here, I have a lot to be getting on with."

The marshal's face fell flat.

"Yes, of course, my apologies, Doctor," he said dejectedly.

He left the office and stood on the boardwalk, trying to figure out where the WPC were going. He hung his head and studied the bloody footprints that littered the wooden boards. He felt the familiar crushing weight of worthlessness as he resigned to the fact that even if he knew where Bader and his men were heading, there would be nothing that he could do to stop them. All that he could do was endure another sleepless night and wait for the sun to rise, so that it might dry out whatever blood had been spilled in its absence.

* *

Bader led his men through the hills to the edge of the Bellamy property, where they dismounted and hitched their horses to whatever they could. They stood together, cloaked in darkness. The men kept low to the ground, hidden behind a wooden fence. They crouched side by side and waited patiently for instruction.

Men like Frank Kelly burned with wild fury, the anticipation of the attack was almost too much for him as he shuffled restlessly and spat, cursing Billy for what he had done. Other men remained quietly on edge, the cool air and eerie silence of night sent chills up and down their spines. Bader stood out in front of the men and paced back and forth, whistling a slow and somber tune to himself.

"Whoever is in that house dies," he said plainly. "I don't want any theatrics. Is that understood?"

The men nodded in unison.

"Well, what are we waiting for? Let's go," he grinned.

He kept low as he led the men along the fence and on up to the house. Crouching, he approached a side window. He looked over his shoulder, making sure that everyone else had followed.

"When we're in, head straight upstairs, that's where they'll be. You two at the back, sweep the downstairs rooms, make sure there's no one else."

Holding his gun by the barrel, he shattered the glass windowpanes and barged his way through. The thin wooden frames snapped like matchsticks as he climbed into the building with ease. The men followed him in, one after another, and dashed for the stairs. Bader led the charge, climbing the steps two at a time. As he reached the top of the stairway, he fell back against the wall and narrowly avoided having a limb blown off by the blast of Abel's shotgun.

The sound of the shotgun ripped Fiona from sleep. She jumped from the bed, her heart hammering wildly. She made her way to the door but fell to the ground as the near deafening sound of ten guns opening fire at once shook through the building like thunder. Just as the shooting had started in unison, so too did it stop. A dull thud sounded and reverberated through the floorboards under Fiona's feet. She covered her mouth to silence her gasp as the air filled with her mother's cries for help.

She pushed herself up and moved to the corner of the room, where she pulled back the rug, revealing two loose floorboards. She lifted both of them and climbed down into the small crawlspace beneath the boards. Lying flat on her stomach, she reached up, straightened the rug and nudged the boards back into place.

One shot rang out and her mother's screams fell silent. The sound seemed to echo and hang in the air for what felt like an age. She closed her eyes tightly and pressed her hands over her ears, trying to block it out. The door to her room creaked as it opened, she fell deathly still.

"Anybody home?" Kelly sang as he sauntered into the room.

Fiona could feel her heart punch against her chest, with every step that Kelly took above her. He approached Elle's bed, slowly at first, then pounced forward, tearing the sheets back and driving his axe down. It buried into the vacant mattress.

Fiona gritted her teeth and concentrated all of her efforts on fighting the urge to throw up. She was breathing too sharply, disturbing the dust around her. The space under the boards was so narrow that when she tried to breath normally, her back pressed into the beams above her.

"There's no hiding from me!" Kelly screeched as he lurched around the room, hacking wildly at wardrobes and checking under the furniture.

Underneath the floorboards, time warped and it felt as though the ordeal went on for hours. All around her, dust motes floated up and down and tickled her nose. She fought against the need to sneeze as hard as she could. She pushed her arms out in front of her and buried her head into the crook of her elbow, ready to silence the inevitable sneeze. She winced and sneezed just as Kelly kicked out at a bedframe, muffling the sound entirely.

"There's no one here!" he shouted and kicked at the bed again as the others filed into the room.

"Sure looks that way," Bader agreed. He held out some matches. "Who else has any?" he waited as seven other men presented their own. "Oil lamps, alcohol, hell, anything that will burn, light it up."

He picked up an oil lamp from a nearby table and lit the wick. He turned the valve and watched as the flame grew and danced. He threw it as hard as he could into the corner of the room, where it shattered and spewed flames out over the walls and floorboards.

"Let's go! Quickly now! Torch the place!" he commanded.

* *

Stacks woke to the sound of gunfire and screams, and immediately understood the severity of the situation. He noted that Billy was not in his bed, which most likely meant that Elle was not in hers, but little Fiona surely would be. He prayed that she was smart enough to hide, or that whoever was leading the assault would be merciful enough to spare her young life.

He was waiting, crouched down at the side of the house, debating whether to risk entry and confront the men head on. Based on the gunfire, he guessed that there were between ten and twenty men inside, but he could not be sure. To challenge that many armed men would mean certain death. He wanted to help the Bellemys, they were like family to him, but he was not so foolish as to rush in.

He heard the crash as Bader threw the oil lamp and saw the light of the flames, flickering and casting shadows against the window. It was not long before he could hear further sounds of shattering glass as the men moved through the house, starting fire after fire.

"God damn it, watch yourselves!" he heard Bader bark at his men. "You'll end up roasting each other!"

Stacks took his chances and ran to the back of the building. He climbed onto a barrel and hoisted himself up to a ledge, where he drove his elbow through a back window.

Humans Are the Ugliest Creatures

The sound of the shattering glass was masked by the snarling and snapping of the flames as they grew and spread throughout the house.

He entered through Abel and Martha's bedroom window, where the flames had swallowed most of the bed and were already licking at Martha's dead body. He tugged at her shoulder and tried to roll her away from the fire. His stomach turned and he fell back against the wall, when he saw the bullet hole in her head. Letting go of her, he noticed a chunk of flesh had been removed from her arm. Puzzled by the wound, he almost failed to notice the growing flames. Suddenly becoming aware, he kept low as the smoke started to thicken and sting his eyes.

He crossed the room, opened the door and saw Abel's body lying on the floor. There was no doubt as to his employer's condition, his body was riddle with bullet holes, and his arm featured the same peculiar cut.

The hallway was empty, all of the invaders had moved downstairs. He stepped over the body and into Fiona's room, where the flames were now moving at an alarming speed. Thick black smoke filled the room and every breath scorched his lungs. He crouched even lower and scoured the room for any sign of the young girl. He focused and tried to block out the hiss of the flames.

"Fiona," he called out. "Where are you, Fiona? It's me!"

The space under the floorboards was quickly turning into an oven. The heat was unbearable and made it hard for Fiona to think straight. With the fire growing in the room above her and flames spreading in the rooms below, she feared that though she was going to be cooked alive. Sweat poured from her as she wriggled, trying to turn onto her back. She though that she could hear Stacks' voice calling to her. Was he really there, or was it the heat playing tricks? Either way she had to get out.

"Stacks!" she screamed and pounded against the floorboards. One of them came loose and she was able to wave a hand. "Stacks, help me!" she yelled again.

He pulled the rug back and grasped her hand, helping her out of the hole.

"They killed them! They killed them both!" she cried as he held her.

"I know, I know," he soothed, "but we have to get out of here right now! Stay low and stay close," he instructed.

They made their way to the door, where Stacks paused for a moment.

"Come on, we have to go!" Fiona urged, pushing against his back.

"As soon as I open this door, I want you to close your eyes. It's very important that you do that," he said sternly.

She nodded and waited for him to open the door. She did as he told her and closed her eyes tightly. The heat bit at her and she thought her skin was going to melt away. They made it halfway across the hall, when she opened her eyes and immediately saw what Stacks had been trying to conceal her from. She stopped moving and stood, staring blankly at her father's bloodied corpse. Stacks noticed that she had stopped and grabbed by her hand.

"Fiona, hurry!" he pleaded.

"Where's Momma?" she said flatly.

"Fiona, please!"

"Show me!" she cried.

Stacks hesitantly turned to the door to Abel and Martha's bedroom. She pushed past him and opened the door. Just as she did, a wave of flames erupted from the opening. It was as though the fire itself was a cracking whip. Stacks tugged at Fiona's arm and dragged her back, just enough so that she missed the worst of it. She shrieked in terror as the flames curled up and lashed at her shoulder and neck. She fell back onto the floor and tried to touch the rapidly reddening skin. She winced with pain and recoiled, almost as quickly as she touched herself. The young girl coughed and whimpered as the smoke choked her and reality of the perilous situation froze her with fear.

"You're okay!" Stacks told her, lifting her to her feet, "this is not the time to give up."

He pushed on towards the window at the end of the hallway, trying to recalculate an exit route, while the men outside watched the flames rise.

Bader stood with his hands on his hips, almost in awe of the destruction he was witnessing. Fire spilled from windows as the thin panes of glass cracked and shattered in the heat. Smoke rose up into the sky, an ominous spiraling column of black, a monument to their chaos.

"I think that about does it," Bader announced quietly, fixated on the swirling blaze as it fed on everything in its path. "It's time to leave."

His thirst for vengeance satisfied, he rounded up his troops and they started to make their way back to the horses.

"I doubt it will be too long before…" he paused and trailed off as he saw Frank Kelly, crouched low and approaching the side of the house.

Kelly flattened his back against the wall and felt the sheer heat of the building against his skin. A sickening grin spread over his face as he drew his gun and waited, listening intently.

On the opposite side of the building, Stacks was lowing himself down from the second story window and trying to convince Fiona to follow. She climbed over the window ledge and clung hesitantly, afraid to drop down. The pain in her shoulder was intense and penetrating. She felt it throughout her upper body and it completely sapped the strength from her.

"Fiona, please hurry. I know you're in pain, but you have to get down. Drop down and I'll make sure you don't hit hard," Stacks did his best to coax her down.

"Okay," she agreed feebly.

She looked down to Stacks and slowly lowered herself. When her arms were at full stretch, she let go. As promised, Stacks caught her and broke her fall, dropping to the ground as he did. She winced and whimpered as the burned skin of her shoulder rubbed against him. He rolled her over and sat her down behind the outhouse.

"Stay here and hide until I come back," he said firmly. "I'll find us a way out of here."

She nodded briskly and slouched low, leaning back against the beams. Stacks slunk away and disappeared behind the corner of the house. Fiona shuddered as a gun fired and gripped her knees tightly, sobbing in silence.

Kelly tilted his head and studied Stacks as he veered from side to side, trying to remain upright and stable. He managed four steps before he crashed into the side of the house and slid to the ground, leaving a large bloodstain streaked along the hot wood paneling. Kelly holstered his gun and spat dismissively. He returned to Bader, who received him with a warm smile.

"Good work," he praised, "I didn't think there'd be anyone left by now."

"Not anymore, anyhow," Kelly joked.

Along with the last of the lingering WPC men, the pair of them headed back to their horses and fled the scene.

Fiona crawled along the floor, giving the building a wide birth, and saw the men riding away in the distance, illuminated by the hellish inferno that had been her family home. Her eyes were red, they stung from the heat and smoke as much as the tears.

She grabbed Stacks' arm and tried to pull him away from the building. He was much heavier than he looked. She struggled to move him, repeatedly falling over and having to fight against the unrelenting pain of her burns.

Looking at his wound and the amount of blood that had pooled beneath him, she knew that he had no chance of survival. He had taken a bullet to the chest but was still managing shallow breaths. She looked at his calm, peaceful expression and wondered how there could be no pain.

"Fiona," he whispered meekly, "put me down and get out of here."

She ignored him and carried on trying to drag him back from the house.

"I mean it, Fiona. You need to save yourself. I'm already finished."

"No," she barked through gritted teeth, with tears streaming freely down her cheeks. "I ain't leaving you to burn up too."

"You never were one to argue with," he murmured and forced a smile.

She tripped over herself and fell again but was too exhausted to carry on. She shuffled forward and rested Stacks' head on her lap.

"You have to go," he said softly.

She ignored him and sat silently, looking up at the blaze. Not a thought passed through her head as she watched on, both physically and emotionally spent.

She was not sure how long it had been since Stacks took his final breath. She began to sob again but there were no more tears left to give. From where she knelt, she stared up at the house, taking increasingly shorter and sharper breaths. She felt the anger and pain course through her like venom, spreading throughout every conceivable part of her, and let out an anguished scream, until all the air had been expelled from her lungs.

* *

"Billy, you hear that? It's Fiona, it has to be her!" Elle cried, her face full of terror.

"Stay behind me," Billy instructed as they ran through the fields toward the burning building.

The house creaked and groaned loudly as the beams and floorboards withered and struggled to maintain shape. Billy stopped at his and Stacks' outbuilding and picked up his gun.

"Fiona!" Elle called out, her eyes franticly searching for any sign of her sister.

She waited for a response but there was none. A loud crack sounded from the house. The ground seemed to tremble beneath them as the second floor gave way and fell in on itself. Flames and sparks spilled forth from the shattered windows. Elle watched on in horror, gripping Billy's arm tightly, unable to speak.

"No!" she cried finding her voice. "No! Fiona, where are you?"

"There!" Billy pointed. "She's over there!"

The pair ran as fast as they could. When they reached her, Billy shuddered upon seeing Stacks' body. Instantly understanding what had happened, he held up his gun and swept the area.

"Fiona!" Elle shrieked and held her sister.

Fiona remained motionless and unresponsive. Elle pulled back and noticed the burns to her sister's shoulder and neck. She covered her mouth and her eyes welled up once more.

"Jesus, Fiona, your skin," she murmured in horror.

Fiona offered no reaction and continued to stare blankly at the building. Billy returned, satisfied that they were alone.

"We saw the light from the fire and came as fast as we could. Fiona, where are the others?" he asked urgently.

"Dead," she mumbled impassively.

Elle dropped to her knees, pressed her forehead to her sister's and wept. Fiona's expression stayed vacant as she slowly raised her arm to hold Elle. Billy rubbed his face and looked at the burning building in absolute disbelief. He crouched in front of Fiona and tried to intercept her empty stare.

"Who did this? Did you see them?" he questioned calmly.

Humans Are the Ugliest Creatures

She shook her head slowly. Billy sighed and relented. He put his arms over both of their shoulders and sat with them until Elle stopped crying.

"What are we going to do?" she asked and cleared her throat.

"I haven't quite worked that out in my mind yet. Until I do, I suppose we'll have to stay at the Grand," he suggested.

"But we don't have any money," Elle pointed out.

"The sheriff and the marshal can arrange it. I'll make sure of that," Billy said adamantly. "If they can't protect us, it's the least they can do." He studied Fiona's burns, "we need to get her some help. Those burns need to be cleaned and dressed." He lifted Stacks' body away from Fiona's lap.

"Where are you taking him?" she asked, turning her head and making eye contact with Billy for the first time since they arrived.

"I'm going to lay him down in his bed. We will have to make arrangements and come back," Billy explained.

"He saved me from the fire. He didn't have to," she sniffed and trembled. "He could have left me, then he wouldn't have died."

She started to sob again, triggering Elle to join in. As the sisters held each other in the light of their burning home, Billy laid Stacks' body down in the bed and said goodbye. He gathered his belongings and readied two horses. He returned to the newly orphaned girls to find them hand in hand, waiting for direction.

"It's not safe to stay here any longer than we have to," he started, "we need to ride to Good Rock and get that burn taken care of. Then find somewhere to stay, and tell Marshal Andrews what happened." He lightly laid a hand on Elle's shoulder and kissed her forehead, "are you okay to ride, Elle Belle?"

"I'm a better rider," Fiona mumbled sullenly, with no enthusiasm.

"Can you even lift that arm?" Billy asked her.

She made an unconvincing attempt at raising her arm, then stopped and shook her head, accepting that she was unable to ride.

"I'll be fine if we don't ride too fast," Elle said confidently as she wiped her eyes with her sleeve.

Billy helped Fiona up onto the horse and sat behind her in the saddle. Elle climbed atop the second horse and rode at their side.

Elle and Fiona wept intermittently as they looked back at the still burning building. The building that was the only home they had ever known, the place where the bodies of their parents lay burning.

Billy kept his eyes focused forward as he tried to process what had happened. He tried to detach himself from the situation and figure out what to do. He contemplated his part in all of it and choked back the tears, fighting against the overwhelming tide of guilt as it swept over him and threatened to drag him down.

Humans Are the Ugliest Creatures

9

Billy, the Marshal, a Phoenix and Blood

Dawn was threatening to spill over the horizon as the trio's mournful travels came to an end. The landscape was still blanketed in darkness, while the farthest distances boasted an iridescent glow. The cool night air would soon revert to the familiar dry heat of day. Shrill calls and songs of the earliest rising birds, filled the air with sound, killing the peaceful silence of night. The moon's light was beginning to dull, and the scattered stars were gradually fading into obscurity. Wisps of thin clouds were smudged across the sky in an endless variety of shapes, lying in wait for the sun to rise and burn right through them.

Fiona hung her head and allowed it to bob limply as they rode. Billy kept a gentle hand on her, steadying her in the saddle and keeping her safe. Elle could hardly take her eyes off her sister. She was too concerned to look away for more than a minute at a time. As Fiona's head gently bowed and rose with each movement of the horse, Elle was sure that her sister was asleep, but it was not long before she caught the reflection of the moonlight on her glassy eyes. From time to time, Fiona would straighten up and observe her surroundings, as though faintly alarmed by something in the distance. When she saw nothing of importance, she would again hang her head and revert to the same catatonic state.

For the duration of the trip, Elle tried to bury her grief for Fiona's sake. There would be time enough to mourn after her sister was taken care of. Elle was worried about the burns. She knew little about medicine, but it was clear that they would not heal well. Fiona's burns covered her left shoulder and ran up her neck to her jawline. The night shirt she wore was charred and ripped open around the wound. Billy had doused a handkerchief in water and laid it over the damaged area to try to sooth it, but Fiona did not seem to be registering any pain at all.

When they rode into Good Rock, they turned and trotted slowly along Main Street. There was no one else awake save for a storekeeper sweeping in front of his store, pausing to watch them pass.

"Which one is the doctor's office?" Billy asked Elle.

She pointed further along the street to Doctor Faulds' office, where a seemingly frail man was on his hands and knees scrubbing the boardwalk.

"I think that's the doctor," Elle said, puzzled by what she saw as they got closer.

When they neared the office, Doctor Faulds stopped and looked over his shoulder.

"Yes? Can I help you?" he spoke feebly.

Elle looked down at what he was scrubbing, saw the bloody footprints and felt the color drain from her skin. The doctor noticed her reaction and rose to his feet.

"Don't mind all this," he said, trying his best to offer a reassuring smile, "there was an incident in the night is all."

Elle nodded politely, climbed down from the saddle and hitched both horses. Together, Billy and Elle helped Fiona down from the horse, and Billy dismounted after her. Fiona stood somewhat unstably, still in a daze. Billy walked her forward and lifted her up onto the boardwalk. Elle stepped up next to her and took her hand. Doctor Faulds immediately saw the burns.

"It's my sister, Fiona, she got burned pretty bad," Elle stammered, with tears in her eyes.

He frowned, looking at the injury in the limited lamp light. He waved a hand in front of her and clicked his fingers.

"Is it painful, Miss Fiona?" he asked but received no response. He rested his chin against his fist and looked thoughtful. "Has she been unresponsive the whole time?" he asked Billy.

"She's been in and out since it happened," Billy told him.

"And just what did happen?" he probed. "This is a nasty burn."

Billy turned and looked the direction of the Bellamy ranch, where, in the weak light of dawn, a faint column of black smoke could be seen twisting into the sky beyond the hills.

"That's what happened," Billy said and pointed.

"Lord have mercy," the doctor muttered and rubbed his forehead with a shaking hand.

"Doctor?" Elle asked.

"It's you," he mumbled as his eyes darted about, searching for nothing in particular. He turned to Elle with a dejected look, "your parents, Mr and Mrs Bellamy, where…" his question trailed off into silence as Elle bowed her head and closed her eyes. "Lord have mercy on us all," he whispered under his breath.

"Do you know-" Billy began and stepped forward but was cut off by Doctor Faulds' sudden alertness.

"Quickly, let's get her inside and take a good look at those wounds," he announced and ushered the girls inside, smiling kindly. He turned to face Billy, with a much more dower, grave expression, "I doubt you want to leave these young ladies alone right now, but when we're finished here, you need to speak to the marshal at once." Before Billy had the chance to even think of a response, the doctor wheeled and entered his office with haste.

Fiona sat on the table and waited. Doctor Faulds readied all of the items he needed and began to treat the young girl's wounds. Elle held Fiona's hand tightly throughout. For the most part she remained impassive but every few minutes or so, she would wince or shudder and occasionally whimper. The doctor noticed the look of distress on Elle's face at one such whimper, and tried to comfort her.

"It's a good sign," he told her, "it would be more worrying if she acted as though she didn't feel a thing. These sorts of tragedies often cause people to react in unpredictable ways." When he was finished, Fiona slid down from the table and assessed the doctor's work.

"Thank you," she said quietly.

Humans Are the Ugliest Creatures

He smiled kindly in response.

"How long until it heals, Doctor?" Elle asked.

"Providing you keep it clean, a few weeks. I imagine that as she becomes a little less withdrawn, and more responsive, the pain will increase. Come back each day and I'll change the dressing. In the meantime, she needs plenty of rest, fluids and keep her in loose clothing. You don't need to worry about payment."

Billy and Elle thanked Doctor Faulds again as they left. They made their way to the Good Rock Grand, only a few doors up from the doctor's office. Billy paid for the room for one night and assured them that the marshal would be paying for their stay indefinitely.

They had one small room at the back of the building, with one bed. Billy placed his things in a wardrobe and hid the rifle under the bed. He found a blue shirt and cut away the sleeves with his knife. He sat on the corner of the bed next to Fiona and handed it to her.

"I know you might not be so keen on dresses, and maybe it's not the prettiest thing to wear, but it's loose and it will do until we find you something more suitable," he said sympathetically. Elle placed a hand on Billy's knee and smiled, "sorry I don't have one for you," he laughed.

His laughter stopped abruptly when Fiona leaned forward and hugged him. He paused, a little shocked, then returned the embrace.

"Thank you for the shirt," she mumbled quietly, "and for finding me."

"Well, you're welcome," he joked. "Elle Belle, are you going to be alright here if I go speak to the marshal?" She nodded surely. He stood and waved as he left. "Try to get some sleep," he said, pulling the door closed.

Elle and Fiona held each other and sobbed gently. After a while, they lay back on the bed, holding each other's hands tightly.

"I don't know how you did it," Elle said, shaking her head and staring at her sister. "I know I wouldn't have made it out of there," she admitted.

Tears fell from Fiona's eyes but she made no sound, other than the occasional sniff.

"I'd have probably froze in place or tripped up or something. You've always been so much stronger than me, much more capable. Elle Belle and Fiona Fire," she smiled.

"Fiona Fire?" Fiona wiped her eyes and smiled back.

"It sounds good don't it," she giggled. "What happened?" Elle asked softly and added hesitantly, "you don't have to speak about it if-"

"I woke up to gun fire," she interrupted in a flat tone, her voice husky from the smoke, "first one big shot, and then a lot more, I don't know how many. It was like there was a thunderstorm in the hall. I hid in the floor space, I didn't even know if I'd fit but I did, just about," she paused and looked away, a fresh wave of tears flooding her tired and swollen eyes. "I heard Momma screaming, until they shot her."

Elle covered her mouth as she cried.

"Someone ran about our room, looking for us. Then they started fires and I didn't know what to do. I was just waiting to get up, but I didn't know if they were still there. Stacks came in and found me. I got burned when we were trying to get out," she stopped again and looked puzzled as she thought to herself.

"It's okay," Elle comforted her, "you made it out and you're here. I don't know what I'd have done if I lost you too."

"I saw Poppa," she said coldly, "I saw what they did to him, but I didn't see Momma. I tried to, that's how I got hurt."

They lay in silence a while longer, holding each other and thinking about the lost lives of their family.

"Will you help clean me up?" Fiona asked timidly.

She hated asking for help, but she was exhausted and her wounds were beginning to ache.

"Of course," Elle replied graciously. She pulled the old iron wash basin from underneath the bed, "I'll go fill this up," she said, picking it up.

She returned shortly after, just about managing to lug the water filled basin through the door. She took the torn sleeves of Billy's shirt, soaked them in the water and used them to lather a bar of tar soap. Fiona sat on the floor next to Elle as she gently wiped the dirt, dust and soot from her face. She soaked the rag and cleaned her sister's arms and legs. She lathered the soap again, massaged it into Fiona's scalp and helped her dunk her head into the water to get it all out.

Once Fiona was dry, Elle helped her get dressed. To their surprise, the sleeveless shirt fit nicely. It was too short to wear outside of the room, finishing just above the knee, but Elle was sure that they would be able find her some britches to wear with it. Fiona studied herself in the slightly warped and stained mirror. Elle stood behind her and smiled.

"Fiona Fire, the girl who escaped from hell itself," she announced proudly.

Fiona smiled back and turned to face her sister.

"Can I come with you and Billy when you leave?" she asked.

"Of course you can," Elle answered without hesitation. "Did you really think we'd leave you here alone?"

"I don't know," Fiona said. "I guess, I haven't thought about much yet. Can we sleep for a while?"

Elle nodded, sharing her sister's exhaustion. They lay down on the bed, holding one another and closed their eyes.

* *

Billy made his way over the road to the marshal's office. The sun was finally nudging its way beyond the horizon and washing away the remnants of the night. With the steadily brightening morning, more and more of the townsfolk were emerging and going about their business. Store front signs changed from closed to open, and a young man on a street corner called out headlines from the newspaper.

Distracted as he was, Billy narrowly avoided treading on a cat, as he absently stepped up onto the boardwalk on the opposite side of the street. He approached the main entrance of the town hall and pounded his fist twice. He was taken by surprise as the door swung open almost immediately. He paused for a second and looked around, then entered the building.

"Hello," he called out, "Marshal Andrews?"

The marshal was sitting at his desk in his office on the second floor. He had not slept during the night, instead he had remained at his desk and waited patiently for the morning. When he heard Billy's voice, he leaned his head back and closed his eyes tightly.

"Good morning," he shouted loudly, "I'm up here!"

Billy had not expected the marshal to greet him at the door, excited and eager to talk, but he thought that the man would at least surface from his office to greet him. He climbed the stairs and opened the door to the office.

"Good morning," Billy greeted, with a tired sigh. "May I sit? I'm pretty weary."

Marshal Andrews held out a hand and gestured at the chair. When Billy sat, he noticed the man's dull and tired eyes. In front of him on the desk, a mountain of ash piled high in a brass ashtray. A glass with a half shot of bourbon sat next to a near empty bottle and a polished revolver.

"It's early," the marshal said, as though he had only just realized. "This must be a visit of some importance, Mr?"

"Earl," Billy finished, "Billy Earl. I work…" he paused, forgetting himself, "I worked at the Bellamy Ranch."

The marshal nodded as he lit a cigar.

"You're the one, aren't you?" he said aloofly, through a cloud of smoke.

"I'm sorry?"

"The one who wants to go after Ed Bader," he clarified, while looking up at the ceiling.

"Actually Marshal, that's part of the reason I'm here. I've killed Ed Bader. Yesterday evening, I shot him with a rifle. I got him in the chest, I think, and I saw him fall from his horse," Billy explained, trying to remain respectful and tone down the pride, that had begun to resonate in his voice.

The marshal chuckled to himself, a chuckle which was alien to Billy. It sounded empty and joyless. It was not the sound of mirth, but the sound of hopelessness and futility.

"You killed White Price," the marshal corrected him.

"I killed Ed-" Billy began adamantly.

"You killed White Price," he repeated firmly, interrupting him, "his body is in the room below us."

Billy stared at the desk in disbelief. He was sure that he had killed the right man. He had replayed it over and over in his mind. His dreams of running away and starting a new life with Elle, were hanging in the balance. Had the blaze not orphaned the girls, and forced Fiona into their plans to elope, the reward for killing White, although significantly less, might have been enough.

"What did he do?" Marshal Andrews asked.

Billy looked up at him, puzzled as to what the marshal meant.

"Bader," he clarified, "what did he do? I saw him and his WPC posse ride out of here last night, after White finally bled out."

He tapped the end of his cigar and watched the ash fall into the tray. Billy lunged forward and slammed his fists on the table. The marshal flinched only slightly at Billy's sudden aggression.

"You saw them ride out of here and you did nothing?" he growled.

"I didn't know where they were going," Marshal Andrews replied plainly.

"You couldn't ride after them? Or try to stop them?" Billy raged.

"Listen to what you are saying, Mr Earl," the marshal urged him, "one man? One individual, against fifteen or so men?"

"They killed Abel and Martha Bellamy and the ranch hand Johnson Stacks, and then they burned down the house," Billy said through gritted teeth.

The marshal sat forward and rested on his elbows, his brow furrowed and hands restless.

"And the two girls, what of them?" he asked apprehensively.

"Miss Fiona was in the house, she got hurt but she's alive. Miss Elle is fine, her and I were elsewhere" Billy told him, returning to his seat. "We're staying across the way, at the Grand. You'll be reimbursing us for our stay. That's the penalty for your inaction," he added firmly.

"Fine," the marshal said. He waved a hand dismissively and leaned back in his chair, breathing a sigh of relief. "I'll wire for White Price's reward money, it'll be here in a few days. Where will you go?"

"Nowhere," Billy shrugged. "I'm not done yet."

"You know, I was like you once," he scoffed. "I was full of optimism about this place, its potential excited me. I was young and I was foolhardy. Justice is not a simple concept in these lands. I tried, I really did. Do you know how many ghosts walk those streets? I lost count a long time ago…" he trailed off and held a shaking hand to his brow. "If you stay here in Good Rock, no good will come of it."

"Someone has to try," Billy offered, "someone has to stand up for what's right-"

"Is that really what this is?" the marshal cut in, narrowing his eyes. "Or is this vengeance?"

Humans Are the Ugliest Creatures

"Does it matter?" Billy asked. "Either way, the people here finally have someone on their side, and I get what I want."

"And what's that?" he asked flippantly.

"Enough money for me and Miss Elle to start a new life. Well, that was the original idea, now it seems Miss Fiona will be coming along with us too. We are in love, Marshal, and I will do anything to make that happen," Billy said passionately.

"I don't want any more blood," he pleaded. "It's the senseless deaths, the pointlessness of it all…" he fell silent and stared at the window, dejected. "The blood flows through the dirt like a river. The current traps you and pulls you down," he puffed on his cigar and frowned, "there's no escaping it."

"You may have lost your way a long time ago," Billy said as he got to his feet, "but I haven't. I got more fight in me than ever." He crossed the room and stopped at the door. "You know where to find me, when the money arrives. Get some sleep, Marshal," he said scathingly as he made his exit.

Billy took the stairs step by step, feeling the muscles in his legs ache with each movement. He saw a bag of groceries on a side table near the door, assuming that they were intended for the marshal, he picked them up on his way out. He crossed the street and returned to the hotel room, to drop off the food.

The two sisters were sound asleep on the bed, hand in hand. Billy smiled at the sweet scene, a smile which slowly faded as he considered the circumstances of the situation. He poured himself a glass of milk, making sure to leave enough in the bottle for the girls and left them to sleep.

Humans Are the Ugliest Creatures

He took a seat on a bench, on the boardwalk in front of the Grand, and sipped from the glass of milk. He squinted against the harsh morning sunlight and felt the burning fires of fatigue around his eyes. The bruises on his body pulsed with a dull ache as he twisted and stretched. The stubble hugging his face, persisted with a nagging itch. He tilted his hat, to shade his eyes and leaned back against the bench, watching the people of Good Rock as they went about their business.

His head was swimming as his thoughts raced. Each thought giving way to the next, before he had even had a second to contemplate them or break them down. The fire, the Bellamys, Stacks, Fiona's burns, Elle's beauty and Bader's wrath, all these thoughts and more seemed to be flooding and spilling over within his head.

He sipped at the milk, it was much warmer than before. He wondered how long he had been sitting. It seemed as if he were only half awake, watching as people passed and dreaming with wide eyes.

"Billy Earl?" someone inquired.

Billy had been swirling the milk in the glass for an indeterminate amount of time. He had no idea how long the man next to him had been there. He looked up to see Sheriff Manning sitting by his side. He had a cheerful and well rested look about him. Holding out a hand, he smiled and squinted against the sun as it peered from behind Billy's head.

"Sheriff Manning, good morning," Billy greeted, shaking his hand out of courtesy.

"I thought it was you," he said wistfully. "White Price's body is over there with a big hole in his side. That's some handy work. You've already fared better than I expected."

"Well, Sheriff, it wasn't White I was trying to kill," Billy sighed tiredly.

The sheriff nodded absently and slouched on the bench.

"I spoke with Marshal Andrews this morning, I heard about the fire. Very sad news," he commented, watching a stagecoach as it rolled by in front of them. "I tried to warn you. Maybe now you'll see it."

"Please, Sheriff," Billy paused, "I've already had enough of this from the marshal."

"I'm sure," he smiled jovially, "I wouldn't expect anything less from old Ellis, trudging around under that rain cloud. He just wants everyone to get along. I think it's guilt that makes him that way. Guilt over what, I'm not entirely sure. I'm not here to talk you out of anything," he paused and checked his pocket watch, almost as if he were bored of his own conversation. "I believe that most men can serve a purpose, especially in a place like this," he chuckled, "you can always find a use for a willing man. Such was the case with Ed Bader."

"Sheriff, that-" Billy began as he straightened up.

The sheriff held up his hands defensively and Billy fell quiet.

"I know you have your opinions on that, but it was what worked for a while. His recklessness means that his purpose has ultimately been served and we'd be better off without him. I know I tried to talk you out of it, and I still think you must've been out in the sun a little too long, but if you are hell bent on killing him, like you damn sure seem to be, then I wish you success," he finished with a smile.

He stood, held his hands behind his back and slowly made his way up the street, smiling and greeting people as he did. Billy finished the glass of milk and, feeling the weight of his of his own body, decided that he could no longer avoid it, he needed to go inside to rest.

As he entered the small room, neither of the sisters woke. They were still sleeping peacefully, arm in arm. Billy took off his boots, for what felt like the first time in years, and lay down on the floor at the base of the bed. He rested his hands underneath his head, closed his eyes and waited for sleep.

He woke up later that evening, shaken from his slumber and alert to a noise in the hall. Billy wondered what time it was, the sun had set and the light had all but drained from the room. He kept his eyes on doorway, watching a shadow as it moved back and forth in the hall.

"Been there for a couple of minutes," Fiona whispered behind him.

Billy turned to see Fiona sat cross legged on the bed, aiming a rifle at the door.

"I was just about to wake you," she told him.

Billy noticed her eyes as he looked up at her. Each one looked swollen and sore, encased in a sharp, striking, red ring. Whether irritation from the smoke or her tears, Billy was not sure, but there in the near darkness of the room, it was unsettling to see.

"There's only one of them. He came and went, now he's back," she whispered as Billy lifted his head to check on Elle. "She's fine. It'd take a stampede to wake her."

"Have they said anything?" Billy asked her in a hushed voice.

Fiona shook her head, the two crimson rings swaying from side to side in the low light. Billy picked up his gun and got to his feet as quietly as he could. Then came a knock at the door. Billy pressed his back against the wall and edged closer to the doorframe.

"Who is it?" he called.

"It is Deputy Yeun, Mr Earl," he announced in a thick Chinese accent.

Billy waved his arm at Fiona to lower the rifle and opened the door. Yeun saw Billy holding the gun and smiled.

"Very wise. It is not possible to be too careful in such times," he said.

The deputy's clean shaven face looked youthful, he could not have been much older than Billy. He wore a black shirt and a colorfully embroidered, burgundy waistcoat. His shaved head was ornamented with a black bowler hat.

"I apologize if I have caused a startle, or woken you from sleep."

"It's fine," Billy told him, "I've had quite enough rest for now." He looked over his shoulder to Fiona, "stay with Elle Belle. No one in, no one out. This won't take long."

Fiona nodded firmly and locked the door behind Billy.

"Follow me," Yeun instructed as Billy tied his belt and holstered his gun.

"Where are we headed?" Billy asked apprehensively.

"For a drink at the Silver Boot," Yean said and then casually added, "where Wilbur Woods currently is."

"Wilbur Woods?" Billy repeated, stopping in his tracks. "You're taking me to him?"

"No," Yeun smiled, "we are simply going to where he is."

Billy studied the deputy suspiciously. Yeun stared back at Billy blankly.

"You said before that you couldn't get involved. The sheriff told you not to," Billy puzzled.

"Either do not begin or, having begun, do not give up," he told him. "I am like you, a man of actions. Now follow," he demanded as he turned and made his way to the bottom of the stairs.

When they entered the Silver Boot, Billy immediately spotted Wilbur and his posse of three WPC men. Yeun pointed at a free table towards the back of the Saloon, near where Billy had sat with Stacks on his previous visit.

Billy lowered his hat, slightly obscuring his face, in an attempt to remain anonymous. He took a seat, while Yeun headed to the bar, spoke with the barkeeper and returned with two drinks. He leaned in toward Billy and spoke softly.

"They handed in their guns at the bar, but that doesn't mean they are unarmed. I've instructed the barkeeper that the weapons are to remain in his possession until morning."

He turned his head and looked at the group as they drank and laughed, while one of them acted out a joke. Wilbur was stone faced and dower, standing in the center of the gang members.

"It makes me angry," he said to Billy. "They are wanted men in this town. But they come here and mock us by behaving in this way. It is an insult. Unless someone does something to restore the integrity of this town, things will never change."

They sat quietly and sipped from their glasses, keeping a close watch on the WPC group. The men got louder and rowdier as the night wore on and they steadily became more intoxicated. They waited until the men had finished their last drinks and watched them cross the smoke filled room to the bar, to retrieve their weapons.

Yeun signaled Billy as the WPC men started moving. They got up from their seats and slipped out through the door, unnoticed by the gang members. Yeun stood in front of the saloon, in the middle of Main Street, while Billy hung back in the shadows of an alley, in-between the Sliver Boot and the adjacent building.

Billy crouched and listened. He focused and through the static chatter and laughter of the patrons. He could hear the gang members arguing with the barkeeper about their weapons. He heard cries of "those is ours" and "you ain't in charge here". After a few more moments, the WPC men emerged from the saloon together.

"Your damn right, we'll be back in the morning!" one of the men yelled back to the barkeeper, "and you can bet we'll be bringing the Cook with us! Maybe you'll be more cooperative then!" he slurred his words and spat as he shouted, clearly inebriated.

"Shut your God damn mouth, Pup," Wilbur growled angrily.

He looked up and stopped at the edge of the boardwalk. He saw Deputy Yeun, standing ahead of them in the street, ominously illuminated in the dim light of the streetlamps. He tilted his head and grunted. The man called Pup read the signal, jumped down into the street and approached Yeun.

"You ought to know better than to be standing in our way, Mr," he warned, his voice in sync with his lumbering, aggressive movements.

Yeun stood motionless, allowing the man to approach. When Pup got to within one step of him, the deputy lashed out. He clobbered the man with the butt of his pistol, instantly rendering him unconscious as he slumped limply to the ground.

"You are wanted men in this town and should not be here. This man is under arrest," Yeun informed them authoritatively.

"Jesus," Wilbur muttered gruffly and turned to another WPC man.

The second man drew a knife from his boot and lurched into the street.

"Should've stayed in China, kid," he cackled as he stepped forward confidently.

Yeun moved swiftly, side stepping and keeping one eye on the knife wielding man. He danced from side to side, dodging attacks, while remaining alert of the other men.

"Quit messing around," Wilbur shouted, almost incoherently.

The man lunged forward, Yeun slid to the side and ducked. As the man stumbled, Yeun drove his foot into the back of his knee, took a firm grip of his arm and wrenched it back against his hip, snapping the arm in two. The bone cracked loudly as the man dropped the blade and cried out in pain. Yeun drove his elbow into the side of the man's head, silencing and subduing him. He left him on the ground next to the first aggressor.

"Under arrest," Yeun proclaimed.

Wilbur spat on the floor.

"End this now," he grumbled.

As the deputy had expected, despite handing over weapons at the bar, the men were still armed. On Wilbur's command, they drew their pistols. Before they managed to straighten their arms and take aim, or realize the mistake they had made, they met their demise. A bullet ripped through one man's neck, filling the air behind him with a fine scarlet spray. Billy turned his head away as he felt the blood rain down on him. The second man took a bullet to the chest, he staggered in place and fell sideways into Wilbur.

Wilbur moved quickly and caught the dying man in his arms. He straightened up, using the man as a living shield and took aim at Deputy Yeun.

"You've made some error," Wilbur barked.

"Wilbur Woods, you are under arrest," Yeun announced, stepping forward.

"You take another step forward and you'll be soaking the dirt like the rest of these poor wretches," Wilbur threatened.

Yean paused where he stood and held Wilbur's gaze. Billy crept out from the shadows and aimed at Wilbur's head, standing less than a foot away from him.

"Jesus Christ," Wilbur muttered, "I knew we should've killed you at the camp. Should've waited at the house and killed all of you," he lamented.

Behind Yeun, Pup stirred on the floor and reached for the knife. He took it in his grasp, rose to his knees and lunged forward, driving the blade into Yeun's thigh. Yeun cried out and fired his gun. Wilbur's human shield shuddered as the bullet buried into the dead man's back. Instinctively, Wilbur fired in response. The bullet crashed into the young deputy's skull, killing him instantly.

It all happened in the blink of an eye, but to Billy, time seemed to pass by at a tenth of its normal rate. Yeun's body had yet to hit the floor, when Wilbur dropped his shield and was turning to face Billy. Billy pulled back on the trigger and watched as the bullet burrowed into Wilbur's remaining eye and disappeared. He fell back, slammed into the boardwalk and rolled into the street.

Billy stood at the edge of the boardwalk, looking over Wilbur's lifeless body. He watched as the blood flowed freely from his shattered scalp and quenched the parched earth.

"Drop that knife and get on your knees, before I paint the dirt with the inside of your head!"

Billy looked up to see Fiona standing near Pup, with a rifle aimed squarely at his head. Initially he did not recognize her voice. It had developed a low, raspy tone since the fire, but it was the visceral anger which threw him off, he had never heard such anger in her voice. Pup stared back at her quietly. A grin spread across his face as he realized who Fiona was.

"Looks like you got mite too close to a fire, little girl," he laughed.

"You want to get burned next?" she hissed.

"Fiona!" Billy shouted as he jumped forward into the street and stood at her side, leveling his gun at Pup. "Get down now," he growled at the outlaw. He turned and gave Fiona a stern look, "go back to your sister. I told you to stay put."

Fiona looked up at Billy, his face and clothes splattered with blood, and for once chose not to argue. All she wanted was to help and she saw that she had done as much as she could.

"I'll come for you first, burned bitch," Pup warned and spat into the dirt at Fiona's feet.

She jerked her arms forward and jabbed the barrel of the rifle forcefully into the center of Pup's face, breaking his nose with an audible crunch.

"It's Fiona Fire. Come and get me, I'll be waiting for you," she growled angrily.

"Get back," Billy ordered Fiona, pointing down the street.

Obediently, she lowered the rifle and ran back to the Grand, passing the sheriff and the marshal on her way as they emerged, having assumed the gunfight to be over.

"What happened here?" The sheriff asked Billy as he approached.

He knelt down next his deputy and shook his head.

"Everyone if you would please head back inside and continue with your evening. Everything is under control here, thank you," the marshal addressed the crowd beginning to gather in front of the Silver Boot.

"Both of you cowards should hand your badges over to this man!" someone heckled from the doorway.

The marshal sighed and turned away, refusing to be drawn into another argument over his character.

"Cowards!" another voice called as the crowd slowly funneled back into the saloon.

"Yeun tried to take them on," Billy explained, "he took these two alive, then the shooting started. Wilbur shot him, so I shot Wilbur," Billy said absently and pointed to where Wilbur's body lay in the dark shadows of the boardwalk.

Marshal Andrews stood with his hands on his hips, shaking his head, a frustrated look painted across his face.

"I told you not twenty-four hours ago, I don't want any more bloodshed," the marshal vented, "now I find myself stood in the middle of Main Street, with the bodies of three young men and Wilbur Woods."

Billy chose not to respond.

"It's not the time, Ellis," the sheriff said passively as he covered Yeun's face and picked up the body. "My deputy captured two and slayed two, the reward money can go to the sheriff's department, to help find a new deputy. Billy shot Wilbur, he gets the reward.

"Jon, if you think you're just walking away from this mess-" Marshal Andrews began angrily.

"I warned you, Ellis," Sheriff Manning cut in, "I warned you about putting up those posters. This is your mess to fix, not mine. Now if you'll excuse me, I need to clean up my dead deputy and make arrangements."

He cradled the body in his arms and walked away. Billy lowered his gun and cracked it across the back of Pup's head, leaving him in an unconscious heap.

"I'm sure even you can manage moving them to the cells, Marshal," Billy said snidely.

He walked away, leaving the marshal to drag the unconscious men to the cells and deal with the bodies of the slain.

Billy trudged along Main Street and returned to the Good Rock Grand. He knocked on the door of the hotel room and announced himself.

"Fiona, open up, it's Billy."

The door opened and he stepped inside. Fiona returned to her post at the edge of the bed and rested the rifle across her lap.

"You still got blood on you," she said, looking up at him.

He touched a hand to his face and looked the bloodstains on his fingers. His hands quaked as he held them out. He tried as much as he could to steady them but failed to regain control. Watching him, Fiona held out her hands for comparison. They were steady as a rock.

"There's some soap and a bucket over there, if you want to clean up," she suggested.

Elle stirred in the bed behind her and sat up, rubbing her eyes.

"Jesus, Billy!" she shrieked as he came into focus.

She darted up from the bed and started checking him over.

"Calm down, it ain't his blood," Fiona informed her coldly.

"What happened?" she asked, clearly shaken by his appearance.

"I just shot Wilbur Woods," Billy told her, frowning and staring at the floor. "and Bader's not dead, I got the wrong man. I got White Price instead."

She placed her hand on his cheek and looked into his eyes.

"I'll help you clean up," she said, full of compassion.

She hurriedly picked up the wash basin and squeezed past Billy and Fiona, to get to the door. She returned and set it down on the floor. Billy removed his shirt, sat down next to her and closed his eyes. With a gentle, loving hand, she wiped the blood from his face. As she dabbed at his skin and slowly restored the face that she loved so deeply, the face that she saw every time she closed her eyes, she smiled fondly.

"Deputy Yeun died," he told Elle, causing her to gasp in shock, "Wilbur shot him."

"It's all so awful," she mumbled despairingly, ringing the blood-soaked cloth in her hands.

"Three days ago, I'd hardly aimed a gun at a man, never mind taken a life," he reflected.

"What's it like?" Fiona asked.

"There's a weight to it," he replied after some thought.

Fiona was not sure that she had understood but she nodded as though she had nonetheless. He placed his hands on Elle's shoulders.

"They're going to pay me for shooting Wilbur," he explained. "That, along with the money for White, should be enough for the three of us to get away and start fresh somewhere. I know it's not as much as what we originally planned, but things have changed and at least it's something."

Elle kissed him passionately.

"As long as it all stops, Billy. As long as we're safe. I can't take any more heartache. Every time you leave my side, I worry to no end. I just want to leave it all behind and carry on," she told him. "We can start again," she held her hand out to Fiona, "together, all three of us."

"It's settled then," he concluded with a smile, "when the money comes through, we'll move on and leave all of this behind."

Humans Are the Ugliest Creatures

10

Billy, the Marshal, Bader and a Betrayal

Billy, Elle and Fiona woke as the sun rose and poured the light of a new day through the window. Fiona was the first to get up. She had slept in-between Billy and her sister, and suffered a poor night's sleep due to the heat. She stood at the end of the bed and stretched. She had briefly allowed herself to forget about the injury to her shoulder and winced as the pain flared with a fiery intensity.

"How's it feel?" Elle asked, through a yawn as she sat up and saw her sister's pained expression.

"It's fine, Elle Belle," Fiona said defiantly, her voice still harsh as gravel, "I hardly even notice it."

"Fiona Fire, strong and stubborn as ever," Elle smirked.

"The bandage feels a little damp," she said, lightly laying a hand on it.

"That'll happen in the heat," Billy offered, without lifting his head from the pillow. "How about I take you down to Doc Faulds, to get it changed?"

She nodded, picked up an apple and took a bite. She picked up a second and offered it to Billy as he sleepily raised his head. He held his hands open and caught the apple as she tossed it through the air. Fiona recoiled at the sharpness of the fruit. She looked at the makeshift dress that Billy had made, where it lay draped over the back of a chair.

"I need some britches," she announced, "and some boots too," she looked down at her feet and wiggled her toes. "I don't know if anyone noticed but I ain't got any shoes."

Billy frowned as he realized that he had indeed not noticed.

"We can purchase some things after we see the doctor," Elle told her.

"And I want a hat," Fiona declared, "one like Poppa had."

"I could do with one or two dresses," Elle added.

Billy looked at her in mock disapproval.

"Billy, I need more than one dust covered dress. It is not befitting of a lady such as myself, to wander the streets in a tarnished outfit," she joked.

"Fine," Billy agreed, "we can forward the payments on to the marshal. He can think of them as reparations." He hesitated and stood up in front of the girls, "at some point we need to return to the ranch, to bury Stacks, to say goodbye. I can speak to the pastor and arrange something for tomorrow."

Humans Are the Ugliest Creatures

The sisters stared at the floor, struggling to hide their emotions.

"That'd be nice," Elle eventually spoke. She stood and wrapped her arms around Billy, "thank you."

"That's what I'm here for, Elle Belle," he said and kissed the top of her head.

"I miss them," Fiona said quietly. "I always talked about leaving and how I didn't need anyone, but this is so permanent. I think maybe I was wrong."

Elle let go of Billy and stood next to her sister, taking her hand.

"I've had this horrible feeling since it happened, and for a while I couldn't work out what it was. Something deep down here in my stomach," she explained and pointed, "I think it's guilt. Guilt that I wanted to leave them, that I was going to leave them. Now they've been taken, and I feel in some way responsible for that."

"You didn't do that," Billy said firmly, "you shouldn't blame yourself for it."

Elle nodded, with tears in her eyes.

"I know," she mumbled through a forced smile, "and I think that one day I won't."

They got dressed and made their way down to the street. It was mid-morning and the town was already bustling with people. The air was cooler than it had been and offered a refreshing break from the ever-persistent dry heat.

Across the street, outside the town hall, the bodies of the two WPC men shot by deputy Yeun were on display. Wanted notices for WPC gang members had been posted above each of them. The morbid scene had already been tampered with. Both of the men's yellow sashes had been removed and nailed to the building, with the words "*Murderous devils*" etched into the green cladding of the town hall.

Elle stared and held on tightly to Billy's arm. Billy looked to the window above, where the grim faced marshal stood, studying the flow of people as they moved up and down the street. By the time that Marshal Andrews noticed Billy and the Bellamy girls, they had already begun to move on.

They walked along the boardwalk at a leisurely pace, pausing to look in through the windows of the various store fronts. Elle picked out two dresses, while Billy helped Fiona find something to wear. She decided upon two pairs of gray britches and a shirt. Elle suggested she chose another, so that she would not have to wear Billy's handmade garment, but she resisted, claiming that it was one of her favorite items of clothing that she had ever owned. She spent some time standing before a mirror, trying on various hats before she finally settled on one. It was a tan, leather hat, the closest thing she could find resembling the hat that her father had once worn.

They stopped off to purchase some more provisions to tide them over until Billy's bounty payout arrived. Fiona felt her stomach rumbling as she walked around the store, studying each of the items on sale and imagining herself eating them.

"Can we get a pecan tree when we leave?" she asked, staring wide eyed at a jar filled with nuts.

"I'm sure we can try," Elle replied. "Do you think it will be hard when we leave?"

"I don't know," Fiona frowned. "When I think about it, all I want to do is get away. I'm sure I'll feel something.

This was our home," she paused, full of thought, "but it's not anymore."

"That's true," Elle said glumly. She hugged her sister, "wherever we go, we'll make a new home."

Fiona smiled and tipped a handful of nuts into a bag.

"Hey, not too much," Billy told her as he noticed how many she was putting in the bag. "Only take what we need for now."

Fiona understood and put half off the nuts back in the jar. She left the store feeling the happiest she had felt since the fire, stuffing her mouth with pecans and enjoying the feel of her new clothes.

As they made their way back to the Good Rock Grand at a relaxed pace, enjoying the day's generous breeze, a man stopped and shook Billy's hand.

"Good job, son," he congratulated, still shaking his hand. "It's about time someone stood up for the people of this town. Shame about that little Chinese though. I couldn't understand him much, but he had guts and that's admirable."

"Thanks," Billy said apprehensively, unsure of what else to say.

"Well, I can see you're plenty busy. Please don't let me take up no more of your time," he said gracefully, "I just wanted to say thank you is all. You folks have a nice day now."

"Sure will," Billy smiled, "you too."

The man patted Billy on the shoulder and disappeared back into the busy street. Elle latched onto Billy's arm.

"Is my love a hero?" she joked, fluttering her eyelashes.

"That had better be a one off," Billy said grumpily, "the sooner we get away from here the better." He stopped as they reached the Grand and looked back at the bodies in front of the town hall. He let out a heavy sigh and shook his head. "The sooner the better," he mumbled.

* *

Marshal Andrews remained statuesque in his favored spot at the window. He watched as Billy and the Bellamy girls returned and disappeared through the open doors of the Grand. He considered their recent tragedy and how the newly orphaned girls must be feeling. At whose feet did they lay the most blame? Was it Bader, for his revenge? Was it Billy, as the catalyst? Or was it the marshal himself, for his inaction? He attempted to ease the cutting sensation of guilt, by apportioning blame equally amongst all the players involved. He understood his own role in all of it. As much as he felt that his hand had been forced, it was nevertheless he who had set events in motion by issuing warrants for Bader and his men. He had protected the outlaw for too long and deeply regretted doing so.

He puzzled back and forth over the timeline of events for a while longer. It was shame, combined with anger, rather than hopefulness, which led him to the idea that he could still do something. He could be of some use to the people of Good Rock, who had come to resent him so. There was no need for more bloodshed. It was a wild and dangerous place, where violence was prevalent, but there was always room for diplomacy, there had to be or they would be no better than animals.

The marshal extinguished his cigar and drank the last of his bourbon. He gathered his effects and went to ready his horse. The overcast sky and gentle breeze were welcome. There was a persistent throbbing in his skull, deep and central. Whether from lack of sleep, dehydration or stress, he was not sure. He was not even sure that he cared, he was determined that it would not stop him. He rode out of Good Rock, under the far reaching, thick swells of gray, experiencing a sense of urgency and confidence, the likes of which he had not known in years.

As he rode, sweat began to flood the ravines of his furrowed brow. His rare bout of confidence waned and withered. He slowed his pace and started to question his judgement as the familiar feeling of ineptitude slowly crept back in. Then it hit him like a bullet, causing pangs of dread to surge through his body like shockwaves.

He paused atop the crest of the hill and looked back over the town. His hands shook. He tried balling them into fists, in an effort to regain some semblance of control. The land beneath him was flat, but he felt as though he were on a tilt and might fall away at any moment. He coughed into his hand rhythmically and tried to draw in air as slowly as possible. He leaned forward and rested his head against his horse's neck, trying to focus on the course hair as it brushed against his skin, and the cool sweat as it ran down his neck.

Time seemed to affect him intermittently as he carried on along the road and left Good Rock behind. The land was subdued. The birds were few and the ground dwelling animals seemed to have rejected the day in favor of remaining in their nests.

Marshal Andrews gripped the reigns tightly as he rode and blinked slowly. Each time he closed his eyes, he tried to hone in on his other senses and distract himself.

He did not understand the affliction, nor had he revealed it to anyone else. He felt ashamed and weakened by it. In recent months, the frequency of these unpleasant episodes had dramatically increased.

The effects seemed to fade as he reached the WPC camp. He climbed down from his horse and handed the reins to Lyle Dixon, who hitched the animal near the camp's entrance.

"Morning, Marshal. I think the boss is at the back, by one of the fires," Lyle stammered awkwardly.

Marshal Andrews nodded his thanks and made his way through the camp. As he did, the WPC men would nod and greet him, almost as if he belonged there himself.

"Well, good morning, Marshal," Frank Kelly greeted as he got up from his seat.

"Frank," Marshal Andrews acknowledged coldly.

"To what do we owe your presence?" Kelly mocked.

"That's enough, Frank," he snapped, "Where's Ed at?"

Kelly held his hands in the air and frowned crossly.

"Is there some sort of problem here, Marshal? Some reason you have to behave so discourteously?" he stepped forward, squared up to the marshal and placed a finger on the handle of the hatchet at his waist. "I think maybe you are miss-remembering who I am."

Marshal Andrews stood his ground and held Kelly's stare. Slowly, a grin spread across Kelly's face and he took a step back.

"Looks like you're finally getting a little stonier," he laughed. "The boss has been out hunting, he won't be too long. You can take a seat over there at the back."

The marshal nodded and walked past Kelly without speaking. He maintained his unfazed demeanor and made his way to the campfire to wait for Bader. It took all of his strength to stride through the camp with apparent confidence. The reality of it was that Kelly had shaken him to his core and he felt that at any given moment, his legs were going to give out beneath him.

He took a seat by a campfire and waited for Bader to return. He held his hands together, to make the trembling less apparent and sighed deeply. He looked into the fire, let his shoulders slump and allowed his thoughts drift to the darker corners of his mind. He wondered once again about what he was doing. Was there really any point in it, considering the risk involved? Further to that, was there any point in anything that he did? As he stared vacantly, he was sure that he could not come up with a way to justify his own existence and it crushed him, just as it did every time he reached the same unavoidable conclusion.

"Ellis," a booming voice sung out from behind him.

It took him by surprise and wrenched him from his grim introspective thoughts. Bader stepped out in front of the marshal, dressed in his usual all black outfit and took a seat nearby.

"Well, you look as happy as ever," Bader laughed. "Hunting was fruitless, so I'm hoping you have some good news for me. Judging by the look on your face, I'd wager against that being the case."

"I asked you to stop, Ed," Marshal Andrews said and shook his head in dismay. "I asked you to stop and you didn't listen. You just keep pushing and pushing. I should have followed you the other night and tried to stop you."

"I'm not quite sure what it is you're referring to," Bader narrowed his eyes and grinned.

He removed his hat and fanned himself lightly. The nearby men were ordered to leave them alone, with a commanding wave of his hand.

"Would you gentlemen give us a moment, please? I need to catch up with our trusted friend here."

The men looked at one another briefly, then dispersed into the camp as instructed.

"I don't want to play games, I'm tired of it. I'm tired of all of it," the marshal said, exacerbated to the point of despair. "You're only making things worse for yourself."

"Do you expect me to just roll over?" Bader asked. "Lie down and let that boy claim me as a prize? Maybe you'd like to strip me down and tie a little bow around me, leave me out in the open-"

"The honorable thing at this point would be to turn yourself in," the marshal cut in angrily.

"Turn myself in," he scoffed, "might as well hang myself. Save your boys the trouble." He paused as though in deep thought, "no, I don't think I'll be doing that."

Marshal Andrews pressed his hands to his face in frustration and groaned softly.

"Look, Ellis, I like you, that's the only reason you aren't on the floor bleeding like a stuck pig. You are talking to the wrong man here. It's that Billy you need to rein in, not me. I tried to speak to him, I brought him here showed him around. I explained how we do things and demonstrated why it is imperative that people do not cross me. Obviously, the message didn't quite sink in, so I had to revisit the issue and provide a little more clarity."

"Clarity?" the marshal derided.

Humans Are the Ugliest Creatures

"Yes, clarity," Bader reiterated in a raised voice, his patience wearing thin. "Some of the men wanted blood from the start. They couldn't understand why I forbade it. Then once White died, I had a real storm to quell, so quell I did, and you should thank me! Some of the things these men wanted to do were frankly inhuman. You are someone who sometimes exhibits rational thought, so why do you think it is that I don't just ride into town and split his skull open, right in front of all those nice people?"

The marshal shrugged, resisting Bader's attempts to draw him into a dialog, and waited for him to continue. Bader waved his hat and tutted dismissively.

"If I kill him, the next challenger appears," he explained. "Pretty soon hunting me will be a sport, which people travel from far and wide to participate in. Deterrence is the objective. I need to show people that choosing to come for me, means losing more than just your life."

"And if he won't back down?" the marshal asked.

"He will," Bader replied, confidently.

Frank Kelly approached the campfire, knelt down next to Bader and spoke quietly in his ear, so that the marshal could not hear. Bader kept his eyes locked on Marshal Andrews and studied him as he fidgeted nervously.

"Thank you," Bader said, patting Kelly on the arm.

Kelly nodded and walked away, leaving the pair alone again. Bader leaned forward, resting his arms against his knees. He pulled a small dried piece of meat from his pocket and bit down on it. The marshal recoiled in disgust as Bader tore a piece off and chewed.

"Ellis, I'm going to expect total honesty from you," he started, "if I suspect anything less," he waved the piece of meat in his hand, "well, you know how it plays out." He chuckled to himself, then stopped abruptly, "why are two of my men lying dead in your street? And where are Wilbur and the others he was with?"

"The other two are jailed and Wilbur is dead," the marshal replied grimly.

"What happened?" Bader asked quickly.

"The young Deputy Yeun enlisted Billy Earl and tried to arrest them," he explained, "he paid for it with his life."

"That little Chinese boy is dead?"

"Yes," the marshal confirmed.

"Shame about that. Who killed Wilbur?" he demanded and got to his feet.

Marshal Andrews hesitated.

"Who killed Wilbur?" he repeated, throwing the remaining dried meat at the marshal's chest.

"Billy Earl," he blurted out, losing his nerve, "Wilbur shot Yeun, so Billy took him out," he finished, avoiding eye contact.

Bader laid a hand on Marshal Andrews' shoulder, causing him to flinch.

"We both want the same thing," he sighed, "we want this to be over. I think I know now how to make that happen. You are going to help me do that, Ellis."

The marshal opened his mouth as if about to protest but was silenced by Bader tightening his grip and squeezing his shoulder painfully.

"My sources tell me that he has a relationship of an amorous nature with a young girl. Is that correct to your knowledge?" he asked.

"I wouldn't…" Marshal Andrews stuttered, "I'm not entirely…"

Bader applied more pressure to the marshal's shoulder, causing him to wince and buckle.

"You are going to tell me where I can find this girl," Bader told him and dragged him from where he sat, forcing him onto his knees.

The marshal coughed as he inhaled dust and dirt upon impact. Bader knelt down next to him and spoke softly.

"Listen, Ellis, I don't want to hurt this girl, I really don't," he pulled the hammer back on his revolver and held it to the marshal's head, "but I will hurt you. So, I'll ask you nicely one more time. Where can I find her?"

"You swear won't hurt her?" the marshal asked shakily, his voice rattled with fear.

"I swear it, I won't. There's been far too much blood spilled already. I will hold her here and throw about a few threats. When Billy eventually agrees to back down and disappear, she walks free. Without a hair out of place," he grinned. "So, you want this all to be over? All you have to do is tell me where to find her. It's that easy."

The marshal stared at the dirt, on all fours, frozen by fear. The sweat rolled from his head and dripped into the dry earth. He closed his eyes tightly and shook his head.

"The Grand," he mumbled meekly.

"I'm sorry?" Bader mocked, holding his hand to his ear and twisting the gun against the marshal's temple.

"The Good Rock Grand!" he shouted.

"The Good Rock Grand, thank you, Ellis!" Bader boomed as he got to his feet and holstered his gun.

Marshal Andrews dropped his head forward and pressed his forehead into the dirt, trying to control his breathing. When he stood up, Bader held an arm out and pointed.

"Sit down, Ellis. Take it easy and have some water." He threw a canister of water to him and watched as he drank gratefully. "You want something to eat?" he asked. "You're going to be here for a while, you need to keep your strength up," he smiled.

"What are you talking about, Ed?" the marshal asked, anxiously looking around.

"You have a role to play in this," he said, implying that it was obvious.

"I don't want any part of this, Ed," he spoke defiantly, "I've already done too much."

Bader sat down next to the marshal and spoke quietly.

"Now is not the time to grow a backbone, Ellis. You are not in a position to negotiate. Either you choose to help me and find some way to justify it, within that gray, cloudy, little mind of yours, or you keep up this bold, noble persona, and I hold you here and force you to do it anyway. Only one of those options ends with you going home without injury." The marshal stiffened as Bader patted him on the back, "I'll let you think about what you want to do," he said smiling.

Bader stood up, leaving the marshal alone by the fire, to mull over his limited options. He sat, holding out his hands and staring at his palms, hoping to see something, some sort of sign of what to do. As he sat thinking, he knew deep down that it was all a charade. There was no choice. He was always going to help Bader rather than resist, he was spineless, as Bader had rightly said. Spineless and pathetic, too weak willed to do anything about it. He felt sick to his stomach. He could not tell if it was from the idea of helping Bader, or the idea of himself.

Most of the marshal's day was spent sitting quietly by the fire. He puzzled over his lack of options and how to accept the kidnapping in which he was going to be complicit. He ate when given food and drank when given water. Bader did not return to him until early evening.

The light was slowly draining from the sky as another day slipped seamlessly into another night. He noticed Bader and Frank Kelly approaching the campfire from a way off. Bader stopped near the fire and watched as Kelly marched on and dragged Marshal Andrews forward by the collar.

"Jesus Christ, Frank, what the hell are you doing?" the marshal screamed, struggling against Kelly as he was hauled along and dropped at Bader's feet.

"This is an interactive demonstration," Kelly hissed, "just in case you were not entirely sure who was in charge of the situation."

Bader stood, unwavering and whistled a low flat tone. Kelly stepped back from the marshal, drew his axe and tossed it back and forth between his hands. One by one, the rest of the WPC men slowly advanced from the less visible edges of the camp and fell in line behind Bader. He stopped whistling and offered a hand to the marshal.

"Get up, Ellis," he ordered.

Marshal Andrews slapped away Bader's hand and pushed himself to his feet unaided. He straightened his collar and jacket.

"Enough with the theatrics," the marshal hissed.

"You know me, I love a good show," he chuckled. "So, what's it to be, Ellis? Are you coming willingly? Or does Frank here have to shorten the rest of your fingers a little?"

The marshal snorted and shook his head, fed up, frustrated and above all frightened.

"Yes," he said softly, "I'll do it."

11

The Marshal, Bader and the Hostage

As the WPC group and the marshal made it to the edges of Good Rock, the sun's slow retreat was nearly complete. The invading light departed and the land's long drawn out shadows faded into obscurity. The clouds, which had loomed large throughout the day, still hung heavy and swollen. The vast sprawling landscape always gave the illusion that the clouds were much closer to the ground. They bulged as they rolled arduously overhead, threatening to split at any moment and unleash a torrent, the likes of which the land had not known for months. The day's gentle breeze had mutated into a blustering wind, its erratic gusts hurling dirt and dust along the funnel of Main Street. The streetlamps sung together like a discordant choir, their lanterns swaying, the sound of metal grinding on metal ringing out into the night.

Bader walked his horse out ahead of the small troop of five and halted. He looked up to the dark, endless sky as the first few drops of rain descended. He held out his gloved hand and watched as the droplets fell and exploded on impact.

"Ellis," he beckoned the marshal forward.

Marshal Andrews looked at the men around him. His gaze was mostly met with indifference, until he looked at Frank Kelly, who was leering at him in an almost demonic fashion.

"Don't go soft on us now, Marshal," Kelly warned, loosening a coat button and resting a hand on the heel of his gun. "It'd be a shame if a little rain washed away all that spirit."

The other men sniggered but the marshal did not react to Kelly's intimidation. Acting unfazed, he broke away from the group and joined Bader.

"It's time," Bader said plainly. His eyes were hidden under the brim of his hat, all that the marshal could see of the man was the excited grin slowly spreading across his face. "I know I've kept you in the dark about a lot of this but don't worry, it's very simple. All you have to do is draw Billy boy away from that building," he explained. The marshal nodded and Bader continued, his tone wry and playful, "but first, we need to pay a little visit to the good Sheriff Manning."

"What for?" Marshal Andrews asked anxiously.

"To get our boys back," Bader replied incredulously, "and you are going to help facilitate that." The marshal shrugged abjectly. "Good," Bader beamed, "let's get moving."

They steadily advanced along Main Street. There was no one else to be seen in the street, everyone had sought shelter from the elements in either their homes or the saloon. The rainfall was gradually worsening and limited their visibility to just a few yards. They dismounted outside the sheriff's office and hitched their horses. Bader urged the marshal ahead of him and Kelly, while the remaining men followed close behind.

"Jon," the marshal greeted somberly as he walked in through the door.

"Ellis, I don't usually see you after sundown, what…" Sheriff Manning trailed off into a perplexed silence as he saw the outlaws piling in behind the marshal. "What is this, Ellis?" he asked sternly.

"We're turning loose the prisoners," the marshal announced calmly.

"The hell we are," the sheriff protested, "them boys killed my deputy!"

Bader drew his pistol and aimed it at Sheriff Manning. Frank Kelly unsheathed his hatched and drove it into the sheriff's desk, causing him to lurch backwards in fright and very nearly fall from his chair.

"This is not up for debate, Sherriff," Bader said coolly. "Where are the keys?"

The sheriff opened a drawer at his desk and held out a set of keys, which jingled lightly as his hand trembled. Kelly, who was leaning so far over the desk that he was almost on top of it, snatched the keys from him and made his way to the cells. The sheriff gave Marshal Andrews a scornful look. Bader noticed the silent exchange as the marshal bowed his head in shame.

"You know, Sheriff, if you were half as affable as your colleague here, things wouldn't have to be so…" he paused searching for the right word, "unsavory."

Kelly hooted as he unlocked the cells and set the men free. They smiled at the sheriff as they passed.

"Thanks for the hospitality, Sheriff," Pup laughed.

Kelly took the hatchet by the handle and removed it from the desk. He held up the keys and dangled them in front of Sheriff Manning.

"Sheriff, if you'd like to follow me to your room," he joked, "just in case something comes over you and you start to feel a creeping sense of bravery." The sheriff remained in his chair, unresponsive, until Kelly offered the alternative, "we could just as easily riddle your legs with bullets, if you'd prefer?"

The sheriff slowly stood up from the chair, picked up a bottle of bourbon and took a long swig.

"And I suppose, you're not going to do anything about this?" he asked the marshal, who seemed to recoil deeper into the mob.

He shook his head in disgust and made his way to the back of the office. He sat on a bench in one of the cells and waited for Kelly to lock to door. The WPC men left the sheriff's office and walked out onto the rain-soaked boardwalk. Bader put his arm over the marshal's shoulders and pointed at the Good Rock Grand.

"Time for your big performance, Ellis," he smiled wickedly. "Me and the rest of the boys are going to be dotted around, crouching in the shadows." He pointed up at the window of the marshal's office. "Stay on your usual perch and keep an eye on the street, one of these boys will give you a signal. We will bolt out of here quick, so you'd best be hot on our heels." He paused and place a hand on the lawman's chest, "I really don't want to have to come back for you, Ellis."

The marshal clenched his fists nervously and offered Bader the vaguest of nods. Bader patted him on the back and clapped his hands together enthusiastically. He held his arms up and pointed forward. The gang of WPC members fanned out across the street, dropping into alleyways and deep doorways.

* *

Billy was sitting on a small wooden stool in the corner of the room, watching over the girls as they fell to sleep. They were still yet to recover from the events of the past few days. Billy tried to empathize and understand how they felt, but he could not conceive of it. Their emotional toll was so great that it manifested physically. He had nothing to compare. He had not experimented anything remotely close to what they were going through.

He sipped from a glass of bourbon, leaned back against the wall and rested his eyes. At the sound of a knock on the door, he dropped forward, suddenly alert. Fiona opened her eyes and lifted her head slightly.

"Go back to sleep," Billy told her. He pressed close to the door, "who is it?" he asked.

"Mr Earl? It's Marshal Andrews," the marshal spoke softly, "I need to speak with you in my office."

"It's a little late isn't it, Marshal?" Billy countered. "Besides I'm not dressed for it."

"I assure you, Mr Earl, it's quite urgent. If you need time to dress, I'll wait for you in my office. Please be as quick as you can," he insisted.

Billy listened to the sound of the marshal's footsteps softening as he moved further away. He knelt down next to Fiona, whose eyes were half open in a sleepy squint.

"I've got to go across the way and speak with the marshal about something," Billy explained. "I doubt I'll be too long."

"Sure," Fiona yawned sleepily.

Billy buttoned his shirt and picked up his gun belt. He left the room and locked the door behind him. He held his hands over his head as he ran across the rain-soaked street and entered the town hall.

The marshal was in his office waiting for Billy's arrival. As Billy entered the room, he was standing at the window, gazing down upon the dark street, as he so often did. The marshal watched as Bader, Pup and two other men crept out from the shadows of the narrow alley and entered the Grand. He turned to face Billy and offered an uneasy smile.

"What is all this about, Marshal?" Billy asked impatiently.

"Please take a seat, Mr Earl," he said politely, "I apologize for the unconventional hour of my visit, but it could not wait."

Billy sat down in the chair opposite the marshal and rubbed his eyes.

"It's fine, I haven't really been sleeping anyhow," Billy admitted.

"Of course," the marshal sympathized, "it's surely a difficult time. Would you like a drink?"

"No, thank you," he replied, "I have one waiting for me back at the Grand, so maybe we should just get on with this. What do you need to talk to me about?"

"Certainly," the marshal said, quickly taking another look down at the street. "I need to talk to you about the bounty money, the logistics of it all and things like that," he babbled nervously.

* *

Across the street in the Grand, Fiona stirred, lost in a confusing semi-dream world, teetering on the edge of sleep. She could hear a faint rustling sound, flowing in from the hall. She rolled over dozily and tilted her head so that she could see the door. Her eyes heavy with the weight of sleep, she peered through the narrow gap of her eyelids. She noticed that there was no longer a sliver of light to be seen at the base the door. She sat up and forced her eyes open a little more, trying to focus.

She could hear the sounds of hushed voices. She listened closely, trying to shift the haziness of fatigue. Then she heard it. One of the voices from the night of the fire. A voice she was sure that she would never be able to forget. She scrabbled forward, but two thunderous cracks froze her in place as the thin wooden doorframe splintered and the door swung open.

"Rise and shine," Bader boomed as they forced their way into the room.

Humans Are the Ugliest Creatures

Two of the men went straight for Elle, pinning her down and tying a gag around her mouth. Fiona dropped from the bed and tried to reach for the rifle but was pulled away before she could get to it. Pup flung her into the wall and pressed a hand down on her bandaged shoulder. The pain, which felt like red hot daggers burying their way into her shoulder, caused her to shriek.

"I told you I'd come for you," he sneered.

She lashed out at him, but he saw it coming and easily dodged her attack. Pup threw a heavy punch, which landed hard over her right eye, knocking her unconscious and sending her spinning to the floor.

"Cool it, Pup," Bader commanded sternly, "we aren't here for her."

"But, Boss, she-" he protested.

"You want to beat on little girls, you can do so, but not with that yellow sash on your arm. You hear me?" he threatened. "You shouldn't be letting children get the better of you anyhow," he smirked.

Reluctantly, Pup backed away from Fiona and left her on the floor in an unconscious heap. Bader drew his gun and stood at the side of the bed, where Elle was being held in place. Her wide eyes were streaming with tears and darting about the room fearfully. He pulled a handkerchief from his coat pocket, spat into it and began cleaning the gun.

"We are going for a little ride," he said absently. "I want to be very clear, just to make sure that we don't have any unfortunate misunderstandings. I need you to remain as silent and as calm as you can be, I know that may be difficult given the circumstances but nonetheless, I politely request that you try," he smiled courteously. "Should you try to escape or call for help, I will personally put a stop to it in such a way that will make the savages look like kittens. And then I will return to this room and I'll use your young sister over there to paint the walls red." He paused to study the gun. Satisfied with its cleanliness, he holstered it and looked down at Elle, addressing her directly. "Do we have an understanding?" he asked.

She lay unmoving, paralyzed as much by fear as by the men who held her down. Bader leaned forward and gently removed the gag from her mouth.

"Do we have an understanding?" he repeated softly.

"Yes," she whimpered, the terror causing her voice to wobble and break.

Bader smiled, replaced the gag and lightly pinched her cheek.

"Good," he said cheerfully, "well, let's get going."

The men picked her up and carried her out of the room. She did not struggle or try to break free of their grip, just tilted her head to the side and tried to get a glimpse of Fiona, who was yet to move from where she lay near the wall. They carried her out into the street and placed her up on a horse in front of Bader. The other men moved quietly as they unhitched their horses, mounted up and followed their leader out of Good Rock.

Kelly stayed behind and walked out into the middle of the street. The thick heavy mud clung to his feet as he walked. He turned to face the town hall, looked up to the marshal's window and waved his arms in the air.

Marshal Andrews peered down at the street, again pausing midsentence. When he saw Kelly waving his arms and disappearing into the obscurity of the stormy night, he lost his train of thought entirely.

"Marshal?" Billy asked, the frustration in his voice plain to hear.

The marshal turned to face Billy, with a look of confusion on his face.

"I thought you said this couldn't wait. So far all you've done is repeat yourself about what I already know. The money is on its way and I'm only getting it for White and Wilbur. I know this," he paused and calmed himself down. "I'm tired, Marshal, and you seem to be getting bored of hearing your own voice, trailing off and staring out that window like you're either drunk or simple," he snapped.

The marshal looked down at his hands shamefully as the guilt of his complicity in the kidnapping overwhelmed him. When he eventually looked across the desk at Billy, it was as though he could feel himself drowning.

"I'm sorry," he murmured wearily, easing himself into his seat.

Billy frowned at the man in front of him and slowly shook his head. He got up from the chair and headed toward the door.

"Marshal, you need to quit your drinking and get some damn sleep. You're turning into a bumbling old fool," he said reproachfully.

"I'm sorry," the marshal repeated, raising his head and looking directly at Billy this time. "I really am. I…" he fell quiet and looked back down at his hands.

Billy studied the sullen lawman for a moment, then left the office. He walked down the stairs and into the lobby. He stopped by the door and looked up at the rain, it was heavy and thick, almost violent, its noise drowning out everything else.

Humans Are the Ugliest Creatures

He ran into the street and up onto the boardwalk on the other side. He paused to try and scrape the mud from his boots. He froze when he noticed all of the mud that had been traipsed into the Grand's lobby. He turned his head left and right, looking up and down the street but it was vacant, there was not a soul in sight. He drew his gun and stood near the doorway, surveying the lobby for threats, but it too was empty.

His breathing quickened and his heart raced as he turned to look back at the marshal's office, only to see no light emanating from the window. His stomach dropped and his eyes widened in disbelief as he saw the marshal on horseback, galloping away and fading into the grainy static of the rain. He ran into the lobby and headed up the stairs. He paused by the broken door and peered inside.

Fiona, with her one eye swollen shut, pulled the trigger on the rifle as soon as she saw movement at the door. Sparks and splinters spilled into the air as the bullet connected with a broken door hinge.

"Fiona, it's me! It's Billy!" he cried out, hardly able to breathe from the shock.

He heard the clatter of the rifle as Fiona dropped it to the floor, followed by the desperate sobs of a frightened child. He holstered his gun, slowly moved into the doorway and entered the room.

"They took her," Fiona cried, "they came and they took her! I tried to stop them!" she bawled.

When she looked up at him Billy saw the purple-black stains of bruising on her skin and the swelling that had forced her eye shut.

"It was the men from the fire! The same ones, I know it!" she cried.

"Jesus, Fiona," Billy exclaimed and dropped to his knees to hold her.

He held her in his arms and tried to process what he was seeing as she wept and wailed into his chest. Elle was gone. Bader had taken her, and the marshal had betrayed them. It was almost too much to stomach, he thought for a moment that he was going to throw up. He closed his eyes and tried to slow his breathing, counting to four with each inhale and exhale. Letting his mind race and going wild would help no one. He knew, however hard it was, that he had to retain some semblance of calm.

"Let me see your face," he said to Fiona, leaning away from her and studying her eye.

"I'm fine," she protested, pushing his hands back. "What are we going to do about Elle?" she asked desperately.

"I don't know. I don't know yet, I need time to think," Billy muttered as he tried to come up with a plan. "The sheriff," he snapped, "maybe the sheriff knows where they went, but I don't know if we can trust him. Hell, I don't know if we can trust anyone in this damn town. The marshal is in on it. He's Bader's man. He tricked me," he told Fiona. "How did I not see it? God damn it!" he shouted and pounded his fist against the floor.

"We have to try something," Fiona whimpered, standing up and trying to lift Billy.

She walked shakily across the room and put on her britches, her boots and her hat. She picked up the rifle and winced as her shoulder stung painfully.

"Your shoulder," Billy said concerned, "it's bleeding under there."

"I don't care," she sniffed defiantly and fought against the pain to hold the rifle up. "Get up," she ordered him, "we have to do something and if the sheriff is the only hope we've got, then we have to at least try," she pleaded through tears.

Billy's expression remained blank as he nodded firmly and got to his feet.

"I'll lead," he said jadedly.

They walked out of the room and cautiously scanned the hallway for any sign of danger. Outside, the street was still and quiet. The only sound to be heard was the constant din of the rain as it clattered into the roofs and overhangs of the street's buildings. From where they stood, under the protection of the Grand's balcony, they could hardly see the sheriff's office through the downpour.

Fiona staggered forward woozily and gripped Billy's arm for support. She shut her eye and gently swayed her head from side to side, desperately trying to overcome the throbbing ache of her bruising as it pulsed with every heartbeat.

"We ought to get you to Doc Faulds," Billy told her as his concern grew. "I can take you there, then go talk to the sheriff myself?"

"After," she replied, "you ain't leaving me and I ain't leaving you. That's the rule now." She opened her eye and looked out over the thick mud, which had been turned into a viscous brown sludge by the deluge. "I don't know if I got it in me to cross that," she told Billy honestly.

"Can you hop on my back?" he asked and got down on one knee in front of her.

She held the rifle in one hand and latched onto his back. He carefully stepped down from the boardwalk and plodded through the mud, taking measured steps so as not to lose his balance and fall.

When they made it across, Billy eased down and allowed Fiona to drop from his back. As they walked along to the sheriff's office, Billy stepped ahead of her and gazed in through the window, accessing the situation.

"I don't see anybody," Fiona said as she peered in next to him.

"Me neither," Billy agreed, with mounting suspicion.

He drew his gun and gradually opened the door, trying to remain as quiet as possible.

"Where is he?" Fiona whispered as she slunk in behind him.

They both turned quickly and aimed at the back of the room upon hearing a strange gargling noise. Using the furnishings in the room for cover, they stayed low and approached the cells. Billy stood and held out a hand, instructing Fiona to lower her weapon. She rose up from where she was crouched and saw the sheriff sleeping on a bench in one of the cells, an empty bottle of bourbon cradled in his arms. The sheriff's hat had fallen to the floor, exposing his bald head. His mouth was wide open in a careless drunken slumber, the noise sounded more animal than human.

Fiona looked disgusted as she watched his body laboring to draw in each breath. Gripping the rifle tightly, she slammed the butt into the cell. The discordant jangle of the bars stirred the sheriff from his sleep.

"Wake up, Sheriff!" she shouted as she clattered the bars of the cell again.

He sat up on the bench and recoiled in fright as the empty bottle fell from his lap and shattered on the floor.

"Jesus Mary!" he exclaimed, slurring. "What are you doing?"

"What am I-" she stopped herself, dumbfounded by his lack of awareness.

"Sheriff, what are you doing in there?" Billy asked directly.

"Ellis, that wretched pig. He's a God damn snake," he shouted, scuffing at the broken glass and mumbling to himself incoherently.

Fiona's eye was wide with fury. She kicked the iron bars and leveled the rifle at him.

"You'd better wake up and get wise to what's going on, Sheriff!" she seethed. "The marshal may be a snake like pig, but you're the yellow-bellied worm in my sights! Tell us what the hell happened?"

Sheriff Manning held his hands up and pressed his back to the wall.

"That's an awful big gun, Miss Fiona," he stammered. "You want to watch where you point that thing."

She stood silently and waited for an answer.

"Marshal Andrews came by. He had Ed Bader with him and a whole bunch of his guys. They threatened me and freed the prisoners, the ones who killed Young," he babbled nervously. "There wasn't nothing I could do, they locked me in here. Ellis just stood there and let them. He didn't say nothing," he spat angrily.

"They took Elle," Billy told him.

The sheriff looked at them both with sadness in his eyes.

"They do that to you too?" he asked pointing at Fiona's face.

Humans Are the Ugliest Creatures

She stiffened up and remained mute.

"I thought as much," he muttered.

"Tell us how we find them," Billy demanded.

"The camp?" he questioned. "I've never seen it."

Fiona lurched forward, driving the gun between the bars.

"You'd best stop your lying right now!" she screamed furiously.

He slipped from the bench and scrabbled across the floor to the far corner.

"I swear it, I've never been!" he insisted. "You think I would go up there, put myself in that situation, with those devils?"

Fiona sniffed and tried to choke back tears. She realized just how futile questioning the cowardly sheriff was. The bars clanged as she let her arms go limp and lowered the rifle. Billy stared at her, his eyes hollow and despairing.

"What are we going to do?" she asked, her lip trembling.

"Give me your badge," Billy said, approaching the cell.

The sheriff looked up at him, confusion strewn across his face.

"Give me your badge now!" he shouted, driving his boot into the bars of the cell and drawing his gun. "You ain't fit to wear it," he accused the sheriff, disgusted by the man cowering before him.

The sheriff fumbled at his jacket, removed his badge and tossed it toward Billy. Billy bent down and picked up the small tin badge from the floor. He studied it for a moment and slid it into his pocket. He put a comforting arm around Fiona.

"Come on, there's nothing for us here," he told her, sounding completely deflated. "We can figure out what to do, while Doc Faulds looks you over."

She wiped the tears away and whimpered as her hand brushed the swelling around her bruised eye.

"This makes you no better than the others," the sheriff called after them as they walked toward the door.

Billy spun in a rage and grabbed the keys to the cells. He sorted through them clumsily, trying to find the right key.

"Hey, watch it," the sheriff shouted fearfully as he backed further into the corner.

Billy flung the door open, held Sheriff Manning by his collar and dove his fist into his face again and again. Fiona stood in the doorway and watched passively, seemingly apathetic towards the violence in front of her. When the sheriff's protests had ceased, Billy loosened his grip and let him slide semiconsciously to the floor.

"This makes you no better than the others," Fiona mimicked sinisterly, standing over the beaten man as he spat out a broken tooth. "If that bullet had gone straight through your skull and killed you, instead of winging you and making you the cowardly invalid you are, the people of this town would be better off."

She took Billy's hand and led him away. They left the sheriff lying on his back on the floor of the cell, wheezing and groaning softly.

* *

Humans Are the Ugliest Creatures

Despite the rain, Bader and his men made it to the camp in good time, with Frank Kelly and the marshal arriving shortly after. When they rode in, Lyle Dixon met them and took the reins of Bader's horse. He climbed down from the saddle and helped lift Elle down after him. He picked up a length of rope and placed a hand on her back, guiding her forward. Completely terrified in every sense of the word, her eyes flitted about wildly as she was marched through the camp. She shook and stiffened, while the men whistle and leered at her.

"Sit," Bader ordered, placing a hand on her shoulder as they reached an iron pole jutting from the ground. "This is just a precaution," he said, wrapping the rope around her waist and tying her in place. He knelt down at her side. "Hey, look at me," he spoke softly, "I know you're scared but none of these men are going to come anywhere near you. You can believe that." He stood and spoke loudly so that everyone could hear and heed his warning, "If anyone so much as comes within five feet of her, I will see to it myself that they don't ever walk again." He returned his attention to her and smiled, "thirsty?"

She looked up at him and nodded feebly.

"I'm cold," she mumbled.

Bader looked up at the rain.

"Yeah, doesn't look to be stopping, does it?" he mused and scratched at his chin. "Hey Dutch, come over here and demonstrate a little gallantry in giving this young lady your jacket."

"Boss, I-" he began to protest.

"I won't hear it," Bader hissed.

Dutch immediately removed his jacket and handed it to the WPC leader.

"We'll move you up under that, canopy over there near the fire. We may be outlaws, but we aren't savages," Bader laughed.

He loosened the ropes, helped Elle to her feet and walked her through the rain. When she was under the canopy by the warmth of the fire, he draped the jacket over her shoulders and handed her a flask of water.

"Thank you," she whispered, the fear still plain in her voice.

"This is unfortunate, but it needn't be unpleasant," he told her as he took back the steel flask and bound her hands behind her back.

"Ed!" a voice called out from the rain.

"Well, if it isn't everybody's favorite town marshal," Bader bellowed joyfully.

Elle's eyes lit up with hope at the arrival of Marshal Andrews. She was sure that they would be forced to let her go, now that the marshal had arrived. She pictured him cutting the ropes and taking her back to Good Rock, back to Billy and poor hurt Fiona. Tears came to her eyes when she thought of her injured sister lying in such a helpless heap as they left. It was torture for her to think of how sweet, caring Billy must be losing his mind with worry. She leaned her head sideways and tried to listen to them as they spoke.

"Ed, you've made your point," the marshal barked, "it is clear to the boy now that you are the one who's in charge here."

"I don't know about that," Bader grinned, "I think it's pretty clear to him what sort of a man you are though."

Elle frowned intensely as her stomach turned and the fleeting feelings of hope faded into the void.

"You're an animal, Ed!" the marshal shouted.

"So are you, Ellis," he replied bluntly, "so is she and so am I. And animals kill each other. Have you ever seen someone, mortally wounded, scrabbling around in desperation? You observe them, even just for a little while, and you'll know beyond any doubt that we really are just animals striving for survival!"

"This has gone on long enough," the marshal said authoritatively, pushing past Bader towards the canopy where Elle was being held. He stopped moving and froze on the spot as he heard the cold, metallic click of a hammer locking into place.

"Please reconsider, Ellis," Bader asked, approaching the marshal from behind, gun in hand. "You've already picked a side. There's no backing out now."

"But you've done what you set out to do. You have shown him," the marshal remonstrated.

"I haven't shown him anything yet," Bader said grimly.

Marshal Andrews turned to face him. When he saw the look on Bader's face, his disquiet bloomed and he began to tremble with fear.

"Untie her," he ordered quietly. "Untie her, Ed. Untie her and let her go, right now," he persisted as the remaining WPC men came into view. "Untie her, Ed," he repeated feebly as he looked around at the encroaching men.

"You know I can't do that, Ellis," Bader replied flatly.

The marshal paced backward, getting nearer to Elle with each step. His heart pounded so hard against his chest that he feared it might burst. Part of him wished that it would and that everything around him would fade away to nothing. The stability and strength in his legs diminished with every passing movement. He stopped just short of where Elle sat shaking under the canopy.

"Get up," he commanded over his shoulder. "Are you okay to walk?"

Elle was far too fearful to offer a response. Shaking, she got to her feet and stood behind the marshal. The surrounding WPC men looked to Bader for instruction, all seemingly bewildered as to why their leader had yet to act. Bader remained in place and watched the marshal's movements. The aging lawman took slow and cautious steps, with Elle cowering behind him. He drew his gun and held his nerve, edging forward, jerking nervously at any perceived movement. He swung his arm back and forth, aiming at which ever man was closest.

"Steady, Ellis," Bader warned calmly, "bravery is not your forte." He held a hand out, instructing the other men to stay back.

"What's the plan here, Boss?" Pup called out furiously from the crowd. "You're just going to let this traitor take her? Shoot him already."

Bader threw him a reproachful glance but it was not enough to quell the tense and angry man. Pup drew his pistol and lurched forward from the crowd. Marshal Andrews staggered backwards in shock and fired his gun, shooting Pup in the chest.

"Run! Get out of here!" he shouted at Elle and pushed her toward a break in the crowd.

With her hands still tied, she stumbled forward, finding it difficult to balance as she fled. She ran as best as she could, but with no idea of the layout of the camp, she was running aimlessly.

Two more gunshots rang out behind her as she ducked behind a tent. She could hear Bader shouting in the distance and the angry hushed voices of two men as they followed somewhere close behind her. She panted where she knelt, summoning every last drop of courage, before sprinting towards the edge of the camp. As she ran barefoot in the darkness, she trod on a rock jutting out from the earth. She shrieked as it pierced the sole of her foot but fought against it and tried to keep going.

She made it to the upward slopping edge of the camp and started to climb. She only managed to make it several feet up the rain sodden bank, before hands wrapped around her ankle and pulled her tumbling back down to the ground. Winded, coughing and gasping for air, she lay in the puddle where she fell, sobbing and trying desperately to breathe. She felt utterly helpless.

"Please," she begged breathlessly, "just let me go, please."

"No, I don't think so," one of the men laughed.

She was lifted up by either arm and carried back to the middle of the camp. She closed her eyes when they passed the lifeless bodies of Pup and another WPC grunt. Gunned down by the marshal, their blood was draining into the already saturated soil. They dropped her down and she got to her knees, trying to understand what was happening around her. Some of the men were gathered outside one of the nearby shacks.

"Ellis, this has gone far enough!" Bader boomed.

Lyle kicked at the door but it would not budge. The marshal had wedged everything he could against the door, barricading himself inside.

"He's in there good, Boss," Lyle confirmed after kicking the door again. "We should torch it!"

"Shut up, Lyle," Bader told him sternly, "our main stash is in there."

The marshal peered through the jagged broken glass of a window and saw Elle kneeling behind the group. He hung his head remorsefully and covered his face.

"I'm sorry, Miss Elle!" he shouted out to her. "I'm sorry for all of it!"

Fresh tears fell down her face, when she heard the woe and desperation in his voice. She suddenly grasped the reality of her situation and felt as though she were about to be sick.

"What's your end game here, Ellis?" Bader questioned him. "There's nowhere to go. You planning on sitting in that hut until we keel over?"

The marshal did not offer Bader a response. He sat down on the floor, leaned against a bedframe and rummaged through Bader's stash. There were two bags, brimming with money and a cache of bullets.

"Ellis!" Bader bellowed at the hut.

One of the more impatient men fired his gun at the shack. Bader surged across the face of the crowd, took hold of the gun and drove his fist at full force into the side of man's head, knocking him to the ground in a daze. He spun in a wild fury and hurled the gun at the hut.

"God damn it, Ellis! Get out here and shoot at us! Act like the hero you just showed us you could be!" he roared.

"You said you'd let her go," he finally answered.

"Things change," Bader countered bluntly, catching his breath.

"I may be a fool for trusting you, but I know what happens when I walk through this door," he said with an abject air of defeat.

He moved the bags of money and the bullets, revealing a bundle of dynamite, tucked away at the bottom of the stash. He lifted it out and placed it in front of him. He closed his eyes and ran his hand along it, outlining its shape.

"I tried to do what was right for this place, I really did," he started. "I saw the future, the communities I'd help build, the freedom and pure joy that a place like this could yield. I think that future died a long time before I noticed."

While the marshal spoke, Bader gathered four of his men together, pulling them forward from the crowd.

"Keep low and keep quiet, find a weak spot and force in there, while he's distracted by his own monolog. It can't be too hard. Do not kill him," he whispered, pointing to the small shack.

"It was ugly people like you," the marshal continued, "who came here and saw it as a lawless playground, to do with as you pleased. It was people like you who killed the future that I envisaged," he paused and sighed, "but it was people like me who buried it."

The marshal fell quiet. Elle watched on anxiously as Bader held his hand up, commanding the men outside the hut to wait. The camp was deathly still. Not a sound could be heard above the constant din of the rain.

"Ellis?" Bader called out to no reply. "Ellis, you still in there?"

"I never meant to…" he trailed off, his eyes full of tears. "Tell them all I'm sorry."

He clicked the hammer back on his gun and fired at the bundle of dynamite. Elle turned and fell to the side as a shockwave rippled through the air and the shack erupted in an enormous fireball. The flames reached up into the sky and glowed white with a brilliant heat. Elle cowered as best as she could with her hands tied, while chunks of burning debris crashed around her. Many of the WPC men fell to the ground, some from the force of the explosion, others from shock. Bader turned away from the initial blast, shielded his eyes, then looked back at the flames crawling up into the sky.

"God damn it, Ellis," he muttered to himself.

The flames fell back down and their ferocious roar faded away, unmasking the anguished screams of injured men and the frantic neighing of startled horses. Of the men who had been attempting to infiltrate the cabin, two were dead and two were mortally wounded, missing limbs and bleeding profusely. Bader blocked out the grim cacophony of fear and pain, and stared silently at the burning remains of the shack. The money was gone and so was a portion of their ammo.

"Shut those horses up!" Kelly shouted, ordering the men about, snapping them out of their dazed states. "You and you," he pointed, "get those boys out of there, dope them up and make them comfortable, they don't look like they got too long."

Kelly paced back and forth at Bader's side, mumbling angrily to himself. The WPC leader remained impassive. In the corner of his eye, he noticed that Kelly had stopped moving and seemed to be waiting for something.

"Calm down," Bader said quietly, "there's nothing to be done."

"Nothing to be done?" Kelly snorted.

Bader had an aggravated look about him.

"What do you want to do? The money is gone. The rain will put out the fire. Those men are going to die," he listed. "You want to ride into Good Rock and get revenge? Who's your target? The fool has already blown himself to pieces!" he barked.

Kelly's face reddened, he searched for an answer but came up with nothing. He cursed and stomped the ground in frustration. Bader held out a hand and urged his only surviving general to remain calm.

"Give me a head count of able men," he demanded.

Kelly squinted into the darkness of the camp, partially illuminated by the quickly dwindling flames.

"I'd say nine, including us," Kelly surmised.

"It's been a bloody week," Bader said distantly. "That ends after tonight. The marshal's attempt at derailing was unfortunate and inconvenient but ultimately futile, it doesn't change the plan." He turned to walk away but stopped when he noticed the simmering resentment on Kelly's face. "You want revenge on him, then take no notice of this, of what he's done. He has achieved nothing. A complete waste of a life. He made the ultimate sacrifice and it was completely pointless," he continued walking. "Settle them down, then come and see me," he called back to him.

Elle pushed herself back up to her knees. Almost all of her skin, head to toe, was caked in mud. In the low light, her blue eyes shone distinctly, standing out against the surrounding dirt, two bright points hovering on the edge of darkness. She stiffened up as Bader approached and began slowly pacing in a circle around her.

"Well, that was quiet something, wasn't it?" he laughed.

Elle sniffed and sobbed, mumbling meekly.

"I didn't catch that, pretty girl. What did you say?" he asked, while lighting a cigar.

She murmured inaudibly again.

"Now, you're going to need to speak up, I was recently too close to a particularly loud noise," he joked. He stepped forward and laid his hands heavily on her shoulders, "What was that?"

"Please, let me go! You don't have to do this," she cried out loudly, looking up to the sky.

Bader stood back and resumed his pacing, puffing on his cigar.

"That's better," he told her, through clouds of smoke. "However, it is incorrect. I do have to do this. I have been left with no choice."

Elle hung her head and wept freely.

"I tried to avoid such a situation but young Billy boy persisted," he explained.

He paused and knelt down in front of Elle. He looked at her with an expression, which seemed full of genuine sympathy and compassion. She flinched and held her breath as he cupped her chin with a gentle hand and looked her in the eye.

"It's because of him that I have to do this. It's because of him that you are going to die," he spoke softly. "It's because of him that your life will have had no meaning, no point to it. To make it through all those years… just to die here in the dirt," he said, his voice full of regret. "All for nothing. It's Billy's doing. Let those be your parting thoughts."

Kelly sauntered up behind Bader. Elle looked up and saw them both standing before her, their faces shadowed by the darkness as the last flames were extinguished by the rain. She coughed and choked as she cried, nearly falling face first into the mud.

"Kelly," Bader prompted and gestured to Elle.

He stepped behind her, took her by the arms and held her upright.

"No!" Elle let out a guttural shout as she struggled against Kelly's grip.

"Don't be afraid," Bader said gently. "Ellis, the marshal, he acted out of fear and it didn't get him very far. You are someone who acts out of love, but love blinds you to the fact it's weak." Held his hand out and caught the axe as Kelly tossed it to him. "Hate always wins. It's strong and unforgiving."

Elle let out an ear-piercing scream as Bader flung his arm back and drove the hatchet into her chest. She fell instantly silent and stopped resisting. She lowered her head and looked down dumbly at the gaping wound as Bader pulled the hatchet free and a sea of crimson flowed freely from between her breasts. Drooling and frowning, unable to understand, she blinked and stared blankly.

Her head bobbed rhythmically as she absorbed the shock of a second blow. There was no pain to process, no emotion to feel. Time was almost at a standstill in the dark, wet, dream like world where she knelt.

After the third strike, she could no longer breathe. She pulled in short, sharp, mechanical breaths of air. Her eyes dulled and were unable to focus. The incessant static of the pounding rain dampened and dwindled as she fell deaf to her surroundings.

She tried to think of her beloved Billy and her darling sister, but she could remember neither his face, nor her name. Her vision faded and her head floated, while she sensed a great deal of pressure against her chest. Wholly consumed by a drowsiness which demanded immediate rest, she let her eyelids ease shut. Moments later, she died in the dirt where she lay.

Humans Are the Ugliest Creatures

12

Billy, Fiona and a Broken Heart

Fiona nursed her swollen eye with a cool, damp rag. It ached and throbbed but as the effects of the drugs, administered by Doctor Faulds, crept in, the pain eased. The buzzing sting of her burns felt like a distant memory, a half remembered dream. She sat at the edge of the bed, with her legs crossed and her hat pulled down low. She twisted her head dopily and looked about their new hotel room.

Billy was sat on a stool, taking a generous swig from a bottle of bourbon. He periodically flexed his hand, in an ineffectual attempt to ease the mounting stiffness. The knuckles of his right hand were bloodied and swelling. He stared as he drank, trying to see if he could tell the difference between his blood and that of the sheriff's. The grooves and wrinkles in his skin were dark flooded canyons and red rivers, crisscrossing and intersecting erratically. He pulled the sheriff's badge from his pocket and flipped it in his hand, feeling guilt wash over him.

He leaned his head back against the wall and felt the cool bones of the building against his neck. He thought about his violent outburst and tried to replay it in his mind, but the memory was fogy and muddled.

The ineptitude of the town's protectors fueled a fire within him that burned hot with anger. His inability to do anything to help Elle was bearing down on him. It was as if he was trying to hold up the sky itself.

He looked at Fiona and for a moment, forgot his own emotional misery and focused on her. Watching her as she absentmindedly swept her hand back and forth across her leg, he wondered how she would look and where she would be, had he not entered her world. She would still be happy.

"You hear that?" Fiona asked, tipping her hat back and tilting her head.

Billy dropped forward and listened but heard nothing.

"What did you-" he started to ask but she cut him off, shushing and holding up a finger.

"Wait," she whispered as she slid off the bed and onto her feet. "I'm sure I..." she paused and blinked, second guessing herself.

"It's alright," Billy told her as he leaned back against the wall, "your mind plays tricks. It's the stress or the exhaustion or something."

"But I thought I..." she mumbled, with a lost look about her. "I mean, I just..." she trailed off into a confused silence.

Humans Are the Ugliest Creatures

"Why don't you try and lay down?" Billy suggested. "Let the medicine do its work."

Fiona nodded groggily and crawled up onto the bed. She turned, ready to lie on her back and froze, deathly still. Billy's eyes widened.

"There it is," Fiona murmured under her breath, "I knew I wasn't crazy."

Billy got to his feet and drew his gun as he approached the door.

"It came from outside," Billy surmised.

Fiona pulled the rifle out from under the bed and fell in behind him.

"There's no way in hell you're going without me," she told him sternly.

Reluctantly, he nodded and opened the door. The man at the front desk ducked down out of sight when he saw the armed duo making their way down the stairs. They walked out into the lobby, crouched by the door and listened.

"It's quiet," Billy said in a hushed voice.

Fiona shot him an impatient glance. The sound of the endless droplets of rain, relentlessly hammering into the boardwalk and the balcony above, cloaked any other noise that they might have heard. Fiona closed her eye and pressed her ear up to the thin gap between the door and the doorframe. Fiona focused, searching through the static for any variance. She opened her eye as she heard horses galloping, the sound fading as quickly as it started. She carried on listening carefully. Billy watched as her brow gradually furrowed and her face contorted with confusion.

"You hear it?" she asked him.

Humans Are the Ugliest Creatures

He looked up as he listened, desperately searching for whatever it was that Fiona had heard.

"What is that?" he wondered as the sound finally became clear.

What they were hearing was a soft creaking sound. It was constant and almost rhythmic in its repetition. Billy drew his gun and waited for Fiona to get in position behind him. He held his fingers out and silently counted to three. He stood and laid a heavy heel on the door, swinging it open with force.

They burst onto the boardwalk and simultaneously fell back in horror. Billy rolled to the side and threw up almost instantly. Drooling and spitting, he babbled to himself nonsensically. Fiona tried to get back up to her feet, but her knees wobbled and gave out beneath her.

Above them, swaying gently in the breeze, was the cause of the mysterious noise and the source of their horror. Elle's lifeless body hung from the rafters, suspended by a rope around her neck. Her tattered and torn clothing, almost entirely stained a deep shade of red, exposed a gaping hole which ran the length of her chest, laying bare the internal intricacies of her body.

Placed on the floor, bellow her dangling feet, was her heart, oozing steadily thickening blood. Her skin, in the few areas which remained untouched by the obscene amount of blood, was dull and graying. Across her forehead, the word "*STOP*" was carved into her skin, the vibrant crimson lettering standing out in stark contrast to her milk like skin. On her left arm the familiar missing strip of flesh, that was Ed Bader's signature.

While Billy writhed on the ground in emotional turmoil, Fiona knelt staring up at her sister's corpse as it dangled and swayed. Her eyes focused on the body gently twisting from side to side in the wind. She made no sound as she wept, completely drained by the events of the past week, she had nothing left to give. She had lost everything, her home and her family. Billy was all that she had left, a man who was essentially a stranger. A stranger, who she watched as he wailed and pounded his fists against the boardwalk in anguish. A stranger, who she knew had loved her sister as much as she did, if not more. She dragged herself close to him and held him in her arms. Keeping her eyes fixed on the mutilated body of her once beautiful, kind and caring sister. In that moment, she made herself a promise, a solemn oath, that she would kill everyone responsible.

Billy coughed and spat as he rolled from side to side. Fiona looked into his eyes and knew that it was useless to try to speak. His grief had consumed him, and he was lost in a world of his own.

In response to the commotion, the people of Good Rock had begun to gather along the boardwalk. The men gasped and recoiled in horror, shielding the eyes of their wives and children.

"Good Lord," Doctor Faulds murmured from behind them. He knelt down next to Fiona and checked over Billy. "Are you two alright?"

Fiona nodded vacantly, as though the question had come from a voice wandering on the winds, as opposed to an actual person in front of her. He waved a hand in front of Billy and tapped his cheek. The doctor sighed and turned to Fiona.

"He's hysterical, I'll give him something to sedate him. You'll have to keep an eye on him. Are you able to do that?"

Humans Are the Ugliest Creatures

Fiona did not respond, she just looked up at her sister, took a deep breath and sat in silence as more tears streamed across her cheeks.

"Fiona?" Doctor Faulds paused, concerned for her, "I'll be sure to check in every so often."

He stood and hastily made his way back to his office. He burst through the door and began rummaging through a nearby draw. He held up a small vile and drew the liquid into a syringe. Clumsily, he stumbled back out onto the boardwalk and returned to the scene. He took a firm hold of Billy's arm, jabbed the needle into his skin and waited for him to settle.

"There we are," he said calmly as he released his grip, "that's better."

With the help of the Good Rock Grand employee, Billy was lifted to his feet, which was less than easy in his drowsy and dazed state. He was carried up the stairs and hoisted onto the bed.

Doctor Faulds returned to find Fiona, who remained less than a foot away from her sister's suspended cadaver, craning her neck and looking up at her. With one eye still blackened by bruising and swollen shut, her open eye looked irritated and raw. She flinched as he placed a consoling hand on her shoulder and looked around at the gathering crowd.

"Have you come to gawp? Seeking thrills, as though this is some sort of grotesque spectacle?" he asked the onlookers, his quaking voice full of disdain. "Either you step forward and lend a hand, or you get back in your houses!" he barked.

Faces in the crowd looked to one another passively. For a moment, the doctor envisaged himself having to complete the grim task alone. Finally, one man stepped forward from the front of the crowd, while a second waded through from the back and approached the scene. Doctor Faulds nodded his thanks to the volunteers.

"The rest of you can get out of here!" he shouted to the remaining spectators as he turned his back on them. "You men take a hold of her, while I cut her down," he instructed.

Fiona watched as the men stood either side of Elle and lifted her, while the doctor cut the rope above her. They laid the body on the boardwalk and crossed her arms over her cracked, cavernous chest. Doctor Faulds pulled a handkerchief from his jacket pocket, placed it over Elle's heart and picked it up. He carefully wrapped it in the cloth and placed it under Elle's cold hands.

"I'll talk to Pastor Richards and have a burial arranged. I'll fill you in on the details as soon as I can," he told Fiona. "I'll check in on you both later on tonight and then again in the morning."

"Thank you," Fiona mumbled on half a breath.

"I'm truly sorry for what has happened, Fiona, I really am," he tried to comfort her.

"Why? You didn't do it," she responded absently.

"No, I did not. But still, you don't deserve such pain," he explained, "now, go back inside. Watch over Billy and get some rest if you can. However hard that may seem."

Fiona took another long look at her sister before entering the hotel and disappearing into the darkness of the room.

She closed the door behind her and stood at the side of the bed, where Billy slept quietly. She watched him enviously as he drew in long breaths and exhaled slowly. He looked peaceful, without a care and free of pain. Hers was a pain which consumed every part of her. She lived inside its belly, in constant darkness, with no means of escape. Her sorrow was sharp, present on every breath, lingering on every thought.

She picked up Billy's bottle of bourbon, put it to her lips and let the fiery liquid fill her mouth. She swallowed it down and grimaced, unfamiliar with the taste. She closed her eye and took another swig, feeling a burning sensation as it ran down her throat. The process was repeated three or four more times, until she began to feel the effects of the alcohol.

She felt lightheaded and woozy as she unbuttoned the top two buttons of her shirt, removed her boots and lay down next to him. Her hand searched at her side, until it found Billy's and interlocked with his fingers, gripping his hand tightly. She drew in a deep breath through her nose, slowly exhaled and felt her entire body begin to shudder, each muscle contracting and relaxing violently, as she cried harder than she had ever cried before.

* *

Three days came and went in a grief-stricken blur, before the funeral could be put off no longer. The rains passed and the sun resumed its reign over the clear blue skies. Billy sat at the corner of the bed, swigging from a new bottle of bourbon, while Fiona buttoned up his shirt and knotted his necktie.

Although the swelling around her eye had eased, a large violet bruise, with mottled yellow and blue edges, stained the area. The white of her eye was slowly receding as a ruptured blood vessel leaked red. The pain of her burns had somewhat eased, but they were nowhere near healed. Regular visits to Doctor Faulds had helped keep the dressings clean and the area moisturized.

"Give me that," she snapped at Billy, taking the bottle from his hands. "You're making this even harder," she complained as she loosened the knot, having failed to tie it correctly for the third time. She took a swig from the bottle and placed it on the side table.

"That's not for you," Billy said slowly, "you shouldn't-"

Fiona stepped back and raised her eyebrows in astonishment.

"Sorry," he apologized.

She was wearing a loose black shirt, with a black ribbon tied in a bow around the collar. Billy was also dressed in black. Fiona had gone out during the previous day to purchase the clothes, and had already worn hers once to visit Stacks' grave. She was not sure when, but he had been buried by his family sometime during the chaos of the previous few days.

On the way, she passed what remained of the Bellamy ranch. The horses and cattle were gone, she guessed that they had been stolen. She pictured herself sifting through the tangled mess of blackened wood and brick, searching for a trace of her parents, but knew that there would be little left to find. In her eyes, the remains of the building served as a giant tombstone. She said a quiet farewell and carried on to where Stacks had been buried.

After she had said her goodbyes to the loyal ranch hand, who had so bravely saved her life, she returned immediately to the Grand. The pitying stares and blatant gawking of the townsfolk was almost too much for her to handle.

"There," she announced triumphantly, "all done."

Humans Are the Ugliest Creatures

Billy stood and approached the mirror, studying his reflection. The man looking back at him was not a man he recognized, the thickening stubble and bloodshot, puffy eyes were alien to him. He took another swig from the bottle and sighed, pulling at his collar, in a futile attempt to draw in air and cool himself down.

"Don't mess it up," Fiona scolded him and slapped his hands away.

"We should probably go," he suggested and wiped his mouth with the back of his hand, after a further mouthful of bourbon.

"Hey, ease up on that," Fiona chided.

"You're pretty bossy for someone who doesn't like being told what to do," Billy quipped and forced a smile for a brief moment.

Fiona did the same, the fleeting moment of happiness only serving to remind the pair of them of the misery, in which they were neck deep and drowning. He put his arm around her shoulders and led her out of the room.

The unrelenting sun beat down on the boardwalk, only for the heat to radiate back up into the air. As they made their way along Main Street towards the church, people stepped back from their path and nodded their heads or tipped their hats, offering condolences. Billy halfheartedly raised a hand in thanks to each, while Fiona scowled and kept her eyes down.

When they arrived at the church, there was a small group of mourners gathered at the grave, mostly consisting of people who had known her parents. Doctor Faulds was waiting at one side of the grave. He offered a sympathetic smile, which Fiona made an effort to accept and reciprocate.

After all the help he had given them, she felt she owed him that much at least.

On the other side was Sheriff Manning, who neither Billy nor Fiona were expecting to see. They both stared at him, their eyes narrow and full of resentment. He briefly met their gaze but quickly cast his eyes down to the ground. His face was badly bruised from Billy's assault and he would periodically dab the side of his mouth, where his slowly healing jaw caused him to drool. They turned away from him and stood at the head of the grave alongside Pastor Richards.

The Pastor spoke about God, heaven and hell, the demons which plague the Earth, and the angels who watch over us and keep us safe. His monotone voice rung out over the crowd, low and lackluster. Looking down over the pale wooden box, encasing the dead body of a once beautiful young girl, now butchered and disfigured, made him second guess himself as he reaffirmed that, "there is a plan."

To Fiona, his words seemed almost apologetic towards the evil that permeated and poisoned the land. What sort of righteous God could stand back and allow it? He preached compassion and pleaded for kindness and forgiveness, but she felt none at all and wondered if she ever would.

As the coffin was lowered into the ground and the attendees solemnly sang a hymn, Fiona held on tightly to Billy's hand and lowered her hat, shielding her tearful eyes from the crowd.

"I'm sorry, Elle Belle," she whispered under her breath, "should be me in that box not you. You never even hurt a fly. I don't know what to do without you. I feel so alone."

Billy stared at the coffin as it was dropped down. Tears wet his cheeks as he hummed along to the hymn and said goodbye to the only woman, he was sure he would ever love. With his free hand, he pulled a leather-bound hipflask from his pocket and took a lengthy gulp. Fiona noticed and snatched it from his grip. She took a mouthful herself and handed it back to him, earning her a reproachful look from the Pastor, to which she responded with a disinterested shrug.

After a few more quietly introspective moments, most of those in attendance made their way back to the town, while Billy and Fiona remained in place. Billy shook his head and puffed out his cheeks, exhaling angrily. He pulled his hand away from Fiona and wobbled, slightly inebriated.

"I'm going back," he grunted.

Fiona watched him scornfully as he swigged from the hipflask, loosened his necktie and stumbled into the gate, kneeing it open. She dropped to her haunches and fanned herself with her hat. When she touched a hand to her face to brush back stray hairs, she was unsure of what was sweat and what was tears.

No part of her wanted to be alone at that moment, but she was too angry at Billy and too stubborn to follow him back to the hotel. With a small stick, she drew a picture in the loose dirt of the grave. She drew the old house and her family, all holding hands. She drew Billy with his arm around Elle and hearts bubbling up between them. When she was finished, she looked up and was startled to see a man standing nearby, waiting for something as he nervously turned his hat in his hands.

"That's a nice picture," he stuttered timidly.

She looked down and scuffed at it, erasing it with her foot.

"It's nothing now," she said coldly. "Who are you?"

"My name's Lyle," he answered hesitantly.

She froze as he stepped forward and she saw the yellow sash tied around his arm. He noticed her reaction and looked down at the neatly tied fabric.

"You don't got to be afraid, little girl. I don't mean any trouble."

"Then what the hell are you doing here?" Fiona asked, her courage building as she studied the feeble and clearly dim-witted man.

"I came by," he coughed as he stammered, "I came by and saw the procession. You see, I was there the other night, when the boss brought her up. I didn't see none of it, only the afters. I wanted to come by and…" he paused and looked about as his eyes moistened with tears. "I wanted to tell you, how sorry I am. It weren't right what happened. It was downright ugly, and I don't want no part of it anymore. I thought those men were my friends but it just ain't right."

Fiona squinted as she studied him and remained unresponsive. He twitched nervously while he waited for her to say something.

"What are you going to do?" she asked.

"I've left the camp and I'm just going to go away, leave Good Rock," he answered.

"Not with that sash on," she told him and stepped forward.

He looked at his arm and hurriedly removed it. He dropped it to the ground and stamped on it, twisting it into the dirt under his heel. He stopped and looked up timidly, hoping that he had adequately demonstrated what he felt toward the WPC. Fiona watched him curiously as he hunched and looked away.

"You got a gun?" she asked. "Seems like you won't be needing it anymore. Toss it down."

He drew the gun and fumbled it, his nerves getting the better of him. He dropped it at Fiona's feet, next to the sash.

"I'm sorry I intruded on you," Lyle said, hanging his head remorsefully. "I just wanted to let someone know that I was sorry for what happened. I just thought that maybe if someone…" he paused unsure of what else to say, further saddened that his apology had been met with little to no acceptance. "I'll just be on my way then," he finally said.

He turned to walk toward the gate, dragging his feet as though they weighed far too much for him to lift. Lyle had just laid a hand on the ornate iron bars of the gate, when a shot rang out and he fell forward. He tumbled over the gate and landed heavily on his back. His arms flailed as he tried to get some purchase on the dirt and drag himself away, but it was not long before Fiona was standing over him.

"Sometimes sorry ain't enough," she barked and unloaded four more bullets into Lyle's chest.

His body jerked and shook with each impact, until he lay still, his eyes glazed over and lifeless. Fiona held his jaw and stuffed the yellow rag into his mouth. She tucked the pistol into her waistband and turned to see Sheriff Manning, standing at edge of the boardwalk, with a small group of stunned onlookers behind him.

"That man was unarmed," he accused.

"That man was Western Protection Company," Fiona snorted dismissively, walking toward him.

"He was nonetheless unarmed," the sheriff insisted as he dabbed at the corner of his mouth.

"If you plan on doing something about it, now's the time," she snarled, stopping at his side.

He stared at her for a few tense moments, before stepping aside and letting her pass.

"I'll be expecting my payment," she told him sternly as she moved on through the awed townspeople.

When she got back to the room at the Good Rock Grand, Billy was slumped on the floor, leaning against the side of the bed. Fiona kicked his legs out of the way and slid the rifle out from under the bed. She took bullets from a drawer and reloaded the pistol. On her way back out, she paused in the doorway and looked back at Billy, who stared up at her with a hint of confusion. In his drunken state, he could not see the blood, splattered and drying, camouflaged against her black clothing.

"I'll be back later," Fiona told him crossly and slammed the door.

Billy lay his head back against the bed and closed his eyes, longing for sleep, even just for a little while, so that he would not have to feel the pain.

Fiona took a horse, rode up Main Street and out into the countryside. She roamed aimlessly across the scrub lands, in the general direction of where she thought the WPC camp might be. After a few hours of fruitless, erratic searching, she gave up and stopped to rest under a nearby tree.

She wiped the sweat from her brow and loosened the bow around her neck, stuffing the ribbon into her pocket. She threw her head back against the tree in frustration, her hat cushioning the blow enough so that it was not too painful.

As she straightened her hat, she saw something in the distance, shimmering in the heat of the day as though she were looking up at the surface from underwater. A group of six or so men rode together, led at the front by a man, silhouetted in his black outfit. The darkness of the shadowy figure atop the horse was broken by what could only be the yellow sash of the WPC. She watched the entourage vanish from sight as they slipped behind a hill. Springing into action, she quickly mounted the horse and rode along the ridge to a higher vantage point.

She made it to the top of the ridge and looked out over the arid landscape, baking in the noon sun. She hopped down from the horse and kicked at the dirt in anger. The elevation was not enough to give her a clear view of where the riders went.

She moped around, edging stones toward the drop and watching them as they tumbled to the ground. She wondered what it would feel like to fall from the ledge, to plunge through the air and crash headfirst into the rocks below. How long would the fall take? How quickly would the lights go out? Would there be any pain? Looking down, she reasoned not.

She wondered if anyone would look for her, if anyone would bother to try and find the body. Would anyone even notice? Billy's head was in such a storm that it would take him a while to realize that she was gone. It would take him even longer to do anything about it. She looked back at the hill where the riders had disappeared and put the dark thoughts to rest. She could not leave this life yet, there were still scores to be settled, there was still blood to be spilled.

Tired and thirsty but full of purpose, Fiona climbed back up onto the horse, descended the ridge and made her way back to Good Rock. As she passed the town hall, she saw Lyle Dixon's body, on display for all to see. Sheriff Manning was standing in front of his office, watching her as she rode by. She sneered at him contemptuously and carried on to the Grand, where she hitched her horse.

Fiona strolled along the boardwalk, stopping to look through a window. She saw a black leather gun belt, hanging on a display. Seeing her disheveled reflection, she removed her hat, tucked her hair behind her ears and straightened her shirt, in an effort to appear slightly more presentable.

"Excuse me, could I please get a look at that gun belt in the window, the black one?" she asked as she entered the store and approached the counter.

The storekeeper was a young looking man, with neatly trimmed mutton chops that fed into his moustache. When he turned to face her with a look of surprise on his face, she was struck by his soft green eyes.

"You the little gunslinger everyone's talking about, the Bellamy girl?" he asked her.

"Fiona Fire," she announced gruffly and nodded.

He stroked his chin and looked impressed.

"That's a good name," he complimented. "I'm sorry for all of what happened to you. I never much liked the WPC. I did some business with them but who didn't? We've all got to earn."

Fiona looked disappointed and thrust her hands into her pockets.

"That why you want the gun belt?" he asked. "So you and the other boy can carry on after them?"

"Yes sir, that's right," she confirmed and pointed at the window, "I was up in the hills, over that way. I think I saw them, but I lost sight of them about as quickly as I spotted them."

"Well you couldn't have been far off the camp if you were out there," the storekeeper told her.

"You know how to get to the camp?" she pressed, slamming her palms on the counter in excitement.

"Of course," he chuckled, "I told you I did some business with them. Marshal Andrews took me up there once with a delivery. Here, I'll draw you a map."

He rummaged through a shelf behind the desk, until he found a blank sheet of paper and a pencil. The storekeeper drew a basic map, from Good Rock to the WPC camp and handed it to Fiona.

"That's it," he nodded. "It's not too long a ride. Now, let me get you that gun belt. It might be a little big for you, but I can add another notch or two."

"Thank you," Fiona said, staring at the map, her hands trembling.

The storekeeper lifted the gun belt from the window display and wrapped it around her waist, marking with his pencil where the extra notch was needed. He laid the belt on the counter, pulled a hatchet from his belt and bore a hole through the leather with one of the corners of the blade. Once finished, he tossed the belt over the counter and she caught it in her arms.

"Here you go, that looks like it should..." he paused, startled as someone came in through the doorway.

"Afternoon, Byron," Sheriff Manning greeted as he entered the store. He looked up at the storekeeper and suddenly fell back against the doorframe, struggling to draw his pistol. "Down, girl!" he shouted at Fiona.

He fired three shots as the storekeeper ran out of the room and burst through a back exit, making a clean escape.

Humans Are the Ugliest Creatures

The sheriff steadied himself and drooled as he panted, his body flooded with adrenaline. Fiona stood up from where she was crouched in the middle of the room. She looked at the sheriff, full of bewilderment and waited for an explanation.

"That man was Frank Kelly," he informed her between deep breaths.

Fiona spun and ran to the door where Kelly had fled, but he was already long gone. When she walked back into the room, she noticed the body of who she correctly assumed was Byron, the storekeeper Sheriff Manning had expected to see. The portly businessman was lying face down in a pool of blood, his throat cut an inch deep from ear to ear.

"Sheriff?" she said pointing at the body.

He stomped across the room and took a look, the color instantly fleeing his skin.

"Damn it, Byron was a good man. What did Kelly tell you?" he asked her.

"I've never seen you fire your gun. I don't think I've seen you holding one. You not a coward anymore, Sheriff?" she asked mockingly.

"However brutish and thug like the lesson you two taught me was, I got the message," he explained, wiping the drool from his mouth. "I've thought long and hard about all of it, especially after seeing you this morning and the lengths that you're prepared to go to achieve some semblance of justice. I realized that, however much I tried to convince myself otherwise, I have a lot to answer for in all of this."

Fiona stood and nodded, quietly approving of the sheriff's enlightenment.

"This doesn't mean you're forgiven," she said flatly.

"It's not about earning forgiveness, Fiona. I know any chance of that is long gone," he admitted. "This is about being able to live with myself. Being able to look back over my life and know that at least I didn't get everything wrong. I don't want to end up like Ellis, standing at that damn window all day, sighing like it's the last day on Earth. He told me once, 'to hate the way a part of you looks is one thing, but to hate who you are is something entirely different.' I don't ever want to know what that's like." He dabbed at his mouth again, watching as Fiona struggled to tie the belt around her waist.

"Maybe you could do with brushing up on your shooting, a little," she quipped.

"Frank Kelly give you that?" he quizzed her pointing at the map in her hands. "Let me see it."

She handed it over to him and waited while he studied it, a harsh frown dominating his brow.

"It's a trap, right?" Fiona deduced.

"Smart girl," Sheriff Manning nodded, "most definitely. There's no other reason to give you this. He'd have probably waited and followed you, you'd be surrounded by the time you got there."

"At least we know where to go," she said bluntly.

"Yes, but Kelly got away. He will have warned them and they'll be on their guard," the sheriff countered.

Fiona stared at the ground thoughtfully. She rubbed her irritated, blood filled eye and squinted against the glare of the sun, spilling in through the glass of the store front.

"I got to go," she said suddenly as she picked up a box of bullets from a nearby shelf. "I'll pay for these later. I'll come find you when we're ready."

With the gun belt draped over her shoulder and a box of bullets under her arm, she snatched the map back from the sheriff and hurriedly walked out onto the boardwalk.

Billy woke from his drink induced slumber with a startle as Fiona burst into the room and loudly slammed the door behind her. He sat up, rubbed his head and yawned. Fiona stood at the foot of the bed, her arms firmly folded across her chest, her eyes locked on Billy. He rubbed the sleep from his eyes and met her gaze in confused silence. Annoyed at being disturbed, by what he perceived to be childish behavior, he tried to lay back down. Fiona reacted quickly and pulled the sheets from the bed, angrily tossing them to the ground.

"How long are you going to lie in that bed doing nothing?" she snapped.

"I'm not doing nothing!" he argued back.

"Then what are you doing?" she demanded, the desperation clear in her damaged and husky voice. "Because I'm out there looking for them. Those men, who killed my momma and poppa, butchered my sister, the sister you said you loved!"

"I do love her!" Billy shouted miserably.

"Then you get up out of that bed and show me, because right now, you're acting like you never gave a damn about either of us," she told him through gritted teeth.

He watched her from where he sat and tried to control his emotions, breathing steadily and balling his fists. He pulled himself to the edge of the bed, placed his feet on the cool wooden floorboards and reached for the nearly empty bottle of bourbon.

"You've had enough," Fiona scolded him and snatched the bottle away before he could grasp it. She swigged the remaining liquid, gasped at the taste and threw the bottle from the window into the back alley. "I know where they are and if you don't get up, I will be going out there alone."

"They'll kill you," Billy muttered at the ground.

"Then don't let them," she insisted, "if you want to ditch me after it's done, go ahead, I'll be fine, but right now I need your help."

"I'm not going to leave you, Fiona," he said looking up at her, "why would you think that?"

She looked away embarrassed, her anger and bravado quickly fading, her eyes wet with tears.

"I don't know. Why would you want me around?" she started. "I saw my sister get buried today and you left me alone. I was thinking, maybe I remind you too much of her and it would hurt to have me around." She lurched forward and wrapped her arms around Billy, almost knocking him backward, "I don't want to be alone, Billy."

"You don't have to worry about that. I said I'd take care of you and I will, I promise," he told her reassuringly. "Why wouldn't I want to be reminded of the girl I love? Sure it hurts right now, more than anything ever has, but I don't ever want to forget Elle Belle, and with you around, I know I won't. It's like you said, you ain't leaving me and I ain't leaving you. That's the rule now."

She held on to him for a few more moments, before letting go and wiping her face with her sleeve.

"I killed a man today," she said flatly. "I cried about it after but not because I felt bad about it like you. I didn't feel anything. He was unarmed and walking away from me. I gunned him down and I'd do it again a thousand times."

Billy was unsure of how to respond. He waited for a moment, studying her in silence.

"I'm sorry I wasn't there for you," he apologized uneasily. "It won't be long now before we can try to move on and put all of this behind us," he told her, trying his best to muster a reassuring smile.

Fiona stepped back and practiced drawing her pistol from its holster.

"Pass me my boots," Billy said as he stood up and stretched.

She kicked them over to him and started loading bullets into her gun.

"How do you know where they are?" he asked.

Humans Are the Ugliest Creatures

13

Billy, Fiona, a Coward Redeemed and the Bloody Camp

"How long do we have to wait out here for anyhow?" Wade Willis complained.

"Quit testing me, Wade," Frank Kelly snapped and kicked out at him, from where they lay concealed behind a bank on the edge of the camp.

"I don't get it, why didn't you just kill the little runt when you seen her?" Wade continued to protest. "Now we got to wait out here all day, for her to maybe show up?"

"This is the plan," Kelly replied irritably, "don't question it."

"Don't question it? That's a little rich coming from you ain't it?" he said, chuckling to himself. "For the past few weeks you've been criticizing the boss' every move, to anybody who got the ears to hear it."

"Wade, you best shut your mouth about all that," Kelly hissed.

"Always telling me how it would be if you were in charge. I swear, if I was in-" Wade was cut off, when Kelly slid down the bank and gripped a hand tightly around his neck.

"You want to take charge, is that it?" Kelly questioned, applying increasing pressure to Wade's throat, causing him to cough and redden. "This is what the boss told us to do, so that's what we're doing. You got a problem, you take it up with him but I don't care for it, so if you keep on griping to me, I'll collapse your damn airways."

His eyes bulged with menace as he delivered his threat. He let go of Wade, spat at him and returned to his position on the bank.

"I hope we're all getting along over here," Bader spoke from behind them.

Wade held his hands against his neck, coughing into the grass.

"Wadey-boy here, thinks he could do a better job as the man in charge," Kelly snorted, without turning around.

Bader removed his hat and fanned himself. He kicked out lightly at Wade and studied him.

"I'd sooner let Frank here put a bullet between your eyes, but unfortunately, we don't quiet have the numbers to be picky about personnel," he laughed merrily. "No sign of anything yet," Bader told them, "everybody's spread out around the camp, tucked away nicely. Someone will be by with some water soon. Kelly, get over here for a minute," he ordered.

Kelly rolled onto his back and slid down the dry dirt of the bank, to where Bader was standing. They walked a few steps away, so that they were out of earshot.

"Any trouble while you were down there in Good Rock?" Bader asked.

"None," Kelly lied, "all according to plan. I didn't even have to look for her, she came straight passed me in the street."

"Then where the hell do you think they are?" Bader wondered.

"Couldn't say. Building up courage, I guess," he suggested.

Bader chuckled and continued to fan himself.

"You see Lyle anywhere?" he asked, expressing genuine concern. "He ain't exactly fit to be out there by himself. He'll be taken advantage of."

"Not hide nor hair of him," Kelly shrugged and shook his head.

Bader opened his mouth to reply but was distracted by the fervent whistling and hooting of one of his men. He angrily signaled at the man to drop back down behind the cover of the bank.

"Stay here and keep this end in line," he ordered Kelly, "I wouldn't put it past these idiots to mess up the simplest of plans."

He bent his knees and stayed low, making his way around the curve of the bank to the source of the whistling.

Humans Are the Ugliest Creatures

Joel Garrett was lying flat on his back, with his eyes shut tightly against the brilliant light of the sun, whistling rhythmically.

"Shut your damn mouth, Garrett," Bader commanded, irritated by the repetitive piercing noise. "What is it?" he asked as he took up position next to the man and peered over the crest of the bank.

Garret rolled over onto his ample gut and scrabbled up next to Bader.

"See that over there," he pointed far into the distance, "that little spec is headed this way." He closed one eye and concentrated, staring and squinting, trying to make out shapes on the shimmering horizon, "looks like one rider."

Bader turned his head and looked at the overweight, disheveled heap of a man.

"At least you were blessed with one quality," he laughed, "time and time again, those hawk eyes of yours prove you ain't all a waste of skin."

He slapped Garrett on the back and moved on around the edge of the camp to take his position. The remnants of the WPC waited patiently and kept their eyes locked on the rider steadily approaching the camp. The gallop eventually slowed to a trot as the lone rider neared the entrance.

"Bader!" the rider called out, scanning the deserted camp. "Get out here," he demanded authoritatively.

Bader peered over the bank at the man and was shocked at who he saw.

"Good evening, Sheriff," he greeted Sheriff Manning with a smile. "Welcome to the camp. I never thought I'd see the day," he laughed amiably.

Humans Are the Ugliest Creatures

The sheriff studied the WPC leader. He remained stern and silent, his hand hovering close to the heel of his pistol.

"Come on over here. I need to talk with you," the sheriff told him and watched as the humor drained from Bader's face.

As Bader made his way into the camp, the sheriff climbed down from his horse and waited. Kelly looked on nervously as Bader approached. He suspected that the sheriff had come to question Bader about the storekeeper's murder, something which Kelly had neglected to mention.

When Bader sent Kelly into Good Rock, he had expressly instructed him to exercise restraint and not to do anything to further inflame the situation. However, upon being caught sneaking into the back of the store, intent on thieving supplies, Kelly resorted to violence before rational thought, as he so often did.

He knew that the repercussions for not following strict orders would be severe, especially since Bader had been on such a short fuse in light of recent events. He twitched with anxiety as Bader got nearer and nearer to the sheriff, until he could not bear the tension any longer. He sprung up from behind the mound of dirt and opened fire on the sheriff.

The first bullet whizzed past him, a mere few inches from his head. The second caught his horse in the neck, sending it down to the ground, neighing furiously as it bled from what was surely a fatal wound. The sheriff narrowly avoided getting crushed by the beast as he leapt for cover behind a nearby wood pile.

Bader ducked down behind a tent and assessed the scene for danger, searching for any clue as to why Kelly had started firing. The gunfire was enough of a signal for one of the other men to bolt up over the bank and charge into the camp, laying down fire on the sheriff's position.

Shaking, the sheriff drew his gun and steadied his breathing, lying in wait for the swiftly approaching assailant. When he heard the footsteps come within a few feet, he dropped to the side and shot at the man. Three bullets dug into the man's chest as he barreled over headfirst, crashing into a pail.

"Hold it!" Bader shouted, his voice hot with a thunderous rage.

Kelly fired once more at the sheriff, pretending not to have heard the venomous command. He ducked down behind a tent in silent fury, ruing the missed chance to silence the lawman.

"I said hold it, God damn it! Kelly, you'd better lower that iron!" Bader seethed.

"What in the hell is going on? Call them off, Ed!" the sheriff shouted from where he hid.

"He was moving for his gun, I saw it!" Kelly screeched in defense.

"I didn't see it," Bader replied, still in cover.

"That's because I wasn't never reaching for it!" The sheriff barked angrily.

Bader stood up and slowly crept out into the open.

"It's all quiet now, Sheriff, you can come out. If anybody else raises a weapon at you, I'll floor them myself," Bader offered.

"He shot my God damn horse!" the sheriff complained furiously.

"And you shot one of my men!" Bader roared back at him. "So I guess it's even. Get up!"

Humans Are the Ugliest Creatures

Sheriff Manning cautiously rose to his feet and dusted himself off.

"Now, somebody want to tell me what the hell is going on?" Bader called out holding his arms wide.

"There's been a murder in town," the sheriff explained.

Kelly stood nervously, feeling streams of sweat trickle along his spine. The sheriff watched him carefully, not wanting to be caught off guard, should he attack again.

"Byron Boyd had his throat cut, in his own store, in broad daylight. I don't know who by," he lied, keeping his eyes locked on Kelly.

"Since when did you get tired of sitting around and become a real lawman again?" Bader asked snidely.

"I wouldn't go as far as that," he replied coyly. "The marshal seems to have took off, I ain't seen or heard anything of him in days now. Looks like Billy Earl has moved on too."

"Billy Earl is gone?"

"Yes," the sheriff confirmed, "lobby boy said he was gone sometime this afternoon."

"And the girl?" Bader pressed.

"Gone with him, gone on alone, who knows?" he wondered. "She's no longer in Good Rock though."

Bader held his hand to his chin, stewing in his thoughts as he stared at Sherriff Manning. The sheriff waited for the WPC leader's response, shuffling uncomfortably in the silence. Bader's eyes narrowed as he studied the lawman, wondering about his newfound bravery.

"So why have you come all the way up here? You got up and decided to risk your life, just to tell me about a murder?

Humans Are the Ugliest Creatures

A murder that you ain't even sure who's responsible?" Bader asked.

A triumphant smile gradually spread across the outlaw's face as he anticipated the real reason for the sheriff's visit.

"I'm here to tell you that the wanted notices have been taken down and I will be organizing a repeal of your warrant, on the grounds of mistaken identity," announced the sheriff.

"And why would you go to all that trouble?" Bader teased.

"The town needs your help, Ed. Good Rock needs the Western Protection Company back," he admitted grimly.

"You hear that boys!" Bader boomed, turning to face his few remaining men as they stepped out over the bank. "I told you it would happen. Hell, I told everybody this day would come." He turned back to Sheriff Manning, "Clearly a little bit of recruitment needs to take place but that won't hinder us too much. This time, I want a badge. I can't be clinging to the shadows anymore. We need to be allowed in Good Rock."

"I'll try to sort something out, but I won't know for sure until-" the sheriff began to explain.

"Jon," Bader sang, "I want my badge."

The sheriff conceded and nodded timidly, much to Bader's delight. The remaining WPC members gradually made their way in from the edges of the camp, to where the pair stood near the center. The sheriff walked over to his slain horse and knelt down next to it, offering a silent goodbye.

"Don't worry, Jon, we'll get you a new steed. A better one," Bader Joked and spun on his heel to face his men.

Humans Are the Ugliest Creatures

"Get yourselves cleaned up boys, we will be celebrating in the Sliver Boot tonight!" he cheered. "I think we all owe our new buddy a drink. Ain't that right Sherriff?"

His cheerful demeanor fell flat as he turned to include the sheriff in their revelry, only to find that the lawman was nowhere to be seen. He twisted left and right but saw no sign of the man.

"Jon?" he called out.

He listened intently for a response, his face tight with confusion. There was no reply. The men behind him looked at one another in abject bewilderment, while Kelly lurched forward apprehensively. The only noise to be heard was the soft crackle of the campfire and the sound of the wind blowing through the camp, disturbing the fabric of the tents.

"Garret?" Bader summoned the man.

"Yes, Boss?" he awaited instruction.

"Take those two idiots and find our dear sheriff," he ordered, "seems he's got a little lost."

Garret and two other WPC men cautiously advanced toward the sheriff's lifeless horse. All three froze on the spot, when the sharp sounds of someone whistling ripped through the air.

Bader instantly understood the significance of the signal, dropped down and scrabbled for cover. Billy and Fiona emerged from where they lay in wait at the camp's entrance and opened fire. Garret and the two men standing on either side of him were gunned down before they had a chance to process what was happening. The four remaining men of the WPC managed to keep low and scurry away to separate hiding places.

Billy and Fiona advanced into the camp, making their move while the WPC men were still running for cover. They dropped down onto their backs, behind a stack of railway sleepers and reloaded their guns.

"Did you see him?" Fiona asked breathlessly.

"Sheriff Manning? I think he's over there to the west," Billy replied.

"No," Fiona shook her head, "Bader, I mean. Did you see Bader?"

"I haven't spotted him yet. He must be hiding. They all are. We need to stick together, it's important," Billy warned her, cradling the rifle.

Fiona shut her eyes tightly and pressed the cool metal of the chamber against her forehead. She held it over her eyebrow, above her blood red eye. It seemed to sooth the bruising, which ached relentlessly in the heat. Billy strained to hear what she was muttering to herself, but he failed to make it out. Just as he reached out and laid a hand on her shoulder, she shrugged it off and stood up, firing wildly as she ran forward into the maze of tents.

"Fiona, wait!" Billy called after her but was forced back into cover by the bullets which the WPC rained down in response.

Sheriff Manning was crouched low, moving quickly past the walkways which ran in-between the tents. He heard the sounds of hushed voices nearby, possibly Bader and Kelly. They sounded agitated, frightened, they were on the back foot and disorganized. He held his gun tightly and prepared to charge on the voices, when a boot flew through the air, connected with his gun and sent it crashing into his head. He dropped the weapon and fell to the side woozily. Dutch was instantly upon him, one knee planted either side off his hips, holding him firmly in place and bearing down on him with a hunting knife.

"Seems you're a little hard of hearing, old man," the outlaw laughed and spat at the sheriff.

Sheriff Manning held his arms up and fought against his attacker, whose confidence immediately began to wane as he quickly realized that he was the weaker of the pair. Dutch tried to lift his body and force the knife down on the sheriff with all of his weight. As the two men squirmed and struggled for dominance, sweat poured from the sheriff's bald head and diluted the blood tickling from his forehead. He gripped Dutch's wrists and pushed back, feeling a surge of strength rush through him as he fought against his impending death. He clasped his hands around Dutch's, and pushed back hard. Managing to get a grip on the handle of the blade, he turned it upward to face his attacker. Dutch grimaced and tried using sharp bursts of force to disrupt the sheriff's progress, but his efforts proved futile. As the knife point neared the WPC man's neck, the sheriff gave one great heave of his arms, jolting the blade upwards and burying it deep into Dutch's throat.

Sheriff Manning retracted the knife and blood poured from the wound. He felt the heat of it on his skin as it splashed against him. Dutch's eyes widened and his jaw slacked. He gasped and desperately pawed at the hole, trying to somehow stem the flow.

The sheriff pushed him to the side and held him still for the remaining few minutes of his life. He offered no resistance. His muscles spasmed and he jerked back and forth as he tried to inhale deep lungfuls of dust laden air.

When Dutch finally stopped breathing, the sheriff got to his feet and tried to wipe the man's blood from his face. He reached down, picked up his hat and made to retrieve his gun. He stopped just a few inches short, upon hearing the cold click of a hammer locking in place.

"Don't move a muscle, don't make a sound," Frank Kelly warned him sinisterly. "Drop the knife," he commanded in a low, hushed voice.

The sheriff did as he was told and straightened up.

"You know you can get out of here, right?" the sheriff told him. "You could just slink away, no one would notice until it was too late. I can't guarantee they won't come after you but at least you'd get a head start."

"No, I don't think so," Kelly rejected the suggestion as he circled around to face the sheriff. "See, I'm not so cowardly as you are. I'd rather stand and fight, than hightail it out of here, leaving everyone else behind." He wagged his finger at the sheriff in mocking scorn, "should've put a bullet in me when you had the chance."

"If you're going to kill me, just do it," the sheriff told him flatly, "I ain't got it in me to go another round."

"This is more like it. You surprised me, putting up a fight against Dutch, like that. It ain't what I expect from you. This however, is much more familiar," Kelly laughed. "Lucky for you, you're more use to me alive right now. Let's put an end to this shall we? Please, lead the way." He gestured toward the middle of the camp and jabbed the sheriff with the gun, prompting him to move.

Bader grinned from where he hid, watching as Kelly marched Sheriff Manning out into the open. They came to a halt in the middle of the camp, where Kelly remained behind the sheriff, using the lawman's ample build for cover.

Humans Are the Ugliest Creatures

"Yoo-hoo, little dead boy, little dead girl," Kelly sung whimsically, at the top of his voice. "I got something here for you!"

Billy peered over the top of the railway sleepers and saw the sheriff standing in front of Kelly, his hands raised high. Fiona watched on, crouched in-between the remaining shack and the debris from the marshal's explosion. Bader crept out from cover and stood close to Kelly and the sheriff. He was confidently exposed, but not by any means an easy target, with cover nearby to fall back to.

"Toss your weapons and come on out here," Kelly demanded.

"There isn't much hope for the two of you, but the kind sheriff needn't lose his life too," Bader chimed in.

"Stay where you are," the sheriff blurted out, "he'll kill all of you, just like he killed Byron."

Kelly's face flushed scarlet with rage almost instantly. He stomped a heavy boot on the sheriff's ankle, which cracked loudly on impact. As the sheriff buckled, Kelly drew his pistol and fired a bullet into the lawman's calf. The sheriff rolled around in the dirt blinded by pain.

"Frank, he had better be lying!" Bader boomed from behind them, his voice guttural and full of fury.

"Your way wasn't going to work," Kelly protested crossly, staring down at the sheriff, watching as the dust and dirt drank the blood. "I did what I had to do!"

"And look at how well that's working out for us!" Bader rebuked.

Kelly sneered and locked eyes with Bader. He lowered his arm and held his gun to the sheriff's head, directly challenging the WPC leader.

Humans Are the Ugliest Creatures

"If you'd have killed the boy in the first place like I wanted, we wouldn't be in this mess," Kelly argued. "You got this one wrong from start to finish, Ed, and it ain't the first time! You damn near wiped out the whole gang. Well, I ain't listening to you anymore!"

"Simmer down, Frank," Bader threatened quietly.

"Your time at the head of this outfit is over. Hell, there ain't even no outfit left," Kelly laughed.

"Frank, you'd best quit it with that talk!" Bader yelled from behind him.

"I'm losing my patience!" Kelly wailed turning his attention back to the sheriff, completely ignoring Bader and clicking the hammer of his pistol into place.

Billy took shallow breaths and rocked his head back and forth, holding the rifle so tightly that his knuckles burned white. He peered out from cover but pulled back as he realized that he did not have a clean line of sight from his position. He laid the rifle down at his feet and drew his pistol.

"I'm not going to wait all day!" Kelly screeched.

Billy leapt out from where he hid and opened fire on them. Kelly was initially taken by surprise as the bullets whizzed through the air and passed him in a blur. It was the dull thud behind him, which snapped him out of his shocked daze and forced him into action.

"Jesus Christ!" Bader yelled to the sky as he hit the ground.

The muscles in his neck were strained and prominent as he clenched his jaw against the burning agony in his gut. The bullet struck an inch to the right of his navel. He tapped the small of his back but could feel no exit wound. He pressed his hands down over his stomach and took a deep breath. He dug his heels into the ground and began to push himself along the dirt, away from the clearing and into cover.

Kelly stepped forward and fanned his revolver, firing multiple shots at Billy in quick succession, but what he gained in speed, he lost in accuracy.

Billy ducked and tried to get back to his position behind the railway sleepers. As he stumbled along the ground, he caught one of the bullets in his thigh. He dropped and rolled the rest of the way, until he was safely out of sight. Thinking quickly, he drew his knife, cut away his sleeve and knotted it around the wound, stemming the flow somewhat but in no way reducing the raging torrent of pain. He winced and clenched his jaw, repeatedly slamming his head into the dirt, overwhelmed by a sense of frustration and inevitability. Kelly marched back to where the sheriff lay helpless and hoisted him up by his collar.

"I give you a chance to save a man's life and that's how you behave!" he shouted at Billy venomously. "How selfish," he said poignantly as he pressed the gun against Sherriff Manning's neck and fired twice. He let go of the collar and kicked the sheriff's lifeless body forward.

Fiona witnessed the shooting from the edge of the camp and tried to back away into the erratic jungle of pitched tents and refuse. She desperately wanted to get back to Billy and help him. She realized how foolish she had been to leave him, it was madness for her to launch an assault on her own. She knew that she had been blinded by a lust for revenge.

As she retreated from the cover of the shack, she was tackled to the ground by a prowling Wade Wills. Wade clumsily barreled into her and knocked her down, losing his footing in the process and falling alongside her.

"You two are finished," he snarled as he scurried toward her on all fours, like some sort of deranged feral.

He thrust his hands down, wrapped them around Fiona's neck and began to choke her. She gasped and felt her eyes bulging as his grip tightened. His rough hands caused an intense flash of pain, when pressing against the partially healed burns of her neck. She tried to push back against him but she was far too weak. She stretched but her arms were too short to reach his face.

Fiona started to panic, flapping her arms from side to side. The pressure in the pulsing veins on either temple, made it feel as though her head were about to burst. By chance, her hand brushed against her pistol, on the floor at her side. Fiona took a firm hold of the gun and pressed it against Wade's ribs. She pulled back on the trigger repeatedly, until all she heard was the clicking of empty chambers.

Wade's body fell limp on top of her and jerked violently as blood gushed from the fist size hole that Fiona had blown in his side. She pushed against his shoulders and tried to slide out from under him. When freed, she rubbed her neck, closed her eyes and took deep breaths. Gingerly, she got to her feet and picked up her hat and gun. As she turned to make her way back to Billy, she was confronted once more. Frank Kelly stood ahead of her, studying her with a menacing leer.

"Not so fast," he told her mockingly and leveled his pistol at her.

She held her own gun up, aiming it at his head.

"I think you already spent all them bullets," he giggled, straightening his moustache with his free hand.

"Are you sure about that?" Fiona asked, trying to hold her nerve but struggling to hide the fear in her rattled voice.

"Try me, little girl," he grinned and leaned forward, pressing his forehead against the barrel.

"I ain't no little girl!" she shouted defiantly and slammed the pistol against his forehead, instantly breaking the skin and drawing blood.

"God damn it!" he shouted in blind anger and grabbed Fiona's wrist as she tried to flee. He pulled her back to him and wrenched her arm up behind her back. "You ain't no little girl? Fine, I ain't going to treat you like a little girl! Now come on!" he seethed, spraying her with spittle as he barked each word.

He dragged her through the camp and threw her down forcefully in the center. Fiona quickly got back to her feet. Determined not to give up, she charged at Kelly but was met by his knee as he reacted swiftly and drove it up into her chest. She fell back to the floor, wheezing and gasping for air.

Near to the edge of the camp, Billy heaved himself into place behind the railway sleepers and picked up the rifle. He watched as Fiona writhed on the ground, struggling to regain her breath. Kelly noticed Billy positioning the rifle and taking aim. He lifted Fiona and held her in front of him, his arm wrapped around her throat. She pulled at his arm, trying to free herself as her legs dangled an inch from the ground.

"Put her down!" Billy shouted.

He had to grit his teeth against the tumultuous fire, which seemed to burn throughout his wounded leg with every movement. He steadied the rifle atop the sleepers but still failed to get a clear shot.

"Do we really have to go through this again?" Kelly asked incredulously.

Fiona swung her legs out and drove her heels into Kelly's shins.

"Damn it!" he cursed.

He dropped forward to his knees, making sure to drag her down with him. He holstered his gun and lifted the hatchet from his belt.

"You see this?" he asked Fiona.

He held it out in front of her and turned it from side to side. The meticulously polished metal gleamed and sparkled in the sunlight.

"This is what we used to cut your sister's heart out. You should have heard how she begged and screamed. It was quite a show. But I expect more of you. I expect you'll be a little more dignified," he taunted her, with a sickening grin stretched across his face.

Bader watched on as one of his most trusted lieutenants descended into murderous lunacy. He had defied Bader's specific instructions and dared to lie about it, undermining his leadership. He wondered how many other instances of defiance had occurred over the years.

He assessed the scene and calculated his odds of survival, which he quickly determined to be incredibly slim. Bader reasoned that if Kelly were to kill the girl, Billy would have a clear shot and take out Kelly, then finish the job by executing him. Alternatively, if Kelly got the better of Billy, drunk on blood, his rebellion would continue and he would surely turn on his master. In either scenario, Bader could not see himself getting out alive.

Grimacing he laid his hands against the floor, rolled onto his knees and pushed himself up from the ground. He fought against the blinding pain in his gut and stood, somewhat unstably, on his feet.

Billy noticed Bader, laboredly getting up from the ground and shuffling forward. He chose to ignore him and kept his rifle trained on Kelly, where he stood taunting a petrified looking Fiona with the axe.

"Look at it shine, such a neat little tool," Kelly whispered to Fiona. "It took us three or four swings to crack her open. She didn't die until a while after, just spilled out into the dirt, right where we left her. You can bet she felt all of it, the pain and the terror." He paused and smiled at her, "but you'll know all about that soon enough."

Kelly gripped the handle tightly and pulled his arm back high. Frozen in place and unable to save her, Billy's eyes widened in disbelief as he prepared to watch Fiona's life come to an end. Fiona shut her eyes and waited for the deadly impact.

She shuddered and tensed as a loud bang sounded behind her. She opened her eyes to see the spray of crimson gore float through the air above her. Kelly's arm, which had so forcefully held her in place, went limp and fell to the side. His body followed shortly after and hit the ground with a thump. She remained statuesque, her eyes locked on Billy's, neither one of them fully understanding what was happening. She lifted a trembling hand and wiped away some of the blood that glued her hair to her face.

Bader stood tall over Kelly's body and the kneeling Fiona. He held his pistol close to Fiona's head. She tensed as she felt the heat of the still smoking barrel against her scalp.

"I saved her life," Bader called out to Billy, "that's my bargaining chip. The second you straighten up that rifle, I won't hesitate, so don't test me. I don't want to do it. Toss the rifle."

"Why would I trust you?" Billy shouted back.

"That's a fair point, but you have to ask yourself, do you have a choice?" he paused. "If you can live with yourself, knowing you caused this little girl's life to be cut short, then by all means try me, but I don't think you want that. I've got nothing left to fight for here. I'll quietly be on my way. All you have to do is toss that rifle," he paused and waited but Billy did nothing. "I know you don't want to fight anymore, I can see it," Bader told him. "You don't carry the hate needed for sustained killing, it's not in you. So just toss it."

Seeing no other option, Billy exhaled dejectedly, then threw the rifle away and waited for Bader's response.

Fiona watched him, unable to understand why he would give up. Bader was the last of the WPC left standing and he was wounded. She cursed quietly to herself, wishing that her and Billy's roles were reversed. She knew that if she were in his place, she would have had the courage to take the shot and end it.

Bader popped open the cylinder of his revolver, emptied the two remaining bullets onto the ground and threw the gun into the nearby campfire. Fiona slowly turned her head and glanced at him over her shoulder, confused as to what he was doing. He raised his hands above his head and nodded at her to get up.

Humans Are the Ugliest Creatures

"I'm the last one. I swear to you, it will be like I never was," he said, wincing and lowing one arm to reapply pressure to his wounded stomach. "Feels like fire don't it?" he offered to Billy, who sat clutching his leg. "I nearly forgot what it's like, it's been so long."

Fiona slowly got to her feet, took a few measured steps forward and turned to face Bader. She squinted against the sunlight as she finally faced the man who had taken so much from her.

"Don't you dare waste the gift I've given you," he told her as he untied the yellow sash from his arm and let it fall to the ground.

Bader turned away from them and began shuffling his way across the opening, headed for the horses. He moved slowly, dragging his feet and grimacing with every pained step.

Billy watched on, feeling as though he had lost. Bader's final play had driven the will to fight right out of him. He felt his emotions getting the better of him and tried, with great difficulty and pain, to crawl out from cover.

She was standing completely motionless, her brow furrowed, watching Bader as he hobbled away. Fiona shook her head slowly, still struggling to understand what was happening. She bent down and picked up the two bullets which Bader had ejected. She rolled them around in her hand and looked around, searching for something.

Using her foot, she rolled Kelly's body over and knelt down at his side. She reached across, drew the gun from his holster and loaded the two bullets. She studied his broken, bloodied face for a moment, then spat at him. She straightened up and took confident steps, striding close behind Bader.

"I got hate," she said softly as she reached him.

Bader struggled to turn and face her, moving each foot slowly, trying to keep his abdomen as straight as he could. As he opened his mouth to speak, she looked him in the eye and gently squeezed the trigger. Bader grunted and groaned as he fell backward, sending dirt and dust up into the air. He landed heavily on his back, his hand pressed against the second wound to his stomach. She took his ankles under either arm, summoned all of her strength and dragged him back to the middle of the camp. She stopped next to the half buried iron pole in the center.

"Fiona?" Billy called out to her as he tried to get to his feet.

He stumbled forward from the railway sleepers, managing several uneven steps, before falling back down. The pain snaked through his leg like lightning. Fiona ignored him and went about tying a length of rope around the pole. The opposite end, she tied tightly around Bader's neck, making sure that there was enough pressure to hamper his breathing but not completely restrict it.

"What in God's name are you doing?" Bader croaked through gritted teeth, his face flushed red. "I saved your life, girl."

"You also turned it into the hell it is," she said matter-of-factly, "killing me would have been a mercy."

Bader's eyes widened as he coughed and choked, the movement of his muscles around the wounds, making him feel lightheaded and woozy.

"Why don't you just kill me?" he spat, with more anger than pain.

"Killing you would be a mercy," she said plainly as she finished knotting the rope.

Humans Are the Ugliest Creatures

"You're just going to leave me here?" he asked.

Fiona stood in front of him and tugged at his boots until they loosened. She took them off and threw them into the fire behind her. She drew the dagger that Bader wore strapped to his leg and used the tip of the blade to pick at the dirt under her fingernails.

"You are responsible for a lot of misery and suffering," she told him, without looking up. "You've inflicted pain on many, many people. You're going to have to taste a little bit of that, before you get to die."

She threw her arm down and drove the knife into his calf and twisted it sharply. She kept a firm grip on the handle as Bader cried out in pain. She withdrew the blade and threw it far off into the camp.

"Fiona, stop it! What are you doing?" Billy shouted to her, trying to drag himself along the ground toward her.

"I'm making things right!" she snapped back furiously, tears running the length of her face.

"No, you aren't," Billy replied, straining as he clawed his way along the ground.

"What do you want to do? Take him back, patch him up and hand him over?" she asked accusingly.

"No," Billy said firmly, "he's not allowed to live anymore but prolonging it doesn't bring about anymore justice."

"You know that it does," she muttered, shaking her head.

Bader coughed and wretched, interrupting their argument.

Fiona helped Billy up from the floor as he got closer. She tucked herself under his arm, inviting him to use her as a crutch. Moving awkwardly, they approached Bader, who was quietly mumbling to himself. She looked up at Billy, her eyes stern and cold as she handed him the gun.

"I think I'm starting to believe him," Bader grumbled, staring off into the distance. "Look past all this, strip it all away and it's just raw, rugged beauty. We're lying to ourselves, to say it's tamed," he chuckled softly. "Maybe that's what he was doing at the window. Trying to picture it without any of us, to see through to the beauty of it. I never saw it before, but it's just like he said…" he trailed off into thoughtful silence.

Billy held the gun against Bader's head. The outlaw looked up at the pair of them, squinting against the harsh rays of the sun as they flickered and glowed around the horizons of their skulls.

"We're the ugliest part of this place," he concluded grimly and closed his eyes as Billy pulled the trigger.

Bader jerked forward in agony as the bullet ripped through his shoulder. His eyes bulged and he coughed violently, the rope around his neck collaring and choking him.

"Son of a bitch," he spat breathlessly.

Billy knelt down and sat on the floor, taking the weight off his injured leg. Fiona stood at his side and rested her hand on his shoulder. He folded his fingers into hers, and together they listened to the incoherent mumbles and groans of pain as they patiently waited for Bader to die.

14

Billy Earl and Fiona Fire

In the months that followed, the weather took a turn. A period of unusually prolonged rainfall, gave way to thunderstorms and snow as the cooler months rolled in. The landscape was mottled white and orange, blanketed by thick, undulating gray skies. Green bodies of cacti reached up from the ground, with micro-drifts of snow balanced between the spines on their extended arms. The ground, which had briefly been softened by the rains, had frozen over and if anything was tougher than before.

Both Billy and Fiona stood in awe of the splendorous scene laid out before them. It had snowed lightly once when Billy was a young boy, but he only knew what his mother had told him about it, he had no memories of his own. Fiona had never seen snow, she had never even considered it, but upon the first morning that she experienced it, she fell in love with it. Its purity and cleanliness seemed to impose an element of uniformity upon the rugged land.

Exhaling forcefully, Fiona watched her breath as it condensed on the cool air and slowly dispersed. She pulled the thick padded jacket tight around her and flattened her hands against her ears. The cold was not something which she was accustomed to, and was by no means enjoyable, but the glistening of the snow was mesmerizing. It was as though the stars had fallen from the sky and embedded themselves in the soft white of the ground.

The sun had not been seen for days and Billy was starting to miss its warmth. He, like Fiona, had lived his life under the heat of the sun. The dull gray ocean floating above them and the muted tones of the snow, had rendered his home a foreign world.

He stood in the doorway to the modest farmhouse, watching Fiona as she scrapped her feet back and forth, drawing pictures in the snow. She laughed as the hens gathered at her feet and feverishly inspected the newly cleared ground. She picked one up and held it in her arms, gently stroking its feathers, while she looked out over the peaceful alien vista.

"You don't have a clue what the hell is going on out there, do you?" she whispered to the animal.

The chicken clucked lightly and twisted its head from side to side.

"Probably better that way," she sighed. "You don't have much to worry about, apart from worms and grain. That's not too bad a life when you think about it, not that you can."

She turned and looked back at the house, upon hearing Billy's whistle. She threw up a hand in response, dropped the hen to the floor and made her way back to Billy.

"Food's just about ready," he told her, lifting her hat from her head and closing the door behind her.

She closed her eyes and took in a deep breath through her nose.

"I wasn't even hungry before stepping in here," she said excitedly and removed her overcoat.

The burns to her shoulder and neck had healed, leaving extensive scaring in their wake. The scar tissue flowed up from her shoulder to her jawline, like a pale, rippling body of water. The blood which had filled her eye, had drained away naturally but left the eye noticeably bloodshot and her vision slightly blurred. Her voice had retained its husky quality, permanently damaged since the night of the fire.

Most would develop a self-conscious attitude, to what could be considered unsightly defects, but not Fiona. She wore each one like a badge of honor, they were a testament to how tough she was. It was the scars that one could not see, which were the most damaging. The crippling fear, which set in when she was left alone, and the nightmares, which would frequently wake her from sleep in a cold sweat.

Billy's leg had recovered well. He walked with the slightest of limps, but it was hardly noticeable and did little to hamper his work around the farm. He had struggled emotionally after the ordeal. He felt a great deal of guilt and blamed himself as the primary catalyst for the tragic events that had unfolded. He was grateful to no end that Fiona completely rejected his view and apportioned him no blame whatsoever.

With the reward money from the WPC bounties, they purchased a modest farmstead, nestled in the quiet hills on the far side of East Ridge, an hour or so out from the town. The house was a small adobe building, painted white in the style of the Mexican builds across the border. Surrounded by the snow, it blended in with its environment neatly, the terracotta roof tiles emerging from the white façade of the building, like the deep oranges and reds of the rock protruding from the snow.

"How long until the snow melts?" Fiona asked, taking a seat at the table.

"I don't know, could be days, could be weeks," Billy mused. "Could be that the sun comes out this afternoon and melts it all away. I hope it doesn't stay for too long, the soil is too tough to work."

"Well, I hope it stays just a little longer. Who knows when we'll get it again," she wondered.

"If we don't want to wait that long, we can always just journey up north a ways," he suggested. "Some parts up there snow all year round."

"All year?" she turned and looked through the window at the gray sky and white ground, which caused the horizon to blur and distort. "All year is probably too much. I don't mind a few days though," she reasoned contently.

"You finish your reading?" Billy asked her, ladling the stew into a bowl.

"Yes," she replied quietly.

"All of it?" he pressed.

"No," she admitted, "most of it, but the snow is a special circumstance."

Humans Are the Ugliest Creatures

"I can't argue with that," he agreed, pausing to look through the window. "Finish the rest after you eat." She started to protest but he held a hand up sternly, "if, as you say, you've done most of it then it won't take long to finish. Learning is important. Here, eat up." He placed the bowl down in front of her and she began to eat.

"What have you got to do today?" she questioned him, in-between mouthfuls.

"I was going to fix that chicken coup," he told her. "I think they'd be a little happier if they had somewhere warmer than a bush to huddle up. Maybe then they'd start laying again."

"I could help," she announced confidently, "I ain't as tired today."

"You sleep through the night?" Billy asked, resting a hand on her shoulder.

"Mostly, I think," she said, trying to remember.

"If you feel up to it, I'd be glad of the help," Billy smiled.

By the time that Fiona had finished her reading, the wind had picked up. It blew gusts across the face of the house, whipping up the snow like sand. Whistles and howls filled the air with sound. Fiona pulled her hat tight to her head and tried to tuck her hair behind her ears and down her collar. She saw Billy a short distance away and walked along the path toward him.

"Hold it steady," he told her as he hammered nails into the broken hutch.

He handed Fiona the hammer and a nail and pointed at where it needed to go. When she was done, she returned the hammer and held her coat tightly over her chest, trying to tuck her chin inside the collar.

"It's not so often we get cold here, is it?" Billy said, looking at the pink skin of his hands. "Well, they can just make do with this," he laughed, kicking the side of the coup.

They hurriedly packed it with hay, encouraged the hens inside and shut the door. They huddled close to one another, assessing their sloppy work.

"I give up on today," Billy announced, "let's go."

The pair made their way back to the warmth of the house. Billy stoked the fire, then joined Fiona, who was sitting at the table, wrapped in a thick blanket.

"Here, take this," he handed her a steaming cup of coffee. "Be careful it's about the hottest thing in here," he joked.

"Is there bourbon in this?" she asked suspiciously.

"Just a little," Billy admitted.

"I thought so," she said, taking a mouthful.

She stood and walked over to the window. She peered through the glass, watching the finer snow as it was pushed and pulled by the wind.

"Are we expecting anybody?" she asked, after a few minutes silence.

"No, why's that?" Billy replied, without looking up and sounding a little confused.

"Because someone's coming. They're a way off but they're coming this way," she explained.

Humans Are the Ugliest Creatures

Billy got up from the table and stood behind Fiona, glancing through the window. He scanned the horizons of the hills. Sure enough, there was a rider coming from the valley, headed in their direction. A little black mote, floating in the great white void. Billy picked up his rifle and loaded it. He found Fiona's gun belt and tossed it to her. She picked it up and fastened it around her waist. Just as Billy had, she made sure that her gun was loaded.

"You really think we'll need these?" she asked him.

"Would you rather have them and not need them or need them and not have them?" he answered plainly, while buttoning his coat. "You want to stay inside?"

She straightened up and shook her head firmly in response.

"I didn't think so," he smiled.

The pair waited by the window as the rider made his slow approach, hampered by the unusual weather conditions. He climbed down from his horse and hitched it in front of the house. The rider was dressed in a thick, black fur coat and gray broad brimmed hat. His near white moustache and stubble made him look as though he had taken a dive headfirst into the snow. He stood in front of the farmhouse, with his head held high and his hands rested firmly on his hips.

"Good afternoon," he bellowed, "I'd like to have a word, if I may."

"Stay behind me," Billy commanded Fiona.

Cautiously, he opened the door and stepped through, with the rifle trained on the rider. Fiona followed closely behind, her gun also aimed at the stranger. The man raised his arms in the air and smirked.

"Well, this is quit the welcome. I promise you there's no need for all that," he told them, his voice gravely and harsh. He slowly lowered one hand and tapped a finger against the left side of his chest, "May I?"

"You pull a weapon out of that overcoat and we will shoot. No hesitation," Billy warned him.

"I would expect nothing less," the man smiled.

With one hand still held high in the air, he carefully undid the top two buttons of his jacket. He pulled the lapel back to reveal a sheriff's badge, which was so routinely polished that it gleamed despite the dull light.

"You're a sheriff?" Billy asked the man, and slowly lowered his rifle, while Fiona kept her gun raised.

"That's right, Sheriff Ethan Olson of East Ridge. It took a while to finalize but here I am," he introduced himself. "Maybe we could speak inside? My bones ain't used to this cold."

Billy nodded slowly and turned to open the door, inviting Sheriff Olson inside.

All three entered the house, where the sheriff was invited to sit. Fiona took her place at the head of the table, keeping her pistol leveled at the East Ridge lawman. Billy poured three cups of coffee and set them on the table.

"Is it necessary that I'm conversing at gunpoint, here?" Sheriff Olson enquired with some concern as Billy placed the cup of coffee in front of him.

Billy looked over his shoulder at Fiona, then back to the sheriff.

"You'd have to ask her, Sheriff," he smiled politely. "I've still not learned how to tell her what to do."

Humans Are the Ugliest Creatures

"Miss Bellamy, would you mind if-" his request was cut short, when Fiona swiftly rose from the chair and straitened her arm.

"How the hell do you know my name?" she demanded, the gun trembling in her hand, inches from the sheriff's face.

"If you'd both take a seat, I'll explain it to you," he spoke calmly but his expression was one of anger.

Fiona locked eyes with him and remained motionless, for what seemed like an age in the tense atmosphere. Eventually, she lowered herself back into her chair.

"Go on," she told him, "but don't be calling me Miss Bellamy. It's Fiona Fire. You only get one pass," she warned him.

"I heard about what happened at the camp near Good Rock," he said gravely. "It was just word being passed around at first, but I made my way over to the town and did a little digging myself. Of course, there weren't no sheriff to ask, not even a marshal. Seemed that everyone who'd been directly involved had died. It was the doctor and the pastor who filled me in on most of it, how they patched you up, buried the dead and so on. It's quite a feat, a real achievement to go up against something like that and walk away breathing." He paused and studied Fiona and Billy for a few seconds, "I can see they got a few licks in but you're the ones who are here now. I guess it paid for this place," he wondered to himself, twisting in his chair and looking around the room, slowly nodding his head in approval.

Billy cleared his throat, prompting the sheriff to continue.

"It wasn't easy to find you, even harder to get up here in the snow but I was determined," he said.

"Why?" Billy pressed.

The sheriff smiled pleasantly, held his coat open and started fishing around in pockets. He produced two folded sheets of paper and laid them down on the table in front of him.

"It would appear to me that you two know how to handle yourselves," he told them.

Billy and Fiona watched closely as he began unfolding the papers.

"What I have here are two bounties and a business opportunity."

Humans Are the Ugliest Creatures

Humans Are the Ugliest Creatures

Humans Are the Ugliest Creatures is the first novel by Jack Barnett. If you enjoyed this book, please leave a review with the seller/ GoodReads.

Author Contact:

Email: jackbarnett71@googlemail.com

Instagram: hatuc_book

Twitter: @JackSBarnett

Printed in Great Britain
by Amazon